TOMORROW
WAR

SERPENT ROAD

D0167521

ALSO BY J.L. BOURNE

Day by Day Armageddon
Day by Day Armageddon: Beyond Exile
Day by Day Armageddon: Shattered Hourglass

TOMORROW WAR

SERPENT ROAD

The Chronicles of Max

A Novel by J.L. Bourne

G

Gallery Books

New York London Toronto Sydney New Delhi

G

Gallery Books
An Imprint of Simon & Schuster, Inc.
1230 Avenue of the Americas
New York, NY 10020

First Gallery Books trade paperback edition July 2017

GALLERY BOOKS and colophon are registered trademarks of Simon & Schuster, Inc.

For information about special discounts for bulk purchases, please contact Simon & Schuster Special Sales at 1-866-506-1949 or business@simonandschuster.com.

The Simon & Schuster Speakers Bureau can bring authors to your live event. For more information or to book an event, contact the Simon & Schuster Speakers Bureau at 1-866-248-3049 or visit our website at www.simonspeakers.com.

Design by Lewelin Polanco

Manufactured in the United States of America

10 9 8 7 6 5 4 3 2 1

Library of Congress Cataloging-in-Publication Data

Names: Bourne, J. L., author.
Title: Tomorrow war: serpent road : a novel / J. L. Bourne.
Description: First Gallery Books trade paperback edition | New York : Gallery
    Books, 2017. | Series: The chronicles of Max ; 2 |
Identifiers: LCCN 2017020293 (print) | LCCN 2017021774 (ebook)
Subjects: LCSH: Survival—Fiction. | BISAC: FICTION / Technological. |
    FICTION / War & Military. | GSAFD: Dystopias.
Classification: LCC PS3602.O89274 (ebook) | LCC PS3602.O89274 T64
    2017 (print) | DDC 813/.6—dc23
LC record available at https://lccn.loc.gov/2017020293

ISBN 978-1-5011-1670-4
ISBN 978-1-5011-1672-8 (ebook)

For My Shipmates

You have the watch. May the wind be always at your backs and may your black flags remain stowed—mostly.

AUTHOR'S NOTE

Welcome back to the world of Max, a world possessing DNA very similar to our own . . . maybe a chromosome or two off.

One of the reasons you're reading this is because you want to know what happened to Max, and we'll get to that shortly, I promise.

First, let's deconstruct and analyze some of the other reasons you might be reading these words right now. You're worried. Your candidate maybe didn't get elected. Hell, your candidate maybe wasn't even on the ballot. The economy is still on the ropes and firearms sales records continue to climb almost congruently with your uncertainty about the future of this country. Legislators are trying to outlaw unbreakable encryption while tech giants feign resistance. Less than nine months after *Tomorrow War* hit bookshelves and e-readers, Syria's grid was brought down nationwide by what many experts claim was a cyberattack. You'd like to think that none of the events in *Tomorrow War* could ever happen here, but the news headlines are a little too close to those fictional events for comfort, aren't they?

I don't blame you; I remain concerned, too. This is why I wrote *Tomorrow War* in the first place: to make you and yours aware of what might happen if we do not remain vigilant of the powers that We the People loan to those who govern us and our way of life. As before: "The thought crime ahead goes beyond the paradigm of right, left, Democrat, or Republican, the outdated behavioral placement control mechanisms, forcing us to choose between two heads of the same serpent."

If you are new to the series, allow me to give you the one-minute version.

The first novel began with reading the account of a man identified only as Max as he was sheep dipped by a CIA recruiter to be a member of the Agency's premier "dirty tricks" squad. After meeting up with his mentor, Maggie, Max soon found himself on an unacknowledged deep black mission inside the sovereign border of Syria. The mission for which Max was sent was a straightforward instability operation at first, but the events that transpired in Syria soon spread to a global catastrophe unlike any the world had ever seen.

Taking Maggie's advice, Max returned to his home in the rural hills of Arkansas, where he made last-minute insider preparations with his cousins Jim and Matt right before the United States grid collapsed. As his area of influence began to crumble all around him, so did the oaths of the servants who swore to support and defend the Constitution. Max witnessed a series of heinous crimes committed by a desperate government. Stricken with guilt from his accidental influence on the collapse, Max swore to take the fight to the state-sponsored murderers. Along the way he encountered a man of means by no means named Rich, surviving on an abandoned train loaded full of provisions, hidden in plain sight from the turmoil unfolding in the city around him.

Together Max and Rich eventually brought down the regional tyrannical faction that had a death grip on the throat of freedom, but not without blowback.

Stack deep, load those carbine mags, and be ready for anything. War is just a page away.

Data Recovery

Director,

This data was pretty corrupted; what is meant is that it should have been, considering the circumstances. Spinning metal discs with metal particles arranged to provide binary if/then statements can be fragile when exposed to extreme electromagnetic pulse energy. This tech has utilized all recovery algorithms, but this may be the final chapter in what is known of Max ▬▬▬▬▬▬▬, at least currently known. Most of his original scans, transcripts and support data has been defragmented and chronologically sorted based on encoded metadata.

Everything seems to be in order for your review.

Very respectfully,

▬▬▬▬▬▬

Lead Tech, Big Iron

PART ONE

SHADY REST

Cold.

Alone.

The hills of Newton County, Arkansas, were a remote place before the implosion of civilized society, which was why I chose to hole up here now. The train still exists as sort of a mobile base of resistance in western Arkansas, but I'm far from the reach of the locomotives. It's not that I don't feel that it's a righteous calling; hell, I helped them bring down the federal government in that area. That winter of resistance was harsh, killing many of us off by common cold and infection. With the spring came organization and purpose. After we figured out that we couldn't go past Fort Smith to the south because of fallout from a reactor meltdown near Russellville, we ended up going north. There the feds had blown out a large bridge just outside of Belle Vista. This effectively limited the mobile command center's travel to about a hundred miles of north–south track. It was fall when I decided it was time to leave. It had been long, dirty months since we neutralized the feds at the prison.

My cousin Jim and I took our gear and said our good-byes when the train made its stop back in Fayetteville; we then watched it resume going south to the exclusion zone on its endless back-and-forth route. It was rough to leave Rich; he said he wasn't ready to ditch his comfy boxcar quite yet. I shook his hand firmly before Jim and I trekked back to my shelter, safely buried in the rocky Arkansas ground a half-day walk to the east.

Jim and I held up for about a week when we got word from Rich via Radio Free Ozarks that a federal hit squad was looking for me.

Rich used verified code words, so I knew the threat was real. If they found me, they'd also kill whomever I was with.

It was time to go.

I left Jim enough to get him through the winter, and loaded up some dry goods, water, guns, and ammo into the back of my derelict Toyota pickup that I'd left covered with camo netting since the shit really hit the fan. Despite the cold, the engine cranked over, waking from a long dormancy. I let it run and embraced Jim one last time, promising to see him again soon, then crunched through the woods, down the trail leading to Black Oak Road. Jim had buried my shelter back before all this; I just hope it won't become his grave.

The only one besides me who knows the exact whereabouts of the cabin I now inhabit, Shady Rest, has been dead for a while. My father used to bring me here in summer. Back then there was no electricity here, no running water besides the river down the holler. If you had to take a number two, you did it in the nearby outhouse.

Dad told me I was spoiled to have a magazine rack inside Shady Rest's outhouse, and that it was a fancy structure because it was a "two-seater." I still laugh, thinking about all this luxury Dad used to tease me about when compared to his Spartan childhood growing up in these mountains.

UMBRA

Notice to All Fusion Centers

Target number one in OPERATION HAYSTACK, Max ▬▬▬▬▬▬, will heretofore be referred to as CONDUCTOR in all applicable op-intel reporting and tippers. Your compliance with this intelligence directive is mandatory until such time as CONDUCTOR is apprehended.

Director sends.

CABIN FEVER

4 Nov

I left the confines of Shady Rest early this morning. My food stores are running low (except the emergency stash in my go bag), so I decided to run a trotline. The sky continues to spit flurries, reminding me of the grim fact that I need to stack a few ricks of firewood. I'll go up periscope tonight to listen for chatter. Rich knows I'm listening at dusk on most days I can get to high ground in time.

5 Nov

Three fish on the line! I cleaned them and tossed them in the pan pretty fast. After scarfing them down, I grabbed my axe and felled two medium-sized trees. I had an old chainsaw in the side shed, but couldn't risk the noise. The sun was getting low when I was done hand-sawing the trees into lengths that would fit my woodstove. I split enough to last me until morning and cooked my last can of train soup. Exhausted. Gonna catch some shut eye and take the bolt gun out in the early morning to see if I can't scare up some game.

SHORT ACTION

6 Nov

The wind was blowing a cold breeze when I stepped off the cabin porch in the early black of another Ozark mountain morning. My .300 Blackout bolt gun was secured to my pack along with a set of trekking poles.

I quietly made my way up the mountain opposite the direction of the wind. Crunching through the frozen grass, I concentrated on stalking my way into my hunting grounds. I had a deer blind set up there and planned to be in it before the sun came up. I fumbled around for my night vision device (NVD) and positioned it over my right eye. The Milky Way came into green focus when the device powered on, calling attention in bright detail to Earth's skewed relative rotation.

The blind's IR signature jumped out from its organic surroundings. Inside, I was half tempted to kick on the small propane heater we'd kept at the cabin for years, using it to keep us warm while hunting. Fuel was very scarce, so I resisted the urge to stay warm the easy way. I closed all but one of the blind's fabric windows to keep as much heat inside as I could and waited.

And waited.

And waited.

The sun had been up for an hour when I caught my first look at wildlife through the small binoculars I kept hanging around my neck.

I watched a yearling and a doe quickly traverse the field in front of me. I dropped the binos and cranked my rifle's optic up to 9x. I rested the gun on my crossed trekking poles and began to track the doe as she moved left to right across the blind's opening. They both looked pretty skinny, so I decided to pass. I've been pretty lucky with the river. I've heard no shots in the mountains today . . . not like it's a common thing anyway.

Sundown

Trotline had a fat catfish on it. Not as lucky as earlier with that trio, but it still smells damn good on the fire. I split another rick of wood and stacked it neatly on the cabin porch. Covered in sweat, I built a fire inside and then stripped down to nothing and went to the side of the house where I had a hose running from a 55-gallon steel barrel fed by a larger cistern. The flat black–painted barrel absorbed enough heat to take some of the chill out of the water, but my God it was still brutally cold. I took a thirty-second shower and ran back inside the cabin into the starlike blistering heat of the woodstove.

Time to eat.

Midnight

Keep hearing something outside, even over the wind that's no longer a breeze but now blasting through the valley. Sounds like a woman screaming.

Big cat.

The shrieking sound along with the flickering kerosene lantern light, from which I write this, makes for an unsettling scene. The wind is blowing hard enough to shake the thick wooden door on its hinges. The two-by-fours I have bracing the door should hold any potential intruder back, but I'm still sleeping with my gun.

That hasn't changed. Ever.

Something wild is out there in the dark, and something even more menacing searches for me beyond it.

Should have burned my table scraps.

November 6

Notice to All Fusion Centers

The search for CONDUCTOR continues. Although we know the day-to-day general location of the supply train where CONDUC-TOR was previously located, we can confirm via quadcopter reconnaissance that he has not been operating in the area for some time. We cannot risk flying or engaging our larger Reaper drones in that area as new intelligence reports suggest that the Northwest Arkansas Irregulars (NAI) have received a shipment of Stinger missiles from a group of recently arrived Redstone Arsenal deserters. As our limited Reaper fleet is a high-density, low-volume asset, they do not meet the commit matrix for employment over Stinger threat territories.

We now have CONDUCTOR's agency contact in custody and have been interrogating this individual for actionable intelligence. We will notify the director if any new information comes to light as a result.

FREE MASON

10 Nov

Last night's storm toppled a tree right into my rock chimney, knocking off a couple cornerstones. I've been using the woodstove anyway, but still need to keep up on the repairs as winter sets in. Don't want a heavy snow to put the roof down on me some midnight in January.

I've heard the cat outside every night, so I haven't been getting much sleep. I'll bet a lot of the meat has been hunted out of the territory since the breakdown of just-in-time shipping; that's probably another reason why the cat is hanging out near the cabin. I found half a bag of cement in the small storage shed in the back. Got to go down to the river and get some water for the mix to repair the damage. The repairs won't last without fireclay and type S, but it'll have to do.

11 Nov

The old wooden ladder I was using to repair the rock chimney yesterday is missing a rung. This resulted in more than one near mishap ten feet up on the side of the cabin. After a couple hours of cursing up and down the crappy ladder and dropping my makeshift wooden trowel a few times, I finally got the missing rocks set back into the side of the chimney. I'm no mason like Jim, but it'll hold.

I hope Jim is holding up okay at Black Oak.

Time for a radio check.

11 Nov. (Later)

Bagged a deer.

I was walking up the mountain this morning the same way I always do before a hunt when I saw him limping through the trees. The buck wasn't that big, but he was enough to fill my cooler. I raised my bolt gun, glassed him, and noticed deep claw marks on his flanks.

Injured.

I didn't want to spook him, so I got low and stalked in, circling around to the high ground. The wind was not in my favor. The buck's ears twitched when he caught my scent. One snap of a twig and the deer would run off and probably die anyway. I braced the gun against a nearby oak tree and aimed for the heart.

I slowly squeezed the three-pound trigger.

The suppressed rifle thumped some bass just before the loud thwack of the 208-grain round hitting the deer's flesh. The animal ran ten yards or so before dropping like a sack of potatoes.

Thinking of the marks on his flank, I cautiously approached

the kill. Cats like to attack at dawn or dusk when we humans can't see very well; right now, the sun hadn't been up too long. I quickly made sure the buck was dead and really inspected its injuries before starting my expedient field dress. They were fairly fresh and not yet infected. Four deep claw marks gouged through the deer's left flank; this was clearly the work of a predator. Might be a black bear, but I doubted it, based on the bloodcurdling sounds I've been hearing at night.

I felt eyes on me as I removed most of the animal's organs, tossing the steaming mass into the nearby bushes.

With the carcass now a good bit lighter, I rolled it onto the tarp I was carrying and started dragging it down the mountain. It was a brutal, freezing trip.

My cleaning station was set up a hundred yards from the cabin. I didn't want the smell of blood and guts near where I slept at night. Using some cordage, I strung the deer up at eye level and moved on to butchering the meat for tonight's stew, careful to drop the heart and liver into a Ziploc bag. I then hoisted the animal high to cool it off. The tarp was littered with blood, bone, flesh, and guts; I'd need to dispose of that a good distance away from the cabin before going in for the night.

After a few hours and some struggling, I eventually got most of the meat in an old Igloo cooler that I kept full of chunks of river ice for this occasion. After securely tying the cooler closed, I hoisted it high off the ground using a tree branch.

By midday, I'd gotten rid of the carcass and was cooking deer stew with chunks of heart, liver, and a cup of rice. It wasn't a lot of variety, but it was calories. If the weather stayed cold, I could keep the meat frozen, maybe stretch it a month or two. There was propane in the cabin's tank, enough to keep the freezer running, but there was no use keeping it active until the meat was at risk of being spoiled. I doubted it would warm up in these mountains anytime before February.

After heading back down the hill to get more ice, I saw the impressions clearly in the clay of the riverbank.

Mountain lion tracks.

I gathered chunks of river ice in a canvas rice bag, feeling my Glock on my hip, taking comfort that it was fully loaded with heavy 147-grain 9mm rounds.

Midnight

Candlelight sucks when you're scared and alone.

I'm laying here on a straw-filled mattress looking at the ceiling. I think I can hear something outside trying to get at the cooler full of meat, despite it being off the ground, but I can't be sure. The wind is going at it and there is no window on the back side of the cabin. If I wanted to know for sure, I'd need to go outside in the snow and see for myself.

Not happening.

It's not that I'm afraid of predator cats; it's that if I get hurt out here, I'm a few days from anyone that can help me, probably even farther from anyone that would help me. Pound for pound, I'm just not genetically suited to fight something with claws, fangs, and natural night vision.

If it's out there, and if happens to get the meat, fuck it. You earned it, kitty.

But if it keeps pissing me off, I'll build a blind and sit up in the trees tomorrow night, out of its reach with my own night vision. See how it likes a .300 BLK round between the eyes.

Death from above.

Yeah, it helps to think I can take it out.

Little less scary now.

When the wind blows especially hard, it makes it through the primitive mud seal and causes the candle to flicker a bit. The temperature is starting to drop down well below hard freeze at night, and I might need to start up the fireplace as well as the woodstove to keep things cozy in here. More stacking fucking firewood, and worse, more exposure to the mountain lion.

My 12 gauge is above the fireplace, Glock under my pillow, chambered bolt gun is propped up against the bed, and my M4 carbine is hidden securely under the cabin floorboards. Can't risk losing it.

Bolt gun for four-legged predators.

M4 for two.

HOUSE ARREST

I awoke at 0600 to snow flurries and gray skies. It was just under 50 degrees inside the cabin according to the small digital thermometer, so I stoked the embers and tossed a log on the fire before gearing up to go to the outhouse. I regretted the trip because of the cat noises I'd heard last night, but doing my business inside the cabin wasn't going to happen. Can't risk disease or infection.

I could feel the draft coming through the sides of the door as I pulled the two-by-four drop boards from the door security brackets. Hell, it worked with castles for hundreds of years; it's good enough for my little cabin.

I opened the door and quickly exited as to not lose the precious warm air being built back up from the fresh log. I saw no tracks on the porch or ground in front of the cabin, so I drew my pistol and moved to the outhouse as fast as I could.

Rounding the front of the cabin, I could see the outhouse fifty feet away, with its moon-shaped door cutout, or what my dad would refer to as one of those luxury features, allowing ambient light to accent your sitting experience. As I moved swiftly to the structure, I glanced over at the cooler full of deer meat.

It was not as I'd left it. Small branches and dead leaves covered the now muddy ground in a circle below the meat. Something large had attempted to use the cooler like a rope swing.

My pace quickened as I moved to the tiny outhouse, slamming the door shut. I twisted the small wood privacy mechanism and thought again how Dad would talk it up as yet another luxury feature, inherent to life in Newton County, Arkansas. As I handled my necessaries, I could hear timber crack somewhere out there, probably from the weight of snow and ice. This unnerving sound made me envision impossibly large beasts crashing through the forest, looking for someone to eat. I pulled my pants back up, disinfected my hands, and drew my gun again for the transit back to the cabin.

I worked up the courage and twisted the wooden cog lock and jumped out into the snow, yelling, just in case the cat was out there waiting for me.

It wasn't. Nothing at all in the vicinity.

With some newfound courage, I investigated the cooler full of meat. Claw marks were evident on the outside and some of the cordage was frayed from the beast's sharp claws. The muddy ground below the cooler was clear of snow, as the cat's activities here last night must have melted it off. It had been right outside while I slept.

I took the day's meat from the cooler and hoisted it a few feet higher off the ground before going back into the cabin to prepare some powdered eggs and venison.

We're done, kitty. I refuse to be a prisoner here.

Going hunting tonight.

As the sun neared the western horizon, I laced up my boots and checked my bolt gun, pistol, and NVD batteries. It was going to be another cold night, so I ripped open a two-pack of hand warmers from my dwindling supply to keep in my pockets. The thermometer outside said 12 degrees and the one inside said 55. Still painfully obvious that this will eventually force me to build a second fire in the fireplace in addition to the stove, but this comfort would come at a painful premium. I'll be chopping firewood as soon as better weather blows in. That activity will triple my caloric intake needs. The cooler will empty faster, pushing me back out there where the predators prowl.

After checking the perimeter around Shady Rest, I pulled the broken wooden ladder out of the shed and climbed up on the cabin roof. It was still bone chilling, but the roof provided some reprieve from the ground; the fire I'd built in the stove was keeping the wood shingles a few degrees warmer than the outside temp.

It had stopped snowing and I could see the waning moon as it slowly cut across the sky like a great scythe. My breath clouded the moon's glow as I watched, wondering what Jim and Rich might be up to this evening. Earlier, I checked the RF spectrum for intel but could hear nothing. I was in the middle of nowhere and the surrounding hills probably blocked any communications coming in from the outside.

I pulled my NVD down over my eye and switched it on. The green glow of technologically enhanced vision filled my right side, reassuring me that man still owned the night.

I pulled the bolt back on my Remington 700, checking for the glint of brass in the moonlight, and was comforted to see a round attached to the bolt. Driving it back home, I snugged up against the stone fireplace and waited.

The cooler remained suspended on the bough, now just a little more out of reach than last night. It swung slowly with the cadence of the night wind. The branch holding the cooler was higher than the roof of the cabin. It extended nearly to the edge of the roof where I sat, leafless until spring.

The silver scythe continued to harvest the night as I froze, waiting for the Ozark demon to show itself.

It never came.

I climbed down and hit the rack at about two in the morning, waking at 0600 when my watch alarm began to beep. I rose out of bed wearing only my yellowed long johns and placed my war belt around my waist in preparation for my trip to Newton County's finest toilet facility. I pulled the barricade from the door and went outside just like I did the day before and began to make my left turn.

Tracks. Again, without claw marks.

Lion.

My pace quickened as I rounded the corner.

The goddamn cooler was gone.

I took care of my necessaries and made way back to the cabin to gear up and find out what happened to my calories.

Fuck.

I followed the cat tracks and skid marks up the mountain a few hundred meters until I found the cooler. The plastic was shredded in several places on the outside, but the whole thing remained secured by three frayed circumferences of paracord. The thermometer said 20 degrees when I stepped off the porch, so the meat was still good inside.

As I dragged the cooler halfway down the mountain, I heard the scream coming from behind.

I turned and caught sight of the creature about fifty meters up the trail. It looked to be about a hundred and fifty pounds. Its teeth were the most visible part, sabers of white stretching its light brown lips.

It was clearly pissed about my repossessing the cooler.

"Fuck you, cat!" I shouted up the mountain, raising my pistol to shoot.

The cat came at me full sprint and didn't stop until I pulled the trigger. The ground in front of the cat exploded as the round hit, sending rocks and snow into its face. It growled and shot off to the right, perpendicular to the mountain trail. I wasted no time in opening the cooler, grabbing as much meat as I could fit in my thick canvas coat, and tying the container back up. Leaving the cooler, I ran back to the cabin loaded with venison, hoping the mountain lion wouldn't chew through the cordage and eat the rest of what I'd left behind.

Venison stew is now cooking in the pot on top of the wood-stove, and the smell is no doubt wafting up the mountain and into the big cat's nostrils, taunting it as I write this.

War.

I dragged my fingers across a small ash pile near the warm fireplace and painted my face with streaks of black and gray; then I unbarred the door once more, stepping out into the wild of the Ozarks.

I scurried up the ladder to the cabin roof, putting my back once more against the river-stone chimney, which felt warm to the touch from the fire that burned beneath me. Before nightfall I went back up the mountain and, checking that there was no immediate danger, brought the cooler down the trail, putting it in a good location to snipe the cat from the cabin roof. The white lid reflected brightly through my NVD and the stars shone with diamond intensity in the background, beaming easily through the bare but thick tree branches.

I lay prone on the roof at an odd angle. The cabin was an A-frame, so there were no real flat spots except over the front door. I waited for the predator to show itself, to claim the food from the cooler.

In concentrating on the kill box, I allowed myself to relax and drifted off. Not sure how long.

I awoke to the loud crack of broken branches and got that camera flash effect in my eyes, the one you feel when jolted awake by a loud noise at night. I focused on the cooler again but saw nothing.

I was nearly asleep again when I ~~heard~~ felt it.

Something caused the cabin to, I don't know, bump?

I flipped over onto my back and crept back up against the chimney. My NVD wasn't mounted to my rifle at the moment so I pulled my Glock and raised it up.

Goddamn tritium sights were blowing out my NVD.

I lowered the Glock and waited. I was on the front side of the A-frame. Whatever caused the bump was somewhere on the other side.

Looking up at the crest of the roof, I finally saw it. Its eyes glowed eerily bright through the NVD, and the outline of its ears could be seen against the backdrop of the cosmos.

The big cat was on the roof with me.

It growled, and I brought my Glock up and pulled the trigger, sending splinters of wood through the air. At least one round hit the mountain lion, which was now screaming and roaring as it came down my side of the A-frame towards me. I tried to hit it again, but the cat was rolling down the roof at me. I attempted to back up and let it fall off the edge, but it hooked me with one of its paws, its murderous claws piercing right through my pants and into my calf muscle. I shrieked in agony and nearly shot my own leg as the creature continued to tumble, pulling me off the cabin roof with it.

I fell with the mountain lion, trying to maintain control of my weapon as I hit the ground hard, knocking the wind clean out of me. The pain of my leg and in my stomach briefly stunned me, but I knew that the big cat wouldn't care about that. It wouldn't give me a moment to compose myself before ripping my face off.

I shot into the thing twice before my magazine locked back. Funny, I didn't remember shooting that many rounds. It still had a hold of my calf and wasn't letting go.

I reached behind me and pulled out my trusty pig sticker as the injured animal lunged at my neck for the kill. In a rare moment of luck, the animal drove itself forcefully into the blade. The razor-sharp steel Bowie penetrated the cat's throat all the way to its spinal column. In its final moments of life, it latched onto my other wrist through my canvas coat, nearly breaking it. I pulled the blade and stabbed at it until I couldn't move my arm.

The beast went limp on top of me.

The fight was over.

JIGSAW

There's not even a goddamned aspirin in this cabin.

My calf hurts like hell. My med kit isn't exactly something a doctor would be proud of, but at least there was a suture kit, a useless snake bite suction cup, and some alcohol wipes inside, so I guess that's better than bad.

The first thing I did after dragging myself inside off the icy ground was boil some water to clean out the cat scratch. I poured near scalding water slowly over the three puncture wounds, wincing in agony and screaming loud enough to be heard all the way to Little Rock.

After I was sure the wound was cleansed, I scoured my hands and ripped open an alcohol wipe. Ready for pain round two of many, I began to wipe the wound. I screamed again, causing myself to bleed even more, so I took a hot rag and applied pressure for a few minutes. The blood didn't stop, so I had to go to my sutures.

Craving a bottle of whiskey to chug, I didn't waste any more time starting on the largest of the three cruel holes.

I nearly passed out as the needle passed through the divide of the small wound channel. Blood continued to trickle down my leg and onto my white sock. I gave each hole three loops and cut and tied everything off as best I could remember from my medical training. I again gave my wound a warm ~~sponge~~ sock bath and sucked air through my teeth when the cold alcohol hit. The thread was crisscrossed asymmetrically, but hey, I didn't go to med school.

After I made sure my leg was as good as it was going to get for now, I pulled my left sleeve up to check the damage there. Thank God for tough old Carhartt jackets. My wrist was adorned with blood bruises, but I still had full movement and it didn't hurt as bad as my calf.

So that's a win.

I hadn't noticed it before, but it looks like one of my 9mm rounds grazed my boot. Could have been a helluva lot worse. I mean, the fight could have gone the other way and I'd be the one with the 25-degree body temp right now instead of the big cat. If I'd shot myself in the foot with my nine, I'd probably have died, or at the very least lost my foot out here and then died. The fact that I'm writing this as the morning sun beams through the cabin windows is something to appreciate. Although I felt like Leroy Brown at the end of the song, it's truly not every day you go to fisticuffs with an apex predator and survive.

I can't afford to stay in bed. I need to get up and move around, even if only to hit the outhouse.

It's mid-afternoon. I have a pot of stew boiling in the cabin. My leg is wrapped up in a bandage, but it's burning like hell. That either means my body is doing its job or I'm about to come down with a nasty infection.

My search for crutches is over; I spent some time today looking for trees with the right natural angles so I didn't have to sit on the porch with my pocket knife playing backwoods carpenter. What I was able to cobble together wasn't comfortable, but I could move around with the makeshift crutches without overstraining my calf muscle, like I probably did when I was out looking for them in the first place.

FML.

⬛

My whole body is aching now. I think it's sort of like the day after a car accident type of thing. With all the adrenaline, you feel fine on the first day, but like hammered dog shit the day after. It's night outside and I didn't feel like hobbling down to the river for water.

Mistake.

You'd be surprised how much snow you have to melt to get a gallon of water. I think I spent more calories going back and forth gathering snow than if I'd just bucked up and went down to the river. Lazy man load and all.

It hurts when I squeeze my calf, but that's to be expected. My wrist is sore, but it should heal fine. Right now, my main worry is infection. I'm nearly out of alcohol wipes and I only have enough sutures to fix two of the three punctures if I were to somehow rip them open.

I've got to be careful, as I might as well be on the surface of Mars. No one is coming to help me out here.

I'll check the trotline in the morning.

⬛

Woke up this morning early, bundled up in a pair of waders, and limped down to the river on the crutches. The cat's corpse was still frozen stiff on the ground. I didn't have the patience or energy to skin it and tan the hide. Would be pretty badass to wear a mountain lion pelt around up here, though. Anyone I ran across would know I was the real deal wearing something like that. I'll get around at some point to dragging the thing away and let nature take care of it.

The trip down the draw to the river took me about ten minutes with my improvised crutches. I was sure not to put too much weight on my calf; all I needed was to have that muscle contract and rip open the wounds. I toted an empty, blue five-gallon water jug on my back and dreaded the trip back up the hill.

Down at the riverbank I broke some ice and walked down into the icy waters, thankful again for the waders I'd found inside the cabin when I arrived.

Thanks, Dad.

The line had no fish. I placed a few small chunks of deer meat on the empty hooks because I had nothing else and waded back to the shore, shoving floating ice out of my way as I went. The cold felt good on my calf but not so good everywhere else. I filled up my water container and strapped it back onto the ALICE frame on my back for the trip up.

Twenty minutes.

I was sweating and exhausted when I got back to the cabin. I quickly stripped down to my underwear in front of the roaring fire to avoid hypothermia. I boiled some water and lightly washed out my wounds, using the heat to bring the trapped fluids out. Once the rest of the boiled water cooled, I gulped it down. I was down to about four gallons and would need to go again tomorrow to build up my water reserves, in case I fell ill from infection and did not have the energy to make another thirty-minute round trip.

DIRECT ACTION
November 14

OPERATION HAYSTACK
DIRECTOR'S EYES ONLY

Our intelligence regarding the train's location on November 13 was accurate. We were able to demolish a section of track, delaying its transit north, and giving us enough time to meet our objective. Our direct action team boarded the train just after midnight. Based on small drone reconnaissance, Rich ████████████'s boxcar was previously identified by its prominent antenna array and solar panels.

Our team was able to capture Rich ██████████; however, one of our men was killed during the assault. We are confident that we now have key interrogation assets that will enable us to geolocate CONDUCTOR in the coming days.

Director, Little Rock Fusion Center

Notice to All Fusion Centers

The apprehended terrorist, Rich ▄▄▄▄▄▄▄▄, will heretofore be referred to as TOURIST. Your compliance with this intelligence directive is mandatory until such time as HAYSTACK is deactivated.

Director sends.

RECOVERY

It's been a week since I've written anything in here, and a damn rough one at that. Three nights ago, I spent hours shivering in my bed, out of split firewood, fever raging and teeth chattering. If not for the water I'd stockpiled in days prior, I'm certain I'd be dead. I pounded water for three straight days, taking care of my necessaries in a bedside orange five-gallon bucket, until my fever broke and I was finally able to stand up without passing out.

I have enough meat left to last me about ten days or so (if I don't exert myself), but I desperately need something besides a handful of old rice to go along with it; I'm down to the bottom of the bag and it's full of weevils. The food cooler is stored under the cabin on the north side away from the sun. Heading out in a few to check on it and get water. I'm only one swallow away from dry cabin status.

My trip to the river was arduous and uneventful, but things picked up after I got there. I was still using both crutches, but felt like I could get down to only one crutch if I let myself heal a little longer and was careful. The ice had disappeared down at the river and there was no snow on the ground. A warm front must have been through while I was bedridden, melting everything. Before I got sick I was actually pondering whether or not to butcher the mountain lion instead of just dragging it away but it's too late now. At least the contents of the cooler are still frozen. I just hope I don't get any crazy Arkansas weather where it inexplicably rises briefly into the 80s when it should be around 20.

Back to the interesting part of my trip to the river. As I checked the trotline and filled up my water jug, I detected the thumping of helicopter rotors somewhere off in the distance. I hobbled fast over to the riverbank and hid behind a row of sapling pines. The rotors got louder momentarily before fading off to the point where I couldn't hear them any longer.

Someone's flying around in this area and there aren't too many reasons to do that. I doubt the government cares about all the moonshine stills in these parts anymore, but they damn sure care about me.

I'm a wanted man.

I took the rotor noise as a wake-up call. Make preparations to repel boarders.

It's been three days since I heard the helicopter. Even with the injury, I've managed to move my pickup truck farther away from the cabin and cover it up pretty well. The cabin is set back into the woods and shielded by a thick tree canopy, only visible by air from the east. The rotor noise came from the west, Jim and Rich's direction, but that doesn't really mean anything.

In other news, I'm down to one crutch. I chucked the other one into the river, grinning as the torturous stick spun in the air and splashed into the icy waters.

Yesterday morning, I dug up a handful of worms and took them down to the river with my pole. I was able to snag two small fish and had them cleaned, cooked, and eaten within thirty minutes. I didn't even bother to take them back to the cabin; I did it right there on the riverbank over a fire circle.

I'm down to my last bit of venison, as the meat is starting to spoil. I'm cooking the rest of it in a stew right now, which I plan to stretch out over the next several days.

Happy Thanksgiving.

Injury update: only a slight limp remains. This is fortuitous, all things considered.

Two nights ago, I decided to hunt for game down by the river with my NVD attached to the rifle. Once again, the distinctive thumping of approaching rotors could be heard in the distance. I took cover just as the helicopter hovered slowly along the river a couple hundred yards upstream. Through my unassisted eye, there was no indication the helicopter was nearby except for the obvious noise. Only through the assistance of my NVD could I see the flying machine. The pilot's instruments were set for night vision, so I could easily spot their glow illuminating the cockpit with IR, revealing two pilots. I had previously turned off my own NVD IR illuminator and concealed it with electrical tape, just in case. Sure enough, a giant IR spot beam was slewing along the river as the helicopter slowly hovered in my direction.

I dipped farther back into the tree line, careful to make no sudden movements, as the human eye is a big fan of movement and contrast. My blood was pumping adrenaline and the slight pain in my calf disappeared. Just as soon as I saw two people rappel from the chopper down into the shallow banks of the river, I began to back away and run up the hill to the cabin, hoping my leg would hold out.

Back at the cabin, I shouldered my go bag and ripped the floor rug aside. I was especially interested in the two loose boards there. I wedged them out with my knife and pulled my suppressed LaRue M4 short-barreled rifle (SBR) out from under the cabin. It was still sealed up in its Pelican case, which itself was loaded with full magazines and an extra bolt carrier assembly.

I then filled my thermos with hot stew and tossed everything else I could think of into an empty rice sack. I was out the door in only three minutes.

Outside, I dragged the cooler out from under the cabin and pulled it behind me as more adrenaline pushed my injured body up the mountain. My kit was beating me about the back and chest as I climbed.

I hid the cooler three hundred meters up the mountain. I then moved the NVD from my bolt gun to my M4 behind the red dot in order to provide me night vision combined with 30 rounds of full-auto capability if the need should arise. I also thought now might be the time to put on my load bearing vest full of mags, and after that, slung my SBR across my chest, caching the rest of my kit twenty paces north of the venison cooler inside a hollowed out oak.

As I began to finally calm down, the pang of pain in my calf returned, warning me not to overdo it out here in the darkness.

I began a slow and deliberate arc back down the mountain to set up observation on my cabin. There's no way those helicopter goons wouldn't find it, and they more than likely knew where it was already considering where the chopper dropped them.

It was only two guys.

With guns. But I was ready for them.

SPY VS SPY

Morning

I was sore from sitting up in a deer stand all night, one that was overlooking the cabin. Up in the hills with a line of sight down on its west wall, the back. There are no windows on that side, but good concealment, so I took that trade-off. At about 0900, I took my last swallow of warm venison stew from my thermos and continued to glass the hollow.

Glint.

I noticed a brief but distinct flash through my binoculars and saw a masked figure talking on a radio of some sort. He was beyond the cabin, down the hill a ways. No, not a radio; the large antenna boom hanging off the device indicated a satellite phone.

Reaching up with my left hand, I made sure the can on the end of my M4 was hand-tightened. I drew my legs up closer to my chest and sat in the tree, using my knees as support for the rifle. I kept the red dot trained on his center mass and tracked him as he crept. As soon as he was close enough to the cabin's clearing, he got on his chest and began to low crawl until he reached the very edge of the cabin's cleared area.

I hoped my binoculars had better magnification than his.

I watched him as he pulled his own binos out and began to reconnoiter the cabin. I should have brought my bolt gun; I could have taken this fucker out without his partner even knowing. The M4 was loud, even with a silencer, but it had a higher rate of fire. I couldn't risk taking out this guy now, as I had no idea where the other one was hiding. If it were me, I'd be right up here somewhere, keeping an eye on my partner.

He could very well be just a few trees over.

Some time passed. The guy watching the cabin never moved from his spot. Just lay there on his chest with the binos glued to his masked face.

The problem was that I needed to get out of the deer stand, and he was waiting for me to appear so he could pop me in the face with the rifle I saw sitting to his right.

By noon, I couldn't feel my legs, besides the pang in my calf. This sensation was slowly moving up my body. I needed to at least stand up, but couldn't.

My window of opportunity suddenly came.

Inexplicably, the man began to crawl backwards, retreating into the trees beyond the cabin clearing. I waited a full ten minutes before I carefully started my descent, wincing all the way. I had to watch where my feet landed on the rungs of the ladder; I couldn't feel them at all. Most of the trip down was upper body. When I made it to the ground, I had to hold the trunk of the tree to keep from falling. I did a few painful squats behind the tree to get the blood flowing again and took a long-awaited head call.

There were two shooters out here, and they weren't rookies. They were patient, or at least one of them was.

I quietly fell back to my cache location and picked up my bolt gun. Yeah, it was extra weight, but I needed to put those .300 Blackout subsonics to work on this hit squad or they'd be bringing my corpse back to be put on parade.

What kind of motherfuckers lay in ambush for other Americans? I mean, what would the job application questionnaire sound like? "Are you willing to extrajudicially kill people? Yes? You're hired! Welcome to the goon squad."

Back on topic.

After gathering my bolt gun as well as some Power Bars and water from my emergency bag, I started back towards the cabin, M4 at the high ready.

Staying slow and low was the key to not being detected by the most advanced sensor every created, the human eye. It was painstaking to move like that, but the alternative to a sore back is getting filled in by shooters you've never met.

I rounded the final bend in the trail as the cabin came into view. I set up a shooting point prone, piling leaves underneath me so I didn't freeze to death waiting on my targets.

I lay in wait for an hour until one of the bastards walked out of the woods ten feet in front of me.

He squinted as his brain told him there was a shape in front of him that was abnormal. Not organic.

I raised the rifle; he was too close for the optic I had set at nine power, so I pointed it in his general direction.

"Listen buddy," I said in a stern whisper, "unless you want to die right now, you better start fucking talking."

His response was a little unexpected.

The man pulled a large tiger-striped fixed blade knife from the small of his back and charged. Rage filled his eyes as he sprinted to me.

I pulled the trigger.

The silenced round cracked from the bolt gun barrel like a microwave popcorn kernel and slammed into the man's ribcage.

What did he do?

Remarkably, he stumbled but kept coming.

I didn't have time to chamber another round in the bolt gun, so I went for the Glock. As I rose the blaster to fire, the man grabbed my hand, pulling me fast into his blade. I grabbed his wrist and rotated it out and away from his body, causing him to lean back over the alternative of losing his knife.

Somehow, he caused me to drop my pistol in all the commotion.

I reached down into the small of my back and pulled out the knife I'd liberated last year from that psychopathic biker.

Our knives were out in front of us as we rounded the fight circle. Two weapons from more uncivilized times stood between us, his dark and subdued, and mine gleaming, stainless.

One of us wasn't getting off the mountain alive.

He came at me first in a downward horror-movie-killer thrust. I blocked his initial attack and punched him hard in the ribs where I shot him. He winced in agony and grabbed his wound.

Seeing opportunity, I rammed the Bowie through his mask, up into his chin and through the top of his mouth.

His lights stayed on for a good bit. I stared him down as he died, hoping he remembered my face on the way to hell.

I then searched for my pistol in the bushes, securing it before dragging the corpse off into the woods. Safer behind the cover of the foliage, I wanted to search the body to see if he had anything that would get me out of this shitstorm.

But first things first. Inside the dense brush, I kept an ear open for his partner. The only shot fired was quiet, near impossible to triangulate; I was confident that wouldn't bring attention, but not too certain, either.

After thirty minutes of hearing only the wind and falling leaves, I figured it was okay to get started.

I ripped the mask from the corpse. No one I knew. Just a face without a name. No ID, big surprise.

I put his carbine aside, an HK416, unsuppressed. He was also carrying an HK USP pistol. Pretty high-quality kit for an innocent helicopter trip and hike through the mountains. This guy was a tier-one goon.

He had a handheld radio tuned to a UHF freq, but I sure as hell wouldn't be going out on it; I knew how mistakes like that ended up.

No codebook or communications plan on him, either. Again, this guy was a professional. All the frequencies I wanted to see were in the man's head, contained in the biological zero and one switches that began to decay the moment I rammed the knife into his brain. I tossed everything useful in the goon's pack, slinging it over my shoulder for later.

███████

Goddamn it. Goddamn it.

I need to gather my thoughts. Why would they do this?

███████

Okay.

I set up observation in a different spot, getting the drop on goon number two, who was looking for goon number one. Except. Well.

I took aim through my bolt gun optics and squeezed the trigger. The target was about two hundred meters from me, so the bullet drop was significant, nearly thirty-five inches. It was also pretty fucking windy. So I missed the head and hit the shoulder, the bullet's kinetic force violently spinning the body around.

The figure let loose with a woman's agonized scream, then reached for a blowout kit and began applying pressure to her shoulder with what I thought was most likely a clotting agent.

"Max! Max, you motherfucker, you shot me, you goddamned bastard!" she screamed out.

I knew in my heart who it was the moment I heard her voice.

My head poked up over the foliage like a prairie dog as I watched the woman hurry to save her own life. She still wore the mask.

"You reach for your gun, *any* gun, and I waste you! Are we clear?!" I shouted back.

She was leaning against a pine tree, one hand applying pressure to her shoulder, and tried to reach up with the other to show that she wasn't armed. I slung my bolt gun and brought my carbine to the ready in front of me as I approached.

She peeled the ski mask over the top of her head, allowing her ponytail to fall on her right shoulder.

Maggie.

My former black-ops teammate out here trying to waste me along with the other goon I put on ice.

I stared at her for a long moment, unwilling to speak, gun trained on the center mass that was rising and falling rapidly from blood loss and adrenaline.

Her big blue eyes stared back at me.

I spoke first. "Why?"

"Be-because they have my daughter." She was turning pale at this point from blood loss and shock.

She took a look at the pack I had on my back that formerly belonged to goon number one.

"Oh, no . . . Max? Did you kill him?" she asked, tears streaming down her face. "Now she's dead. My baby is going to fucking die because of *you*!"

"Sorry for not being more accommodating," I said, unsympathetic. "The way I see it, Maggie, this ends three ways. The first is that I kill you right here on this mountain. The second is I let the mountain kill you. The third is that I save your traitorous ass and you answer my questions."

She just sat there against that pine tree, defeated and out of options. I knew in my heart that if the gun was in the other hand, I'd get no such quarter; my body would be cooling to outside air temperature right about now.

I didn't speak for a while, letting her chew on what we both knew was inevitable. Without medical attention, in another hour, she'd be gone anyway.

Finally she spoke. "Okay, Max," she muttered, nearly unconscious.

I cached her weapons behind a nearby tree and frisked her for concealed knives, guns, sharp sticks, or poison lipstick before fireman carrying her murderous ass and her kit up the mountain back to the cabin.

SISTER IN ARMS

I put Maggie on the cabin table and dumped both of the goon back-packs out on my bed. To be clear, Maggie is blood type B+. I know this because I'm also B+ and wouldn't have even been assigned to Maggie in the first place if I wasn't compatible. As an added mea-sure of survivability, they wanted people like us to be able to give each other blood if the need should arise, like now.

I quickly pulled the direct transfusion kit out of its sealed pack and began prepping Maggie to receive my blood. The kit was idiot-proof and the instructions were printed (with pictures) on the anti-coagulant blood bag. I connected the lines and watched my blood stream into Maggie's unconscious body. At resting heart rate, it wouldn't take too long before I'd have to disconnect the line and tape over the holes in our arms. I didn't want to give her too much. As the blood flowed, I tended to her shoulder. The 208-grain sub-sonic bullet didn't tumble, but passed clean through.

Easy day.

I pulled the clotting agent–infused bandages off her wound and cleaned it out with a squeeze bottle of saline from the goon packs. After verifying that the bleeding had stopped, I began to sew her up with her own trauma kit. She moaned and jerked a couple times during the procedure, but didn't wake up. I wasn't sure quite how long it had been, but sometime after I finished with her wound, I started getting dizzy, so I disconnected the transfusion line and let the blood bag continue to pump into her arm.

Her deceased companion had a few packets of electrolyte drink powder in his kit, so I mixed up the recommended ratio for thirty-two ounces and guzzled about a third of it down. I was still feeling a little dizzy, so I decided to tie Maggie securely to the table in case I passed out.

After about an hour, I started feeling a little better, but wanted to hedge my bets here. I continued to take on fluids and eat from the goons' stash of food to get some strength back. Maggie's color looked somewhat better by now, but she was still passed out and breathing deeply.

I took this time to reorganize my kit, taking what I needed from Maggie's and her assassin buddy's and integrating it into my own.

She's still asleep as I write this, and if she doesn't wake up soon, I'm leaving her here.

30 Nov

Maggie woke up after twelve hours of unconsciousness and asked for water.

I mixed up another batch of electrolyte and sugar water and brought it up to her dry lips.

"Thanks," she said in a raspy voice after taking a few gulps.

"Listen, I know you're fucking shot, tired, and weak, but I don't give a fuck. Start talking," I said.

"No grand tour of Shady Rest?" Maggie replied.

My heart skipped a beat and I felt anger flash across my face; only me, Dad, and Rich knew the name of the cabin.

And Dad was dead.

"What the fuck did you do to him, Maggie?!" I barked.

Maggie took a deep breath and began to speak, "I didn't do a damn thing to him. They brought him in, and now he's being held at a multi-agency intel fusion center for questioning."

"Where is it?" I said, reaching for the map of Arkansas that hung on the wall above the table.

No response.

"Fine, maybe I'll just do to you what your buddies did to Rich to get him to talk," I said.

I dug my thumbs into Maggie's shoulder. Yes, I realized what I was doing, but this was also the person who trained me.

She winced and cried out in agony, but didn't give up Rich's location.

"You know that's not going to work. We've both been through the same shit," she said through clenched teeth.

"Okay, we'll play it that way. When does your ride return for extract?"

No reply. I resisted the temptation to go any further. I wouldn't get anything from her no matter what I did to her physically . . . but her mind might be different.

"Maggie. If you ever want a chance at seeing your daughter again, you'll tell me when that goddamn helicopter comes back."

———

01 Dec
Night

The helo touches down in one hour. I'm dressed like goon number one, and he's dressed like me, only dead. I've got Maggie zip-tied to a tree. I plan to cut her loose when I hear rotors. She tries anything, and she knows I'll fucking blast her and the helo out of the sky without hesitation. With any luck, we'll fool the pilots into thinking the hit went off without a hitch.

Maggie finally talked. She's not a stupid person, after all.

My heart raced as the rotor noise got steadily louder. I cut Maggie's zip cuff, checking for spares in my pocket as I did so.

I waited for an eternity for the rotor wash to knock leaves and dead branches down on the river bank. It was pitch black outside, but I was on my NVD, my retinas bathed in the green light of distant stars. The tips of the helicopter's rotors glowed, forming a flickering, violent circle of light above my head.

I watched Maggie as she broke an IR chem light and waved it at the pilots before dropping it onto the rocky river bank. It was too late to whisper threats in her ear; she was either going to do what I told her to do, or she wasn't. Her mouth was taped up under the mask and her injury was in a sling, giving her only one arm to work with. All of her guns and knives were in the bottom of my pack, but I let her sling an empty HK416 over her back for visual effect.

The helicopter hovered a little lower. I approached first with the goon corpse in a fireman carry. The injury from the cat sent a pang up my leg, but I didn't dare show it.

The green glow of artificial eyes were watching as I loaded the corpse into the open helicopter door. The co-pilot watched me place the body as I tried not to appear that I was keeping an eye on Maggie. I then signaled the pilot to hover even lower. The ground was uneven so he couldn't set down, but he complied and the copter lurched down a foot, nearly touching skids to the rocky shore.

I nodded for Maggie to get inside and she did so.

I jumped in after her, feeling the thick zip cuff in my cargo pocket to ensure it was still there.

This was about to go down.

I positioned the corpse between Maggie and myself, bolted it into the airframe with a d-ring, and nonchalantly zip-tied the wrist of the dead man to Maggie's good arm. I then pointed at her and gave the universal signal of a finger across the throat, which in this case meant *If you try anything, I'm kicking you and the stiff out the motherfucking door.*

She nodded.

The co-pilot shoved a green David Clark headset between the seats at me. I had to think fast.

I signaled to the co-pilot that my ears were shot from gunfire, hoping he'd understand the lie I was trying to convey.

Maggie revealed earlier, before we left the cabin, that the pilots didn't know the stiff. He was a contract killer.

The co-pilot stared at me for a few awkward seconds before nodding and returning to the helicopter controls.

The helicopter engines increased RPMs. I could barely make out the wet compass above the cockpit glass. We seemed to be headed west. The digital airspeed indicator read triple digits, probably somewhere in the neighborhood of a hundred and twenty knots. Calculating that airspeed, I had about an hour until the chopper would be circling to land.

Maggie told me earlier where the makeshift intel fusion center was located. Where they were keeping Rich.

Bentonville, Arkansas.

The feds took over the headquarters for what used to be the largest retail chain in the United States and plugged a bunch of industrial generators into the local grid and somehow got some satcom up and other infrastructure up and running. The massive complex was a regional hub of operations for what was becoming the new post-collapse government.

Here was the rub: I couldn't just sit and wait for this no-shit-black helicopter to land on the roof of the fusion center with a zip-tied, compromised CIA operative traitor and the wrong dead body onboard.

I pulled Maggie's NVD off her head, effectively blinding her in the darkness. I then stuffed the device in the top of my pack and latched it to the airframe. Things were about to go one of two conceivable ways.

My heart thumped as I waited for the right time. It had been about forty minutes since we took off, but I could see a pinpoint of artificial light getting brighter on the horizon. The grid was still down, so I had a feeling we were quickly closing the distance to the fusion center. I eased up to the space just behind the cockpit and checked the wet compass.

272.

I tried the direct approach. I tapped the co-pilot on the shoulder and screamed at him over the engine noise.

"Turn left, two three zero!"

Both the co-pilot and pilot cocked their heads simultaneously, like confused dogs. The pilot shook his head and pointed at the light on the horizon. He then pointed at his watch hand and gave me the signal of five minutes.

I tapped the co-pilot on the shoulder again, this time putting the tip of my silenced rifle against his temple.

"*Turn left, two three zero!*" I screamed again, fighting the noise.

The co-pilot jumped and reached for something on the right side of his seat. Not wanting the pilot to crash, I waited until I saw the MP5K before pulling the trigger on my rifle, blasting the co-pilot through his helmet. I noticed the small hole appear through the windscreen in front of the co-pilot at about the same time I saw the blood splatter.

The helicopter jerked and lurched left, pinning me against the side. I could see the treetops below getting bigger.

Maggie fell out.

I thought I was going to die. We were moving at over a hundred knots and were probably a couple hundred feet off the ground. There would be no surviving that.

I held on for dear life, trying to keep the muzzle of my rifle pointed in the general direction of the cockpit.

The helicopter leveled out.

The pilot looked back at me and was met with the same view the co-pilot had moments before.

"*Two two five, now!*" I yelled.

I could hear very faint screams, but dismissed it as the good ole' PTSD talking.

The helicopter turned to the left and the wet compass heading bug settled on 225.

I hit start on my watch chronometer and waited, gun trained on the pilot. As the aircraft headed in the general direction of Fayetteville, I made final preparations.

I reached forward and took the MP5K from the co-pilot; he wouldn't be needing it anymore. I grabbed his two spare mags still full of 9mm rounds and stuffed everything in my pack.

Faint screams again.

I leaned outside the helicopter and saw Maggie hanging there, her hand still attached to the corpse, which was also still attached to the helicopter. After strapping myself into the airframe, I pulled her sorry ass back inside and sat her back down in the seat. She immediately tried to deck me, but forgot her good hand was still attached to the corpse. Blood trailed down her wrist from where the zip tie had cut into her skin. Good.

I caught the pilot looking back anxiously and came to the realization that he was talking on the fucking radio.

I jumped back to the cockpit, communicating to him that he better swing that boom mic off his lips or he'd never leave the aircraft alive. He was scared. I could smell urine and didn't know if it was him or the dead co-pilot. I ordered him to shut down his transponder and all modes and codes as well as his radio, TACAN, and all other navigation. He quickly and efficiently complied. Screens went dark and needles died and disappeared. The fusion center's artificial light was on the right side of the helicopter and getting smaller. I couldn't make out the interstate below. Too much overcast, so I was going completely off of airspeed and time.

"Set her down," I commanded.

The pilot began making engine control, cyclic, and collective adjustments and we began to slow down and descend. Now low enough to see some details, I noticed that we missed a suitable grass field, so I pointed over to a clear spot a few hundred meters away, gesturing the pilot to land there. He was so terrified by now that he'd have probably set it down in the trees if I hadn't said anything.

As the helo hovered over the field and began to land, I grabbed my loaded-down pack and waited just behind the cockpit. Just as soon as I felt the chopper touch down, I hit the cockpit with a three round burst, destroying the radios and navigation equipment. Sparks flew everywhere and a small electrical fire began to smolder under the dash. I pointed my gun at the pilot and gestured for him to take his NVD off, shut down the aircraft, and get out. I followed him with my muzzle, making sure he wasn't about to pull an MP5 out of his ass. He stepped out of the portside door onto the thick grassy ground, and then I told him run. He stood there for a moment, probably in shock, so I shot the ground at his feet to help him along. He took off into the darkness.

The rotor began to slow to a point where I began to finally hear myself think. I watched the pilot through my NVD as he stumbled through the weeds off into the distance. Satisfied he wouldn't be back anytime soon, I then approached Maggie.

"Okay, this is how it's going to play out. If I ever see your ass again, I'm going to kill you. I'm not going to talk. I'm not going to reason. I'll just pull the trigger and end you. Do you understand?"

She looked at me and nodded.

"Good. I'm going to cut you loose. Here's a bottle of water. The helicopter med kit is on the bulkhead near the cockpit. Don't follow me. Remember what I said."

I cut her zip tie and disappeared into the tree line moving south and west.

NWA

I moved hours through the fields, forests, and backyards of northwest Arkansas. It took me a good while to figure out where exactly I was. The first thing I did was find a place to recombobulate. I knew it was a mistake not killing Maggie, but now we were even. She saved my life a while back by telling me to head for the hills and stack it deep, so that was my way of paying her back. That's the way I rationalize it, anyway. My brain was telling me to end her, but my heart was telling me to let her live.

No more of that.

I came across an old tin roof chicken house that seemed abandoned. It was starting to sprinkle and the sky would open up at any moment, so I cautiously approached. Before entering, I covered my nose and mouth with my sleeve to weaken the stench. The smell was overwhelming; I knew what to expect when I found the door and quietly entered.

The place was a chicken tomb. I found a corner with the least amount of dead chickens and started to reorganize my kit. As much as I'd have liked to, I couldn't carry all the guns captured over the past few days. The HK416 was nice, but it was a heavy bastard, probably a pound or two more than my silenced direct-impingement M4 that I now had strapped to the side of my pack.

I loosened the drawstring on the top of my pack and reached inside, pulling out the co-pilot's MP5K along with two full mags of 9mm, not including the one in the gun. I tugged on the side folding stock, allowing it to fold out and snap into place. I pulled the bolt back and locked it to the rear. Confirmed that the chamber was empty. No way the co-pilot could have gotten the drop on me without one in the hole. I performed a quick HK slap, sending the bolt home and loading a 9mm round into the chamber. These old roller lock guns were just badass.

I placed it on safe, folded the stock, and slung the single point sling over my chest, allowing it to sit just above my hip. I'd keep the HK on my body for quick response and the M4 strapped to my pack if I needed to reach out a little farther than the 9mm could.

After reorganizing my pack, I made camp in the chicken house, getting used to the smell before catching a little shut-eye to the sounds of cold rain hitting the metal roof. As I drifted off to sleep, I thought about Rich and Jim and hoped to hell they'd be all right.

The morning sun was beaming through the large fan inlet of the chicken house onto my face when I woke. I downed a bottle of water and shoved the empty into a side pocket on my pack. All in all, I only had six bottles of water and about a dozen energy bars that I'd acquired from Maggie and her partner. That was enough to get me to Black Oak, to the buried storm shelter I had there. Hopefully Jim hadn't eaten everything.

Well, that's not what I was really hoping. More than anything, who knew if I would find a smoking hole in the ground where one of those drones had dropped a few laser guided five hundred pounders. Easier to think about Jim eating all my food, though. Yeah, I'll just go with that.

I stood up and adjusted my pack straps and headed out the door toward the road. I walked slow, keeping to cover until I reached it. I was probably about ten miles from the helicopter, well within a search area, so I knew I had to be careful. I also knew that my photo was probably in the possession of every federal law enforcement officer in the region. Thinking of that made me adjust the brim of my ball cap a little lower.

Once I reached the road, I began to feel too exposed. I walked on the side and still felt uneasy from the openness, so I moved to the ditch, eventually deciding to hop back over the barbed wire fence and just stay in the field and follow the road from there. It began to cloud up at about mid-morning, which was a good thing if you worried about drones.

I certainly did.

The MP5K hung under my arm just above my belt. Its weight was comforting, as was my M4 carbine strapped to my pack. I thought about this for a moment. Civilian ownership of firearms was made illegal months before. The first hungry civilian that saw the outline of a rifle on my pack would immediately rat me out to the authorities; I'd be targeted and they'd be rewarded.

Cursing, I pulled the rain cover and concealed my entire pack from view. This would make things slower if I needed to go for the M4, but at least the HK would be fast and accessible. I decided to put it under my Carhartt and go concealed-carry with the sub gun, too. Desperate times.

I pulled my binos up to check the sign up ahead that read ELKINS 10.

I'd be there by nightfall if I hurried. I still had most of Wesley to get through before then.

███████

I trekked through dense growth alongside the road for miles, not hearing an engine. It was well past noon and I hadn't eaten. My belt was already a couple notches smaller since I was tuned up by that mountain lion; my stomach felt as if it was consuming itself. I kept moving.

Rounding the bend on the road to Elkins, I heard voices. Now in familiar territory, I knew that there was a bridge up ahead that was pretty long, considering backwoods standards. I remembered the bridge from years back, but didn't come out this way often and even when I did, it was in passing at fifty miles per hour in my truck. I decided to cross the road now, as the other side had a hill and denser foliage.

Finally around the corner, I could see the bridge and the checkpoint that was set up on my side. I sat and watched, not wanting to get into another goddamned conflict. I just wanted safe passage.

Making decisions on an empty stomach was bad, so I tore into one of my few remaining energy bars and downed it along with a half bottle of water.

I pulled my binos and glassed the checkpoint, taking note of who was down there, how they were armed, and with what. There was one guy dressed in military fatigues carrying what looked like an M16. I obviously couldn't see the selector switch from that far away, but it didn't matter. The other three men carried pistols on their hips, but one of them also carried a longbow. Not a compound bow, but an honest-to-goodness British-style longbow. Not high tech or modern, but it could still put the hurt on you from farther away than one might imagine.

The water was high and very cold, making expedient crossing on foot without the bridge a no-go. I could try to head up- or downstream to see if there was another way across, but the very presence of the checkpoint told me that these men had the monopoly on river crossing for what was probably miles in both directions. I couldn't stay here forever, and this bridge stood between Elkins and me, and Elkins was what separated my cousin Jim and me in Black Oak.

I decided the best course of action was to just ask, so I did.

I tightened my pack straps and headed back down to the road. I made sure the MP5K was chambered and that the safety was off. Back on pavement, I walked around the bend in clear view of the checkpoint and waved my arms. The guy with the M16 screamed for me to freeze, so I complied. I couldn't hear what the M16 guy was saying to his buddy, but it looked liked he was sending him to me.

My heart rate increased steadily as the man approached. When he got to within fifty yards he drew his handgun, but kept it low. I raised my hands but kept them at chest level. If this guy was even halfway good with a pistol, I'd be dead before I could pull the sub gun from under my coat. Calculated risk.

You should have just sniped them from the hill, I told myself.

No. You're not a fucking murderer.

The man stopped at about ten yards. "State your business, stranger," he said firmly.

"Just want to cross the bridge; my family is somewhere on the other side," I responded.

"You armed?"

"Yeah."

"What else you got in there?"

"Listen, this ain't worth my trouble. I'll just find another way across," I said to the bridge troll.

"Well, this is the only way across for ten miles on either side. We ain't shakin' people down, mister, but the Feds have been creeping into this territory looking for people. We're runnin' low on ammunition. Pretty soon, they'll be able to just walk across the bridge without any thought of us shootin' back."

"I hear what you're saying, but can we make a deal here, or do I need to talk to the guy with the M16?" I said.

"No, I'm his right hand. I can speak for the group. What are you offerin'?"

"The best I can do is a half a mag of 5.56 for your boss's rifle in exchange for safe passage."

I left a little negotiating room just in case they demanded a full mag, but if they wanted more or if they tried anything stupid, I'd dump everything I had into them and leave them bleeding out as I walked over their bodies to the other side.

The man looked at me for a long while before replying.

"Okay, you got yourself a deal. Put the ammo in your ball cap and approach the checkpoint. Don't have anything in your hands except the hat with the ammo, you got it?

"Okay," I said flatly.

I quickly removed the rain cover, grabbed a full mag, and began thumbing rounds into my ball cap.

Sixteen, just to leave no doubt.

I got situated and approached the checkpoint slowly and deliberately, keeping the man ten yards ahead of me. I kept the ball cap with the ammo in my left hand, just in case I needed to reach for the sub gun.

As I approached, guns left holsters and the boss's M16 was brought up into high ready.

I stopped.

"Hey, I mean you no harm. An agreement was made with your guy here. I just want to cross," I said.

"He's right. We have a deal," the right-hand man added.

The boss signaled for the others to holster their guns, but he kept his own rifle high. I began to move again.

At the checkpoint, I approached the man with the M16 and said, "Here's your half a mag of 5.56, as agreed; now please let me pass."

The bossman approached slowly and looked me in the eyes; his facial expressions immediately revealed recognition. He didn't have to say a damn word. He looked down into my hat and grabbed the ammunition, and then quickly pulled the magazine from his M16, frantically feeding rounds into it.

He was empty the whole time.

I walked past him with my hands still open and continued across the bridge, walking backwards with my eyes on the M16. He slammed the mag into the gun and racked the bolt back, feeding a round into the chamber.

I jogged backwards and pulled the MP5K, nearly falling on my ass from the weight of the backpack and the awkwardness of trying to run backwards with it.

"Don't fucking try it!" I screamed.

The bossman raised his weapon at me as I unfolded the stock on my sub gun. I took aim through the diopter sight and squeezed the trigger, tagging the man in the shoulder. My ears rang, but I could somehow hear his M16 clank against the concrete at his feet and the thud of his body as he hit the ground, screaming in agony. I turned and ran across the bridge, noticing the road spikes on the other side. Guess they didn't have enough people to staff both ends of their checkpoint.

Oddly, I didn't hear any pistol fire coming at me, and I was about to turn to see what was going on when it nearly knocked me off my feet.

THWAP! was the sound I heard as the arrow hit my pack. The impact caused me to stagger for a few steps before I finally realized what happened. I kept moving, not wanting to find out the firing rate of the man's longbow. A hundred yards past the other side of the bridge, I broke off into the woods, sixteen rounds of 5.56 and one round of 9mm poorer.

Safe inside the cover of thick Arkansas pines and oaks, I dropped my pack to see what happened. The arrow impacted fairly hard, hitting the stock and buffer tube of my M4. Aside from some cosmetic damage to the polymer stock and a small dent in the aluminum buffer tube, all was good. The gun was still functional, but I had a nice hole in my rain cover. Fuckers.

I didn't kill anyone today, and I made it across the bridge without shooting all my ammo. In hindsight, I think I should have smoked them from the hilltop, but luck was on my side for the time being.

———

After sorting out the arrow situation, I referenced my compass and kept moving through the thick foliage and thorns common in these parts. After half an hour or so, I hit an opening in the dense growth and spilled out onto what I was pretty sure was Highway 16. The road was clear going in both directions, giving me time to make the choice.

Do I go west past Pizza Junction to Shoffner's Corner in order to get home, or east through Elkins and Sulphur City? West put me closer to Fayetteville than I'd liked, but East was a bit farther.

Reluctantly, I tightened my pack straps and moved east in the direction of Elkins, a place I knew well ten years ago. Highway 16 was dotted with vast fields, farms, and the occasional home that butted right up to the road, built in the days that horses pulled carriages.

It was close to sunset when I came upon Elkins High School on my right.

The place looked as if it had been shut down for years. Grass grew tall up between the cracks in the sidewalk, and three startled deer jumped and sprinted away from me past the entrance to the hangar-shaped gymnasium. There was no sign of anyone on the campus and I needed a place to bed down for the night. I followed the direction the deer sprinted through the overgrown courtyard that once bustled with students moving back and forth between buildings. The school looked like a large hotel from here, with the doors to the classrooms facing me from both sides. I saw one of the whitetails jump a low chain link fence up ahead, so I kept moving in that general direction. With half the row of classroom doors behind me, I closed the distance to get to the field ahead. I could now see the goal posts and scoreboard being overtaken by mold and other signs of neglect.

Shattering glass behind me caused me to dive for the dirt. I concentrated, listening for any other signs of movement. I heard more rustling around coming from inside one of the classrooms I'd just passed. I parted the grass in front of me, providing a better view of the doors.

I sat there, watching, waiting, until a bear cub came stumbling out of one of the open classroom doors. I froze in terror, realizing that I only had the HK 9mm readily accessible, and that my M4 would cost me time and noise to retrieve. I slowly reached for the HK and gripped it tightly as another cub stepped out of the classroom and into the muddy courtyard. Apparently all those stories about bears sleeping the whole winter are bullshit.

I froze, staying to gauge the wind direction from the way the tall reeds of grass were swaying.

The classroom doorway darkened halfway just before Mama Bear came walking out. Just as soon as she stepped into the courtyard, she craned her massive head upward and began to sniff. She tensed, swiveling hear head from side to side, scanning her surroundings.

She looked right at me for a moment, prompting immediate flashbacks of wrestling the mountain lion. I didn't move a follicle and just averted my eyes away from hers.

She growled.

I was about to get up and start sprinting for my life just before I saw her swat one of her cub's on its hind end, prompting it to get back inside the classroom. The second cub followed its sibling and Mama Bear followed them both back inside.

Maybe it was the deer smell that woke them up, or maybe it was me. Either way, I decided to take the long way around on my way back to the gymnasium. There was nowhere to run or climb in this little kill box the bears called home. I crawled for fifty feet or so before I had the balls to get up and crouch to the field where the deer escaped.

The field was in pretty bad shape. Only the bleachers, goal posts, and scoreboard signified that football used to be played here. The derelict scoreboard indicated that the Elks were losing 13–21. I walked around the perimeter and under the bleachers, finding nothing that I could use. As the sun dipped below the trees, I pulled out my NVD and climbed to the top of the bleachers. With the MP5K still slung across my chest, I fished the M4 out of my bag, checking the silencer to make sure it was still securely attached.

I waited. The cold aluminum sapped the heat from my body and I began to shiver. I sat on my pack for a while and just kept my eyes trained on the football field through the NVD. After about an hour, I could see the eyes of a rabbit moving through the grass. I brought my M4 up and adjusted the red dot to the lowest setting. The green dot hovered over the rabbit's head. I took a deep breath and exhaled.

Squeezing the trigger, the round thumped from my suppressed carbine and the supersonic crack of the 5.56 bullet followed. The rabbit spun before hitting the ground. I rushed down the bleachers, trying not to fall, as my legs were frozen and numb. Jumping the bottom handrail, I landed in the grass and ran to the rabbit, hoping it was dead. The pain in my leg was barely present, just enough to remind me of the traumatic hand-to-paw bout with the mountain lion.

As I approached the rabbit, I could see that the shot was a clean kill and I was thankful that I didn't have to take a deer instead. It would have been pretty damn wasteful, as I'd have to leave most of it here. I'd have probably dragged it near Mama Bear's den, but still, the rabbit made more sense and I was lucky to have it. I took it by the ears, grabbed my kit, and headed back to the gym, again taking the long way around, as I had no desire to confront an Arkansas black bear at night protecting her cubs.

I cautiously approached the Elkins High School gymnasium. There was no sign of anyone around me, but I could see a faint flickering light far across the road opposite the high school on the elementary school side. It couldn't be brighter than a candle, and was invisible to the night-adjusted naked eye. I checked my light discipline to make sure I didn't have a flashlight on anywhere and crossed the gravel walkway to the front of the gym. The doors were chained shut and the glass was still intact, even though it looked like someone tried to work it over with a baseball bat at the glass panel just to the right of the door. I had three padlock shims in my pack, so I fished around for those for a few minutes until I found them.

"Work the lock," I whispered to myself, hoping that twin Doberman pinschers wouldn't appear out of nowhere. I must have been getting rusty, because the huge brass lock that held the chains around the door handles wasn't going to give in for me tonight. Defeated, I shoved the shims back into my pack and looked for another way inside.

I walked around the parking lot side of the gym, keeping an eye on the flickering light in the window of the elementary school three hundred yards away across the street. I reached the back of the gym and navigated through a maze of old school bus tires and dilapidated gym equipment. Approaching the back door, I turned the knob. Locked. So again I reached into my pack for the lockpick set. I'd long ago replaced some of the raking tools with modified hacksaw blades. Very few original picks remained. After a few minutes of raking the lock, I got frustrated and tried a couple of bump keys, and was finally able to gain entry. Glad the lock was older than I was, as the newer ones could not be bumped.

I slowly entered, listening for any signs of life, human or otherwise. A twig snapped somewhere outside, causing me to involuntarily close the door and lock it behind me. I was committed.

I stepped through some curtains and stage props before climbing a short set of stairs that spilled out onto a small wooden stage. I scanned the dark gym through my NVD, looking for threats, before stepping off the stage onto the basketball court. Championship banners circled the gymnasium's high walls, some ancient, some more recent. As I followed them around the perimeter, I saw the mascot, a massive stuffed elk's head. It seemed to look majestically down onto the bleachers, as if deciding whether or not the fans were worthy enough to watch. I didn't like it; the eyes appeared black through my NVD and seemed to follow me around the gym. I climbed up the steps to the bleachers, noting that they were old and made of wood instead of the more modern aluminum design. With no signs of anything amiss, I did a perimeter sweep of the rest of the gym.

My final stop was the coaches' office. I pulled the glass door open and went inside, out of the laserlike gaze of the stuffed elk's head.

I clicked on my flashlight and raised the NVD off my eye. The office had been hastily ransacked. The small refrigerator door was open, the insides gutted of anything useful. Photos of wives and children hung on the walls above the desks; a banner hung behind the desk in the back that read "Whatever It Takes." A coatrack in the back concealed another door that led to a staircase. I went inside the small landing and followed the wooden steps up.

Rounding the corner at the top of the stairs, I came out inside a bonus room–type space equipped with desks arranged neatly in rows and a foosball table sitting crooked in the back in front of another door. I approached the teacher's desk in the front of the classroom and flipped through the papers.

I WILL NOT TALK IN STUDY HALL WITHOUT PERMISSION.

This was written hundreds of times over several sheets of paper in different handwritings.

Study hall.

I checked the door behind the foosball table. It was unlocked and led out onto a fire escape that overlooked the courtyard between ground level classrooms. The ladder was retracted and secured with a flimsy plastic tamper seal. I wouldn't be using it, as it led down to the ground and not very far from where Mama Bear and her cubs were hanging out for the winter.

As I came back inside, I noticed a cooler sitting under the foosball table. I prayed for warm beer or maybe some soda, but what I found was three full plastic bottles of water with mold growing on the outside.

A whole lot better than nothing.

I decided to make camp in the study hall for the night, so I unpacked my sleeping bag and made a place to sleep, and then brought out my mess kit to prepare tonight's rabbit stew. The rabbit didn't have a lot of meat on its bones, but it was all I had.

After lighting a few candles from my pack, I dumped the tin of number two pencils out onto the teacher's desk and wiped it out with minimal water. I then filled it up halfway and placed it just over my large can of Sterno fuel using some old books to hold up the corners. I dressed the rabbit quickly and knew that adding the brains and eyeballs to my stew was the best survival option, but I wasn't quite there yet. I'd save the bugs, brains, and other disgusting shit for when my little cabin gut was gone. No need to get all reality TV just yet.

Piece by piece, I lowered the rabbit meat into the boiling water and then tossed a quarter of a peanut butter energy bar into the mix for a little sugar flavoring. I watched the bar melt and swirl around in my tiny cauldron and set my watch timer for twenty minutes.

━━━━

I have to say that the rabbit stew was superb. I ate everything in the tin and drank the energy bar broth, trying to ignore the number two pencil seasoning. I normally didn't mind sleeping in weird places like this, but there was just something unsettling about the upstairs gym classroom and the crazy elk's head.

I tossed the guts and bones off the fire escape platform into the courtyard below. Maybe the cubs would find them tomorrow.

I secured both doors with zip ties and placed some empty soda cans from the trash at the bottom of the stairs. Should get my attention if someone decided to come to study hall tonight.

My next move is simple. Make it to the storm shelter and locate Jim. I should get there by tomorrow night if I leave early enough and don't run into too much trouble. There's one large bridge I'd need to deal with, but what are the odds of another bridge checkpoint armed with a longbow sharpshooter?

Right now, I need to blow out the candles and try to sleep. Tomorrow, I'll see a lot of miles on foot, with too many of them exposed. My gear is disorganized right now, so I'll set my alarm a little early and take care of it in the morning. The full stomach of rabbit stew is starting to make my eyes heavy.

SULPHUR CITY

My watch began to beep at 0430, prompting me to climb out of the warmth of my bag and into the cold folding chair next to the foosball table. As the fog began to drift from my mind, I heard strange noises coming from outside. I grabbed my NVD and stepped out onto the fire escape. The two cubs were wrestling over the scraps I'd tossed down last night. The wind was blowing at me from the direction of the animals, so I knew that they wouldn't notice me up here. Mama Bear was nowhere to be seen, but a part of the courtyard was blocked from my view. It was biting cold outside, so I went back in to layer up and get packed and moving.

It was just before five when I retraced my steps through the gym to the locked back door and out into the parking lot on the opposite side of the gymnasium from the bear den. The faint light I'd seen last night in the window of the elementary school across the road was gone.

I followed Highway 16 south, looking for the Sulphur City Road. I'd have frozen if not for the layers and pace I was moving.

The road was long and relatively straight by Arkansas standards, with access to the woods on both sides; I felt safe walking on the actual road until the sun came up. Here it was dark and quiet, with no signs of life. Not even the chirp of morning birds. I was able to make three miles and be nearly upon my turn before it got too light to risk walking out in the open.

The last half mile was a brutal trek through tall, wet grass, soaking me from the waist down with morning dew until I broke out onto Sulphur City Road. I turned west and made it to the outskirts of Sulphur City by about noon. A barn sat half collapsed just off the road, so I climbed up into the loft and set up an observation point, intending to be here for about an hour before moving into the micro town.

The loft floor creaked; its sounds made me think the whole barn would collapse in on me if I stepped in the wrong spot. This was the highest point that overlooked the only intersection and four-way stop within fifteen miles.

I pulled the binoculars from my pack and glassed the area from the crooked loft window. The intersection had score marks on the concrete where it looked like a vehicle burned up. Panning the binos to the right, I could see an armored vehicle sitting half inside the front of a home just up the road from the intersection. No smoke or movement or sounds were coming from any direction except the dilapidated barn structure I was using. After an hour of seeing nothing out of the ordinary, I climbed back down out of the barn and moved low to the intersection, crossing it carefully and quietly.

The armored vehicle up ahead appeared to be a mine resistant ambush protected (MRAP) carrier. The back end was riddled with armor piercing dents and punctures and explosive damage. One of the tires was bent at an odd angle, indicating that this thing wouldn't drive again without depot-level repairs. As I came around, I could see the side of the vehicle.

"GHT" was all that was visible, with the rest obscured by the house it had crashed into.

#FIGHT

This was one of the ghosts' MRAPs, belonging to someone crucial to the liberation of the detention center at the university. My gut sank and I needed to sit down for a moment. Without the help of those armored rebel vehicles last winter, we'd never have taken the prison. Jim would still be held there as a political prisoner.

I leaned up against the back of the MRAP and took a few deep breaths, trying to suppress the debilitating anger and frustration of the situation.

I ended up opening the back door on the vehicle and was hit by the smell of a corpse. Reluctantly, I climbed up into the derelict armored vehicle, wrapped a bandana around my nose and mouth, and leaned my head into the front area of the MRAP.

It was a ghost. The body wore the familiar clothing, but it was too decomposed to identify. I climbed out of the MRAP and onto the roof of the vehicle.

"B" was spray-painted in bright letters.

Blinky, the bravest of all the ghosts. The one never afraid to put his life on the line for freedom of those around him.

I spent the rest of my daylight hours digging a hero's grave.

04 Dec
Early

I spent the night back in the loft of the partially collapsed barn. There was enough old hay to make it a little softer, but I still had to deal with the cold and the creaking of the old hulk. I barely got any sleep, as the barn seemed to shudder every time a gust of wind blew down the valley. I couldn't build a fire without burning the whole place down, so I had to rely on my sleeping bag to fight off the wind that seemed to find its way through the cracks in the barn walls. After a cold, miserable night, I forced myself up and on my feet, tearing into the last energy bar. I still had some water, likely enough to reach the river that would be raging down the middle of the valley a few miles on the road past Sulphur City.

After packing up, I slipped on my NVD and climbed down the rickety wooden barn ladder to the dirt floor. At the bottom, I felt for my only companion, the MP5K slung across my chest on a single point sling, resting on my right hip. I paid my last respects at Blinky's grave and got moving.

I made good time and was at the quarter mile straight stretch right at sunup. At the last dogleg before the straight stretch, I climbed the nearby hill and stopped for a water break. While finishing up my second-to-last bottle of clean water, I pulled the binoculars and glassed the road ahead. I had a clear view for nearly a half a mile across the flat valley to the next hill.

My heart sank again as I saw another goddamned MRAP on its side just before the bridge. I couldn't see anything else but the bottom of the vehicle. It was a clear morning with no trees between here and the bridge. I'd be out in the open for a few minutes before I could cross the bridge, but I had no choice. I had to see the MRAP; I had to know if another ghost had been assassinated here.

It took an hour to go the distance. I kept hearing faint sounds of engines in the sky and worried that a hellfire would go high order nearby at any moment.

I feared my government.

After killing my back and knees by low crawling or crouching the whole way through the tall grass of the adjacent fields, I was finally near the overturned armored vehicle. I held my breath, rounding the wreckage. As the top came into view, I let out a sigh of relief. No markings on top. Someone besides me had taken out a DHS MRAP.

I scanned the skies again before examining the overturned hulk. Small-arms fire riddled the entire vehicle on every visible side and a large hole ripped through the front end. I pulled out my flashlight and checked the damage. The three-inch diameter hole was coated in a green tarnish around the edges all the way through the vehicle into the cab.

Copper.

Someone had been making explosively formed penetrators.

My design had gotten out there. I'd heard it distributed on the pirate stations in between DHS propaganda interruptions before I'd skinned out and headed for the hills of Newton County.

"Someone hit back, Blinky," I said aloud without even thinking.

I was so enthralled trying to examine what took down the DHS armor that I didn't notice the huge gap in the bridge just up ahead. Leaving the rusting MRAP, I carefully stepped out onto the concrete and steel structure that spanned one of the larger branches of the White River and began to piece together what happened here. The DHS MRAP was probably hauling ass down the quarter mile, like I used to do as a teenager. The driver likely didn't see the hole in the bridge until it was too late. I walked back to the MRAP and, sure enough, faded skid marks on the road where this heavy fucker locked its brakes, screeching to a halt right before someone detonated the copper EFP into its grille, instantly cooking the occupants.

Bad day for whoever was inside.

I didn't even want to climb up and see what the driver looked like now. It wouldn't be pretty.

Leaving the wreck, I walked over to the artificial precipice. There was a twenty-foot gap between me and the rest of the bridge and a lot of rushing water below. I backtracked to the wreckage and veered down under the bridge to the riverbank.

I was only three miles from Jim. I pulled my radio and was about to key our private channel when I hesitated, reminding myself of the technical capabilities of the lawless thugs that were running the country now. I switched off the handset, pulled the batteries, and tossed both inside my pack. I couldn't risk the radio turning itself on in my pack and something keying the transmit button as I trekked to my holdout.

I headed down stream over the rounded rocks that the river had polished over thousands of years, long before men like myself walked this area. After following the river's path for an hour out of my way, I saw a beaver dam up ahead. As I approached, the loud slaps of beaver tails on the water warned the others to escape; some large birds squawked and flapped away into the trees. I wasn't desperate enough yet, but now I knew where to find them when I got to that point.

Greasy beavers.

Moving closer to the large dam, I began to see bright contrasting colors intertwined with the branches and tree limbs that made up the structure. It wasn't until I was nearly upon the dam that my brain processed what I had been looking at.

The dam was clogged with dozens of human corpses in varying

stages of decomposition. The birds that were scared away from the beaver's warnings began to return and peck away at the rotting flesh. I moved closer, covering my face.

All civilians.

Bullet holes.

Some children.

I dropped to my knees and struggled to keep my rage in check, staring at the sky, wanting so much to line whoever was responsible for this against the wall—to give them the justice they deserved.

I vomited into the river and watched it flow quickly into the dam. My eyes were watering and my stomach churned for a long while before I was able to compose myself enough to stand.

I said a few private words for the people unfortunate enough to have a beaver dam as their final resting place. I then kept moving, now cognizant of this water source and where it flowed.

FAMILIAR PLACES

Two hours after the dam, I found the path I was searching for across the river. The decrepit steel beam bridge spanned the rushing waters up ahead. It more resembled an Erector Set creation than a working structure. Every piece of its frame was rusted Mars red and chunks of its concrete were missing, forming holes throughout. Many years ago, after school, when this one-lane bridge was still in use, I would jump off into the deep water and swim. The bridge was condemned a long time ago; I thought it had already been torn down for razor blades. Huge berms of dirt and concrete pylons were put in place on both sides to keep vehicles from attempting to cross the abandoned deathtrap. This bridge was long replaced by another, but that was two miles farther downstream and could be manned by another checkpoint.

I'm sure the old girl could handle a couple hundred pounds, even if just one more time. I approached the archaic structure, marveling at its resilience and refusal to collapse. The weld markings indicated that the thing was built in 1913. I climbed up onto the structure and stuck to the edge where I could keep a couple hands on the beams. Aside from a few chunks of concrete falling away beneath my feet and plopping into the rushing waters, it held just fine.

I was across the river in less than ten seconds and safe on the other side. I climbed the steep barrier berm and skirted the concrete pylons and was on the road that used to bring wagons, horses, and people over the one-lane bridge. The abandoned road was dirt for another quarter mile up to the new road and then it was washed out by rain and lack of road-grader maintenance. I jumped the washed-out sections and took comfort in the thick canopy of trees that covered my head, blocking any view from the skies above.

It was cold in the shade of the large oaks, but I wasn't alone. More deer jumped across the road ahead of me, their white tails flashing as they vaulted over the three-wire fence on the left side of the path. Up ahead, I could see the light at the end of the tree tunnel and quickened my pace. Only three more turns in the road until I was on my land again.

Approaching the exit to the old road, I could see more concrete pylons and another dirt pile. I started jogging to those, keeping the MP5K from banging against my side as I went. At the dirt pile, I took cover and pulled out my binoculars to survey the newer road that ran from north to south in this particular stretch.

Easing up over the berm, I was at first startled by what I thought I'd seen. Dozens of people, mostly dressed in white and evenly spaced like they were about to march in a military parade. At second glance, I realized it wasn't people; it was tombstones rising above the grass at a cemetery. I'd forgotten about it, as you couldn't really see the cemetery when driving by on the new road below my vantage point. From up here, the monoliths stood tall against time and the elements. Looking at them through my peripheral vision, I could make myself see a column of people again.

Satisfied that I was alone, I swung my torso and legs over the steep berm. Two turns left.

With only a mile to go, I half jogged, half walked to the next turn in the road, leaving the pavement only to give the farmhouses a wide berth so as to not be detected and reported to the DHS by any quisling traitors looking from their windows.

Now west onto Black Oak Road.

One turn left.

I was moving quickly up the hill when I heard an engine. I took off my pack and tossed it over the barbed wire fence, chasing it over into the adjacent field. I lay low as the sound of the engine told me it was at the top of the mountain, probably three quarters of a mile away. As I lay in wait, another sound began to drown out the approaching vehicle. Electric engines whirred and revved from somewhere.

I peeked my head up over the top of the tall grass and the small drone's gaze immediately met mine. Instinctively, I slapped open the MP5K's stock, bringing the weapon up to my cheek and firing at the drone. It hovered at first but then began to take evasive maneuvers. A round hit one of the quadcopter motors, sending it spinning hard into a nearby tree.

The engine on top of the mountain began to rev.

I had to move.

I sprinted in the opposite direction of my property as the vehicle sped down the hill to the quadcopter crash site. I pulled my M4 off my pack along with some magazines before hiding the rest of my kit underneath an old rusting truck that had been sitting at the edge of this field since long before I was born.

I snuck to the edge of the grass line with a clear view of the road as I caught my first glimpse of the vehicle, a black Chevy SUV with DHS markings on the side along with "K9 UNIT" stenciled on the rear window.

Two men came jumping out of the SUV dressed in body armor, short-barreled M4s at the high ready. One of them opened the back door and yelled what sounded like a German command into the backseat. A large dog jumped out onto the pavement. Its teeth flashed and it wore a saddlebag as well as some sort of shoes that covered its large paws. One of the men gave it a rag to smell and firmly issued another command, and the dog immediately put its muzzle to the road. In a split second, it shot across the road and jumped the fence in the same spot I did a few moments earlier. The men took up defensive positions around their no doubt armored SUV.

I've been taught how to evade dogs, but I simply didn't have the most important ingredient now—time.

With time and distance, evasion can be made possible by not traveling in a straight line but rather in a system of U-shaped paths, with the goal of eventually crossing streams and other terrain that would make tracking difficult.

The large dog was only a few hundred yards away on a straight-line sniff path to me. I could hear it growl as it swiftly navigated through the tall grass and shrubs. I ran up the hill, looking over my shoulder like a wide receiver. The dog broke through the brush fifty yards away and caught sight of me. Its ears perked as it quickened its pace, baring its large white fangs as it closed the distance.

I hated to do it, but I took the shot, hitting the dog in its chest from fifty yards. It flipped end over end, yelped, and then lay still. The shot was suppressed but it was an M4 and loud with the silencer—just harder to triangulate. I looked back one last time to see if the men were in pursuit, and noticed something very troubling.

The dog wasn't there anymore.

I barely had enough time to take the second shot, this time through its head right as it leapt at me. That put its lights out fast, painless. As the dog lay dead on the ground, I verified that it wore body armor, which is what must have saved it the first time. I truly felt bad for the animal, as it was only doing what it was trained to do and didn't know right from wrong, unlike the two men that sent it to kill me.

I worked my way a few yards back to a break in the grass line and got low, observing the men. One of them was missing and the other remained positioned on the opposite side of the vehicle, his rifle atop a bipod on the hood. I backed away a little farther from the edge of the grass when I observed the man lean toward me on the hood, putting the rifle up to his shoulder.

A twig snapped behind me.

I rolled over onto my back and aimed the gun between my knees as I became aware of an electronic beeping sound. The sound seemed to get louder and the frequency higher.

Louder again, the frequency constant.

"They fucking shot Brutus!" I heard a voice yell out.

Again, this time after a radio was keyed: "They fucking shot Brutus. Get your fucking ass over here!"

I heard a car door slam and the horn on the SUV bark once.

I decided that on my back was not a good way to die, so I quickly got up, but not high enough to be noticed by whoever was coming to see Brutus the dog bleed out.

Goddamn, I felt bad about it.

I waited with my gun leveled in the direction of Brutus's master as the one from the SUV arrived on the scene.

"What the fuck?! You see, Tom, this is why guns have been out-lawed. These fuckers can't be trusted with a pair of kid's scissors, let alone a firearm," the SUV guard said.

"Did the drone get facial recognition before it crashed?" the one called Tom asked, nearly crying.

"Yeah, clear view, but the guy was wearing a hat and baseball cap. It might be him, or another lunatic gun nut holding out in these hills. We should just fucking firebomb the whole place," the SUV guard said.

"Fuck, Corey, I'm telling you right now, I'm going to track this piece of shit down; I'm going to fucking make him suffer for this," Tom said.

"Listen, you go back and check on the facial recognition. I'll . . . I'll load Brutus up. You shouldn't have to," Corey replied.

The murderous canine lover headed back to the SUV, leaving me behind with Corey, a man that had no idea I was a snake in the grass three meters away holding an M4 carbine to his ~~chest~~ head. He, like the dog, was wearing body armor.

The moment I was waiting for.

Corey slung the gun across his back and grunted as he put the dog's corpse over his shoulder.

"Stop right there and don't fucking move, or it's over," I commanded.

Corey began to slowly turn to face me.

"I wouldn't," I said.

He froze in his tracks.

"Hey, Corey . . . did you take an oath as a federal law enforcement officer before all this happened?" I asked.

He didn't respond.

"Answer or it's all over."

"Yeah, I did," he said, his voice cracking.

"So what was I supposed to do? Was I supposed to let that dog kill me?" I said angrily.

"Listen, drop the gun and you won't be . . ." Corey said before he was interrupted.

"It's him!" Tom screamed from down the hill at the SUV.

"That's right, it is me, Corey. Turn around. Look me in the eyes," I ordered.

He turned to face me, his face rapidly cycling through hatred, fear, and rage.

"In two hours, this place will be crawling with feds and a lot more dogs. We'll find you and I'll shoot you myself. Count on it," Corey said.

I raised my carbine to Corey's head in response.

"Killing me is a capital crime, you piece of shit!" Corey shouted. "I can kill you right now for pointing that gun at me! You fucking idiot! Civilians shouldn't have ever been allowed to own guns in the first place!"

I shot him in the right knee.

He dropped to his left knee and cried out at the top of his lungs; I waited until the dog lover came to his rescue.

As soon as Tom broke the clearing, I shot him in left knee, making it hard for either of them to help each other move later. Twin shrieking wails competed for airtime as I took their guns and left them to hug it out in the tall grass.

I returned to where I hid my pack and pulled it from under the old truck, replacing it with the two M4s I reverse-confiscated from the two thugs. Might come in handy. I also took the full mags with me; they'd do nicely in my kit.

I rushed from the cache under the rusted truck and over to the SUV that was still running. The men continued to cry out from atop the hill, so I figured I had some time. I pulled on the vehicle doors. Locked. I could tell from the glass that the windows were bullet resistant. The thickness of them refracted the view of the inside like an aquarium. Striking the hood with the butt of my rifle, I could tell that and the fenders were armored, too. The tires were run flat type, so unless I wanted to work on this thing with a cutting torch and a sledge, I wasn't going to kill it anytime soon. I left it running and entered the woods behind the old church.

Final turn.

I was on the heavily wooded path to my bunker. Shrouded by shadow of the nearby mountain, this area still had snow on the ground. Nothing had disturbed the path I was on, at least not for a few days. I did see signs of deer, but thankfully nothing else. My pace quickened alongside my heart rate as I moved. I still had some work to do before I could approach. I made wide arcing turns for hundreds of yards in odd directions. I knew where the streams were in this area, and I made sure to cross them back and forth and travel up and down the streams to evade the dogs that might be coming behind me. Satisfied that I'd done everything I could to slow my pursuers down, I started making my final approach to the shelter. Nothing, not even pepper or any other bullshit, will stop a tracking dog. They'd eventually find the shelter if they put enough manpower on the problem.

I approached from the north, reaching the high pond bank where I'd made nightly radio calls to Rich in the days when this darkness began.

I didn't dare turn on my radio now.

I missed Rich. And those bastards still had him.

The high banks of the pond reminded me of a small meteor crater as I walked around its rim to the southern side and down the pond embankment.

I couldn't see the shelter.

I rushed over to where we buried it and nearly tripped over the hatch. Jim had hidden it well; he'd planted some indigenous bushes all around the thing and repainted the exhaust pipes and access hatches in a camo pattern that blended in perfectly with the area.

I knocked on the hatch, at first not noticing the large hardened lock attached to it. He clearly wasn't here.

I searched for any sign of Jim, but it looked as if the place had been abandoned for a while. No tracks, no sign of food prep or anything. The five-gallon shitter bucket was empty, too.

I checked the lock again for a note. Jim had left me one this way before. Nothing. But when I went to flip the lock over and look at the backside, I could see something written on the side of the hatch, very faint as if scratched with a small pencil. I had to get down on the ground and beam it with my flashlight to read it.

JACK

That was our camping liquor cache behind the old oak tree, buried in a cooler, not far from here.

I hid my pack and moved quickly to the spot where we used to camp. It wasn't long before I could see the old '55 Chevy pickup hood sitting on the ground next to our fire circle. I went behind the tree and moved the rocks and dirt aside, revealing the old cooler where our whiskey used to live.

I was disappointed to see the cooler empty, except for a piece of paper and the shelter lock key.

"You can't drink paper, Jim," I said aloud.

Unfolding the tattered sheet, I read the word "pneumonia" in Jim's handwriting.

I sat there in shock, thinking the worst. My cousin must have caught pneumonia and died somewhere up here in these hills. I began to whimper, and sadness overtook me for quite some time.

I was alone in the woods we grew up in. Even the sun was making efforts to abandon me in light of the news of Jim's demise.

Sullenly, I walked back to the shelter with the paper tucked inside my shirt pocket. Back at the hatch, I dropped to my knees and opened the lock. I slung the hatch open and the smell of charged batteries and stale air hit my face. Defeated, I slithered into the opening like a lethargic snake and scooted down the steps and through the door to the living space. I knew that this area would be crawling with feds tonight, if not early in the AM tomorrow, but I didn't care.

Jim was dead.

What did anything matter? I feel ashamed to even write this right now, so I'll probably end up ripping the pages up and burning them, but I am thinking it. I miss everyone.

Good-bye.

CAPTAIN CAVEMAN

0200

Can't sleep. Haven't heard any helicopters or vehicle engines.

The place is cleared out. There are some essentials here. Case of water, half a dozen cans of food, a couple boxes of 5.56, but there were a lot more supplies when I left for Newton County. I wonder where Jim took it all. Fucking pneumonia.

I had it once. As a matter of fact, I was with Jim when I caught it. We were twelve years old when we finally worked up enough courage to explore the cave at the edge of the property. We were scared when we entered with our old incandescent bulb flashlights and roll of kite string. We must have gone a mile into the cave that day. We ran out of the string we were using to backtrack as we explored. I still remember seeing the lantern marks, initials of lovers torched into the rock a hundred years ago. My parents used to tell me stories about kids getting lost in the cave, never to be heard from again. They didn't want me in there and had no idea I wasn't listening.

We somehow lost track of time exploring the vastness of the cave, and when we finally made it back to the entrance, it was dark outside. I started feeling weak just as soon as I was heading back home. By the time we got home, Mom didn't even grill me on our whereabouts or why we were covered in head to toe with clay (and bat guano). I was that pale. Mom put me to bed that night with a 100-degree fever. I was admitted to the hospital the following night, and diagnosed with pneumonia the next morning.

I spent two days in the hospital with a worried mother beside me the entire time. After I was finally well enough to go home, the cave was an afterthought. She never asked Jim or me about it. We took this as the okay to go back anytime we wanted, and did just that.

Jack—Shelter key
Pneumonia—Cave

Cave . . .
Jim wasn't telling me he had pneumonia.

I packed frantically, climbing out of my hole in the ground at 0500. I hurriedly locked the shelter, placing the key in my pocket, and trekked southwest in the direction of the old cave. Again I took a wide arcing path, crossing streams and navigating briars in a zigzag to slow anything that might be on my trail. As the sun came up over the trees to the east, I heard the unmistakable sound of a helicopter rotor beating the morning air into submission somewhere off in the distance. The power-line clearing was the last open area before I disappeared into the woods, into the cliff face that concealed the entrance to the cave.

Not many people knew of its existence outside the family. One time, a college professor had pulled up some ancient records on the cave from the county archives and came for permission to map it, but nothing ever came of it. All those records had been moved online a long time ago and I doubt anyone would be perusing any basements for the geological records of this region, searching for old caves.

The helicopter noise faded by the time I was at the cliffs. It had been a while since I had been out this way, so it took some time to find the right path up the side. After going up the wrong cliff face once, I finally found the right one and was on the ledge and up the tight path. I fished out my headlamp, stowed my pack behind a boulder, and went over the small hill prior to the entrance.

Someone had covered the entrance with branches, making it difficult to discern unless you knew it was there. The opening was only about three feet across and two feet high.

I yelled down into the first chamber. "Jim!"

No response.

I moved the branches out of the way and crawled, sub gun first, into the opening, my headlamp searing through a darkness that only the cave dweller would comprehend. After making it through the first few feet, I was inside the large first chamber. Jim and I called it the lobby back in the day. Oak leaves from the outside covered the clay and rock, and the temperature and humidity generally mirrored the outside.

"Jim!" I called out. No response.

I clicked my light off and pulled my NVD down over my eye as I followed the path down to the gateway and the second chamber. The crawlspace was tight. I got down on my chest and began to low crawl through the opening, barely fitting. I'd gained a few pounds since I was a teenager. As I transited the five-meter crawlspace, the temperature began to climb. I used to tease Jim when we crawled through the opening, making him go first as I growled like a bear from behind and screamed like I was being eaten alive. It worked a lot more than it should have.

Finally through the opening, I adjusted my NVD and called out again.

"Jim!"

This time my voice echoed through the chamber and the response was the chirp of bats.

The clay was thick in this area. I could see no tracks in the clay, but did note where something had been dragged. I kept moving forward until the chamber opened up to the size of a large living room. Through my NVD, I saw the outline of a partial boot print and clicked on my light. The print was scraped over by something, as if someone was trying to conceal their tracks.

I kept moving to the next chamber. Looking down at my machine gun, I thought how foolish it might be to open fire inside the cave. Jim and I had regularly found evidence of cave-ins within some of the chambers when we explored them years before.

I turned my light off again, observing the local wildlife through night vision device. The small bats hung like stalactites on the cavern ceiling. Covered with what looked like frost and condensation, they seemed frozen in time, impervious to what went on outside the chambers in which they slept like vampires. Most people think of bats as huge black flying rats that would suck your blood as you slept. That might be true in some parts of the world, but these were gray in color, only two inches long, and not very frightening . . . well, unless you were a flying insect that happened to be targeted by bat sonar.

I rounded the next corner and saw what looked like a small base camp. Someone was in the sleeping bag. A radio and other equipment sat on top of a plastic tote on one side of the sleeping bag; a rifle was on the other. I approached cautiously, stepping lightly until I could reach the end of the carbine. I grabbed the familiar gun by the silencer and dragged it slowly to me, placing it behind me a safe distance from whoever was in the bag.

"Jim!" I yelled.

The person in the bag screamed for his life and reached for the carbine that wasn't there. I didn't recognize him; his face was covered in clay and hair. It was Jim, though; his mannerisms gave it away.

"Hey, calm down, it's me! It's Max!"

I flipped on my light and looked at him. His eyes were wild, feral.

"Max? You're alive?!" he said.

"Yeah, cousin, I'm here, I'm alive. What the hell is going on?"

Jim wiped his eyes and shook his head before quickly taking a sip from his canteen and speaking in a less hoarse tone.

"I have a lot to tell you, cousin. None of it good."

FLASH

OPERATION HAYSTACK
FOR BENTONVILLE FUSION CENTER ACTION

Neutralization of HAYSTACK target number one was a failure. Agent Maggie ██████████████'s interrogation continues. Her account stated that CONDUCTOR shot both pilots and that CONDUCTOR informed her that his plans were to leave northwest Arkansas. She was unknowingly being monitored by thermal biofeedback and her claims of CONDUCTOR's intended movement indicated a high probability of deception.

TOURIST has not proven to be a reliable source of intelligence; however, we were finally able to locate records pertaining to his background after accessing DNA databases that have recently been made available under the War Powers Act. His prints were not present in any database, NICS, IAFIS, or otherwise. After running his DNA through the ██████████████ database, a hit came up under a DOD identification number that linked to a sealed personnel file. After that file was accessed, we learned that TOURIST worked for NSA from 1995 to 2015 under their elite MUSKETEER program. As such, he's been trained to resist our interrogation techniques and has been deemed a risk to any and all fusion center operations. TOURIST is being held under War Powers Act authorization and is currently on hunger strike. We will continue to attempt to extract intelligence from him until such time as he expires. Shoot on sight has been ordered for CONDUCTOR and a substantial reward will be given, based on locality need, for any civilian that provides information that leads to the kill or capture of HAYSTACK target number one. This target is the highest threat to the region and must be neutralized by any means necessary.

▬▬▬▬▬▬▬ sends.

ASCENT

In the hours after my arrival at Jim's camp deep inside the cave, he painted a picture of the situation that had unfolded outside our geothermal climate-controlled retreat.

Jim escaped the shelter a month ago, after radio reports of drones and dogs sweeping the countryside started to come over the airwaves.

What was left of the federal government didn't stop at enlisting the help of outlaw biker gangs to secure order in the region; they started to bring in "help" from overseas. Thousands of Chinese troops had been observed coming in via boat on the west coast of the United States and hundreds had already made their way this far east.

Possession of firearms was punishable by swift justice from the barrels of provisional government firing squads. Although limited in scope, the electronic communications that were allowed between citizens was heavily monitored. Any subversive communications were quickly geolocated and met with overwhelming force. Most of the federal law enforcement officers had resigned their position, not wanting any part of the government sanctioned totalitarianism that swept the United States since the grid went dark last year.

Food was heavily rationed, and even the anonymous accusation of food hoarding resulted in immediate search and seizure of private property. This was the guise in which the provisional government confiscated the guns. Hoarding food was deemed such a serious crime that, if convicted via on-the-spot police tribunal, it would be a felony and result in immediate loss of all constitutional rights, especially the right to keep and bear arms.

Stop and frisk, something that was once only a big-city phenomenon, was now prevalent in all fifty states. If a duly sworn officer wanted to, he or she could search without warrant or probable cause under the new War Powers Act.

Habeas corpus had been indefinitely suspended, meaning that under any suspicion, any agent of the state could detain any citizen for an unlimited time for interrogation. Basically Guantánamo Bay rules, but now applying to anyone for any reason.

This is the power under which my friend Rich was made to disappear. Little did the bastards realize that I knew where he was being held.

Jim recounted the transmission he intercepted on the night of 14 November. A distress call was sent from the train. Someone had blown a section of the track, forcing the train to stop. The same crew cut the power to the rear half of the train and boarded Rich's car in the darkness of night. They captured him, but not without a fight. The radio reported that Rich had gut shot one of the hit squad thugs that came for him.

Jim said that he'd heard dogs and engines in the valley below the cave entrance and that he'd been holed up inside with only brief visits to the surface. He looked like shit and needed a shower. Hell, so did I.

After getting the full intel dump from Jim, I took advantage of the cave's warmth and relative security and made preparations to take a long sleep. I tried not to think of all the bad things I was going to enjoy doing as I began to mentally plan Rich's rescue.

---

07 Dec
Day of Infamy

I awoke this morning to the smell of bacon. The small fire seemed to vent up into a crack in the top of the cavern, as the place wasn't filling with smoke. Jim passed me an old rag and placed the blistering hot can of bacon in my hand.

"Rest is yours, cousin," he said, chewing.

I sat there enjoying breakfast when he handed me a steaming canteen cup of instant coffee.

"No freaking way, man!" I said.

"I didn't drink that much of it after you left. Ain't no fun when you're alone," said Jim.

"I know. It was lonely in Newton County, too."

I proceeded to tell him the story of what happened to me up in the mountains, of me fighting that big cat and playing a game of spy versus spy against Maggie and her dumb partner. I ended the story with me hijacking the helicopter that brought me most of the way back to Black Oak by way of Elkins High School, a chicken house, and a barn loft.

"Damn, cuz. How big was the cat?"

I, of course, exaggerated a little.

After breakfast, we left Jim's kit behind, except for my MP5 and his M4, and we crawled back through the crawlspace. I let him go first. About halfway through, I growled and yanked on his feet, and he screamed and crawled with a vengeance I hadn't seen in decades. That felt good.

Back in the lobby of the old cave, I received a pretty good sock on the arm in retaliation for my old cave prank, and we then headed up the walkway through the cave lobby. The temperature dropped like a rock as we approached the opening. We crawled out of the earth's womb covered with clay and grime and into a cold Arkansas morning.

"Think we can make it back to the shelter?" I asked.

"Why in the hell would we risk that?" Jim said.

"The solar shower is still hanging in the tree and we could both use one," I said.

Jim thought about it for a few moments, tugging on his beard.

"All right, but we get the hell back here if we hear or see anything, right?"

"Yeah, of course," I said, lying my ass off.

The sharp pain of bright morning light caused my eyes to water. As they adjusted, I checked that my own kit was where I left it before taking a few things out for our trip back down the mountain to the buried shelter. There was a pretty good overcast developing, so that meant no killer drones dropping hate and discontent on us from above. I let Jim take point, as he was more familiar with troop movements in the area than me. Jim hunted a helluva lot more than I did during our childhood and his ability to move quietly through the woods was uncanny.

It was strange seeing him stalk with the M4; I was used to him wielding a gun with a decorated wooden stock, not a collapsible made of polymer. The sawed-off 12 gauge slung across his back was more Jim's speed, but I'd hate to meet him in the dark woods carrying either blaster. After a few minutes, we were down the cliffs and at the bank of one of the many small creeks between the cave and the shelter. Jim held his hand up, stopping me in my tracks. I instinctively got low when he did.

After examining the ground for a few seconds, he leaned back and whispered, "Dogs."

"How old?" I whispered back.

"Hours, maybe."

I slung my sub gun's stock out with a click and made sure I had one in the hole before stepping through the stream in the direction of the shelter. Jim moved like a specter through the trees. His feet deftly avoided the dry leaves and twigs in front of him while mine seemed to find all the sticks and branches that sounded like bubble wrap. The ground was cold and wet and the trip seemed to take forever.

By the time we arrived on-site, I had mud up to my knees. The solar shower was full of water, so I let Jim go first. He definitely needed it more than I did. I stood watch atop the banks of the crater pond and listened for anything that didn't sound like someone enjoying their first shower in over a month.

Jim signaled with a low whistle that he was done and I came down the bank. Jim was dressed by the time I got down the hill. I pulled the half-dissolved bar of soap from my pack and stripped down. Jim left me a couple gallons of cold but not freezing water and I was happy to have it. I was starting to grow things in places that hadn't seen soap and water in a while. Shivering, I quickly washed, not wanting to get into a naked gunfight or have anything bitten off by one of those German attack dogs.

After putting on my dirty clothes (hey, at least I was clean before I put them back on), I slung the MP5K back over my shoulder and looked around for Jim. He was nowhere to be found, so I started up the trail for a ways.

I smelled smoke. Bringing the sub gun up to my cheek, I moved forward, one foot in front of the other, controlling muzzle bounce as I moved. I broke out into a small clearing where Jim sat around a circle of rocks poking a small fire.

"Time for lunch," he said.

"That a good idea?"

"Well, we're a quarter mile from the shelter and three miles from the cave and the wind is blowing good enough to spread the smoke. Also, I have this," Jim said as he removed the cans from his pack.

Soup.

He pulled three cans out, opened them, and dumped them into the aluminum pan that normally housed his cooking utensils, salt container, and a small camp stove with fuel. He then broke out something really special—a can of Vienna sausages. He dumped them whole into the pan with the soup, mixing a lovely potion of near-pure-sodium-infused processed meat and broth. As our lunch cooked, my stomach grumbled. While we waited, Jim pulled the Buck 110 from his pocket and began to shave away at the unruly beard on his face.

Shaving with a pocket knife in the middle of the woods still earned a "hardcore" from me.

Jim nodded in acknowledgment as I began to recognize the face hidden underneath. After he was done, he pulled off his belt, wrapped it around his legs, and began to strop his Buck back to a razor's edge.

"Your turn?" he asked.

"Naw, I think I'll wait for the barber shop to open."

The soup was beginning to boil over the small fire Jim had quickly started.

Rich had that skill, too. I hoped he was okay, and I felt a sharp sucker punch of guilt hit my gut. I'd been in situations like his before; every minute in captivity is worse than a hundred years out here.

I had to do something. I had actionable intel, but the longer I waited, the higher the chance that they'd move him—perhaps somewhere out of my reach.

"They've got Rich in Bentonville. I've gotta go get him," I said to Jim out of the blue while he sipped on the lunch.

Jim didn't say anything for a long while. We both finished our meal and Jim then stood up, heading back to the shelter. I pissed on the small fire, grabbed Jim's pan, and scrubbed it in the paramecium-rich pond on the way back.

"It's too dangerous to travel that far, but I don't think you'll listen to any type of logic," Jim said.

"Drones?"

"No, they won't fly the big drones here. The NAI saw to that."

"Who?"

"NAI, Northwest Arkansas Irregulars."

I raised an eyebrow and offered a look of skepticism before Jim cut off what I was about to say. "Don't judge. You know a few of those guys. Ghosts."

"I saw one of them, cooked inside his MRAP back near Sulphur City. Buried him," I said, trying not to let my voice crack.

"Which one?" Jim asked, in shock.

"Blinky."

We both began to gather our things and take the long arcing approach back to the cave.

"How'd the NAI put a stop to the drones?" I asked as we walked.

"They came across a shit-ton of shoulder fired missiles. Took down one of the drones a while back. Those government bastards learned from their mistakes and began guarding the airfields pretty good after you said you shot that one on the ramp, so the timeline matches. They were getting pretty bold, dropping bombs on NAI pretty regularly until the missiles arrived. Now they'll only fly small drones with no heat signature. They know that whatever they put in the sky short of a stealth bomber is fair game to the NAI."

"How do I find them?"

Jim looked at me and shook his head, "You don't. They're using the cell structure. Only groups of three with no regular communications aside from passive radio signals and dead drops."

"Damn, Jim, you sound like a bona fide spy talking like that."

"From what I hear, cuz, you're one to talk."

We spent the last mile and a half in silence as we made our approach to the cave.

Crossing the last small stream, Jim swung his M4 around fast. I instinctively shouldered my submachine gun, ready to blast just as soon as I knew what Jim was shooting at. He squeezed the trigger, letting out a suppressed shot that impacted a squirrel near the base of a great oak. The tree rat's head flew apart and it spun in the air, smacking hard against the trunk. Jim ran over and began to gut the thing. He had it strung up and hanging from his web belt in minutes.

"Something different for tonight's stew," he said, grinning. "Usually don't get too many out foraging this time of year."

We disappeared into the cave, slithering deep underground like night things.

PART TWO

KINETICS

15 Dec

I've been planning and gathering intel for a week. This is what I know.

After my encounter with the drone and the two feds on my way out here, I knew that these woods were pretty thick with opposing forces, all looking for little ol' me. They weren't very good and the animals they were using were mostly hunting dogs. I'm sure they treed a few skinny squirrels and maybe found a rabbit or two but, based on the men out here searching for me, it appeared that the government didn't have the resources to take it so seriously. If they did, I'd probably be in a cell next to Rich and bathed in bright lights right now. There was no helicopter or any other air support out here, probably because of the threat of the NAI's Stinger missiles.

My first order of business before I started my reconnaissance mission was to change my appearance. Jim informed me that Rich said over the radio (before he was captured) that my photo was on wanted posters all over local bulletin boards spread throughout Fayetteville. They had the photo on file from my Agency common access card. I needed something to blur my lines, so to speak. Some new clothes, hat, and some glasses. My old house was blown to bits a long time ago, with only the wreck of an MRAP and a blackened piece of ground to mark where it once stood, so I had to keep moving to the Averys' place, who were the nearest neighbors and a good clip up the mountain.

Without the threat of Reaper RPAs orbiting overhead, my trip to the Avery house wasn't as stressful. I left Jim behind with instructions to listen to his radio at the bottom of every hour. I wouldn't be transmitting unless it was absolutely necessary, and he shouldn't transmit for any reason unless he was in serious trouble at the cave. Jim returned the kit I'd left behind. Among the zip ties, ammo, rifles, and spare explosively formed penetrators (EFPs) was a pistol silencer I'd left him but he'd never got around to using. The can was engraved on the side, the words filled in with anodizing. The small letters indicated that it was manufactured by a company called Rugged, and I hoped it would be just that. It added a little weight to the end of the small 9mm machine gun, but it was worth the cost.

I took a different route than the one Jim and I used to get to the shelter. There was no sign of any living thing out here in these woods, not even deer. Most of them had been hunted nearly to extinction last winter. These woods were just too close to Fayetteville and every good old boy with a 7mm mag rifle took to the forest to harvest game after the shit hit the fan.

I stalked through the forest, trying to sound like Jim. Although we were both a good bit Cherokee, I think he got the useful genetic skills. I broke cover out onto the road just after noon, but stayed in the ditch as I walked up the hill to the Averys' place. The gate had once been locked, but someone already worked it over with a chain and truck, pulling it open, bending the metal gateposts. The rust forming where the posts had been forcefully bent indicated that the looting had been a while ago.

I jumped the downed gate, careful not to twist an ankle on the old cattle guard. I approached the house low, gun to cheek. About twenty meters out, I stopped and listened for a long while, hearing nothing but the winter breeze and the chattering of my own teeth. Satisfied, I approached.

The front door was cracked, the jamb splintered from whoever owned the black boot print stamped on the door.

I pushed with my gloved hand.

The door creaked; the sound seemed to echo throughout the empty house. I continued inside, closing the door behind me. The smell of mold and old books hit me. A house that was recently full of life and laughter now was no better than any other dilapidated house rotting in some city on Main Street, U.S.A. Saloon doors separated the ravaged living room from the kitchen. Whoever had been here had flipped over couches, checking every nook and cranny, probably for food. Even the crumbs in the couch were probably fought over and eaten feverishly.

I felt like I was in a Western as I approached the oak saloon doors. I swung them open and immediately changed genres, walking into a murder mystery. The smell wasn't bad, as the body had long ago rotted flat. The corpse was a woman, at least based on the long hair and clothes, but hey, these were strange times and I could be wrong. The way the clothes were laying there as if purposely arranged reminded me of the cult classic movie *Night of the Comet*, except this time there was a mostly rotted human corpse still inside the clothes instead of red dust. I walked over to the body and knelt down. The jeans appeared to be pulled halfway down. Blood covered the denim. Holes dotted the white blouse. They could have been stab marks or bullet holes, but I couldn't tell. I didn't see any sign of gunfire or empty shell casings laying around, so it was a safe bet that the woman was sexually assaulted and then stabbed to death . . . or maybe even stabbed to death first. God. The tongue sticking out of her mouth was odd-shaped, but it was probably the decomposition. Old man Avery lived here alone, so I took comfort that this wasn't his wife, and really hoped it wasn't any kin, even though that wouldn't make it any less horrible.

I searched the kitchen for supplies and, big surprise, found nothing edible. Whoever turned over the house had taken everything down to the breath mints. I opened the empty oven, seeing the crude scrape marks on the bottom. Either someone used a pry bar to clean it or someone had actually scraped the burnt food from the bottom to eat. I said a few words for the dead woman and hoped that whoever did this would someday pay for it.

I headed upstairs. Every hundred-year-old board on the steps creaked as I climbed. As I reached the landing, I saw something that made me tense up again. Bloody handprints were smeared along the rail as well as the walls all around the landing. I brushed the trigger with my finger before pulling it away, maintaining discipline until I decided to storm into the guest bath.

Another corpse lay clothed and covered in blood in the dry bathtub. It was a little more preserved; the leather jacket with motorcycle club patches all over caused my heart to race a little. The run-ins I've had since all this went down seemed to go south when I came across people dressed like this. This corpse's hands were cupped over its bloody crotch and a look of unholy agony was frozen on what was left of its face.

Jesus. I don't think that was a tongue in that woman's mouth in the kitchen below.

Near instant karma, though. This fucker got what he deserved, bleeding out dickless in a bathtub. There was some toilet paper left on the dispenser, so I took the roll and closed the door behind me. What a shitty way to go.

I was checking the rooms for anything useful when I heard the roar of engines coming down the mountain. I raced down the stairs and nearly bolted out the front door when I saw a large convoy roll past before stopping on the side of the road. There must have been a dozen or so armored vehicles and I didn't realize what I was seeing at first. Red stars and a Chinese flag adorned the side doors of them. I ducked back inside the house when the doors of the vehicles flew open and the soldiers began to spill out onto the road. I quickly climbed back up the stairs. After reaching inside the top of my pack for my binos, I looked out one of the bedroom windows that over-looked the road.

The first two soldiers I surveilled were carrying AK-47s and appeared to be Asian. I swept the binos down the convoy line seeing the markings of the Chinese military convoy on every vehicle down the line—deep inside the sovereign borders of United States.

That was the moment I realized that I was no longer inside the United States. I was in some lawless facsimile of my great country. Why were they here? What's the real motivation to transport Chinese troops thousands of miles to the United States? Their grid couldn't possibly be up, or could it?

I felt as if I was trapped somewhere between a banana republic dictatorship and Germany in the late 1930s. While I have some serious reservations on killing Americans, even scumbag traitors like Maggie, I wouldn't hesitate to smoke a foreign combatant on U.S. soil.

One of the Chinese troops gestured to the house, took one last puff on his cigarette before tossing it on the ground, and started walking in my direction. There was no escape. I needed to move fast and be out of the house before he got here, and that type of movement would be heard outside and then I'd be engaged by twenty PLA soldiers with AK-47s.

I slowly allowed the curtain to close and backed away from the window and into the upstairs hall. I quickly scanned for a hiding place until I saw the skinny cord dangling from the ceiling.

I yanked it, pulling the ladder down on top of me along with a few chunks of white spray-type insulation. I kicked the insulation out of sight into the adjacent bathroom and scrambled up the ladder, tossing my pack into the attic before pulling the bottom section of the ladder up with me. I eased the access closed, extinguishing my last bit of useful light up here.

Just as the access door closed, I heard the loud kick at the front door and what sounded like Chinese commands. I leaned over to the attic door, felt around, and pulled the cord into the darkness with me.

If these bastards wanted to come up here, they'd need to find a stepstool.

I lay in a thick bed of insulation crossways across the frame studs, so I wouldn't fall through the ceiling into some Chicom's lap. As I lay still, concentrating, I could hear the house getting tossed below. Unsure of what they were looking for, I waited, hand on the grip of my sub gun, waiting to open fire through the ceiling into whoever was doing the searching.

As my eyes adjusted, I began to see the subtle outline of the attic vent along the ridge of the roof. The silver metallic ductwork appeared when my eyes were acclimated to the gloom.

One of the soldiers was definitely upstairs now.

Doors slammed and drawers were pulled—at least that's what

it sounded like from here. Footfalls stopped somewhere, maybe the bathroom, maybe right underneath the attic door. I heard something scoot across the floor below.

I began to slowly and quietly roll over the wooden beams, farther away from the attic door, back into the recess of the slanting roof, until I was far enough away to barely conceal myself behind a small pile of insulation.

My heart nearly leapt out of my throat as the attic lit up from the light spilling from the open access door. Chillingly, the ladder creaked as the soldier extended it to the floor. I heard it strain as the man climbed. I flexed and constricted on my silenced machine gun grip so tightly that my hand was beginning to fall asleep.

A searing flashlight beam swept through the attic back and forth before suddenly going dark. I heard the soldier climb down the ladder and walk down the hallway and down the stairs.

I got moving, rolling back over to the access point. As soon as I was certain it was safe, I grabbed my pack and climbed down, following the soldier's footsteps, except this time going through the kitchen and out the side door opposite where the convoy was stopped. The door was stuck, so I quietly opened the kitchen window and went out that way.

On the ground again, I rounded the corner of the house to get a peek. The soldiers were milling about their armored vehicles, smoking and talking. One of them had surveying tools out and seemed to be working with another man. After the last few soldiers returned to the convoy, a horn sounded, probably signaling that the convoy was about to move.

And just like that, the vehicles were gone as quickly as they arrived. When the last one departed my view, I moved to the road and watched the green armored reptile meander around a bend before stopping again.

I checked my six and pulled out my binos. The convoy had halted more than a mile down the mountain; again the soldiers got out and headed for one of the old houses. I merely observed, timing them on my stopwatch. It took them six minutes from the time the convoy stopped until I heard the faint sound of the horn again. The convoy disappeared from my sight and the engine noise faded not long after that.

It had to be pretty damn expensive to get them over here. Something had to be worth their time.

From what I could tell, the soldiers weren't looking for supplies. They were looking for people.

———

I headed back to the old Avery house, but this time kept my ears open. I'm not going to lie—I was shell shocked. These scribbles are for me and my sanity, but if anyone were to read this, I can tell you that, rest assured, seeing Chinese troops in a convoy on American soil does something to you besides asking the question as to how this could have happened. It does something I can't explain well, or convey in such a way that you might understand. What I can say is that the emotions I felt were confusion, fear, and then a metric shitton of fucking anger.

I tried to put the image of the convoy aside and climbed back upstairs. The closets were full of clothes that seemed to fit, so I went back and forth between bedrooms until I was able to compile what I needed. New shoes, pants, shirt, coat, glasses, and hat. The glasses sort of sucked, as they were prescription, but weak enough so I could tolerate looking through them without going cross-eyed. I consciously chose clothing that would blend into the local population.

In one of the upstairs bedrooms, I examined my ensemble in a full-length mirror. Through the natural light of the bare windows I looked the part, minus the machine gun slung across my chest. To really project the Marxist bootlicking aura, I decided to use the scissors I found in a drawer to trim my beard to a careless scruff. All I needed was a Che shirt, or perhaps some other sort of political statement. Come to think of it, I'm pretty sure I remember seeing a Che shirt on one of the students that was gunned down on the grassy knoll near the football stadium last year. He certainly didn't deserve it; he was just some poor college kid finding himself and who didn't know any better.

Armed with the right clothing and accessories, I departed the Avery house back to the cave.

The cave.

The cave.

What was I now? Still sapiens sapiens? Funny, it didn't seem that way. Here I was, killing my fellow S2 with modern-day spears and retreating back to a bat-filled cave, where my tribe member waited in the wings for my return. I was even bringing back loot from another fallen tribe to boost our own survival. Not much has changed in 200,000 years. Saber-toothed tigers drove armored vehicles and flew drones.

I trekked back down the mountain and disappeared into the treeline right before the church. My gun remained at the ready up until then as I fully expected to see the green Chicom convoy boomerang back up the mountain at the most inopportune time. But that never happened, and my return trip to the cave was uneventful. As much as I wanted to maintain my disguise for Jim, I had to tuck it away inside my pack as to not soil it with cave clay. I couldn't be walking around in the streets looking like I just crawled out of the ground.

Jim breathed a sigh of relief upon my return.

"A little part of me, in the back of my mind, was telling me you weren't coming back, Max," he said.

He didn't use my name that often. He usually called me cousin, or boy. I knew he must have been worried.

"Don't worry about me—you know I can take care of myself," I said.

Jim smiled, slapped me on the shoulder, and handed me a piece of deer jerky and a half-full bottle of water.

I debriefed Jim on what I'd seen at the Avery house, especially the mystery of the Chinese troop convoy, and what I thought of the situation on the ground.

"All right, what's the plan?" Jim asked.

"Well, I need to head into town to gather some intel and see what kind of battle space I'm going to be operating in. I haven't been in Fayetteville in a good while, and I don't know what it's like right now," I said.

"Yeah, I don't either, but based on what I've been hearing on the radio, it ain't good."

I grabbed Jim's radio from the cave floor near his sleeping bag and headed back to the crawlspace.

"Let's have a listen," I said.

We were in the lobby, feeling the dramatic drop in temperature right before coming out onto the side of the cliffs that concealed our cave's entrance. We rock-climbed a ten-foot face and bouldered the rest of the way to the top of the mountain, eventually finding high ground in a meadow with a pond surrounded by trees.

A startled deer bolted as soon as we came into the clearing. Jim slung his gun in front of his face and took a shot faster than I could extend my sub gun stock. It was instinct to make my weapon ready when I saw Jim move like that; I'd never take the shot on a deer with a 9mm unless I could pass for the main character on a remake of

Castaway. Jim's suppressed shot missed the deer, though, striking some nearby rocks and ricocheting off into the trees.

"Damn, that would have been stew till spring," Jim said.

"At least we know they're still here. Set up a stand overlooking this pond. You'll get him next time."

We extended the antenna on Jim's Sony radio and began spinning through the spectrum. Many of the channels were automated weather reports. The FM channels, once brimming with music stations, were now an RF void of mostly static. We continued to slowly adjust the dial and the antenna until we reached something that sounded like news.

". . . As a reminder, curfew remains in effect in Washington County until further notice. Any citizen on the streets after nine PM will be detained and asked for a valid work permit indicating place of employment and approved working hours. In local news, the Chinese government has graciously provided eighty-five pallets of food and medicine for the local community. Do not be alarmed at the presence of Chinese military personnel in Washington County. They are here to assist and provide security and will be patrolling the streets and back roads of Washington County to augment our strained federal police force. With the emergency ratification of the Firearms Safety Amendment, all citizens are reminded that the possession of any semiautomatic firearm is now a federal crime. Ration rewards will be given to any citizen that provides information regarding private possession of semiautomatic firearms. Text TIP479 and your message to CRIMES. When in doubt, send it out . . ."

"What channel do you usually hear the irregulars?" I asked Jim.

"The one you were just on," Jim responded.

After a long pause, Jim broke the silence. "You're still going after Rich, aren't you."

"Yeah. I am."

Clothes:
Hiking boots
Wool socks
Jeans from Avery house
Plaid shirt (hipster lumberjack) from Avery house
Puffy black winter coat from Avery house
Black glasses with lenses popped out from Avery house

Kit:
Fixed blade knife
Folding knife
G19 pistol
MP5K sub gun w/ can
300 rounds of subsonic 9mm
Night vision device
Flashlight
Hiking pack
Mess kit
Food/water for three days
Charcoal
Yaesu handheld transceiver w/ codebook
Zip ties
Pick set
Padlock shims
Pencil
Paper

Before I departed the cave this morning, Jim and I worked out several comm code words. We'd only transmit one-word codes, only at midnight and only in the event it was a no-shit emergency. We'd say the code word no more than three times before going dark until the following night.

Jim wasn't exactly excited to see me go, so I tried to reassure him that I was only headed into town to gather intel and I'd be back in a few days. Family wasn't something you took for granted anymore; we both knew that.

At the trailhead, I pulled my knife and looked at my reflection on the stainless steel fixed blade. I think I had the look I wanted. Less operator, more defenseless beta male.

Miraculously, my bicycle was still serviceable after being hidden in the bushes for so long. I ripped it from the clutches of the sticker vines and spun the wheels a bit. It was tactical, spray-painted flat dark earth, although rust was now showing here and there. The tires were low, but okay nevertheless. I'd see about getting some air in town. The lock was still attached to the frame with the key inside. I pocketed the key, got on the bike, and began to pedal out of the woods, finding the ruts of the four-wheeler trail that had been blazed years before. My pack was a little lighter than when I made the trip to the cave from Newton County. I'd left some of my heavier kit back with Jim.

It wasn't very long before I was on the road proper. The MP5K was hidden at the bottom of my pack, so I was relying on the concealed Glock for personal protection from the types of people that I might encounter on the way to town.

I pedaled up the mountain until it became a little too straining. Yeah, I could have pushed through it, but it was cold and I didn't want to work up a sweat under my new hipster clothes and get a good ol' case of hypothermia on the way to town. I decided to walk the bike up the hill, until I heard the sound of an engine. Instinctively, I rolled the bike into a nearby ditch and bailed into the woods as the engine noise grew louder.

A convoy of three vehicles approached and zoomed by. The lead vehicle was a black SUV, the middle was a van with antennas adorning the roof, and the last one was another black SUV. I knew that Jim and I had not been on the radio, so I wasn't too worried about the sighting of a SIGINT van speeding down the mountain. Even so, I dug into my pack to make sure my Yaesu was powered off and that I wasn't butt dialing the DHS, or worse, the ATF. With the amount of guns and ammunition I had on me, I'd probably be executed on the spot if I got rolled up on, riding dirty like this.

I broke cover, grabbed my bicycle, and started pedaling.

I soon passed the old, derelict militia building. Word was that the government tried to torch it decades ago, when all the members were warning us about these very times. As I rode past, I could still see the burn marks on the roof, a testament to a period before the collapse, when level heads vigilantly cautioned and were mocked and persecuted openly for doing so.

I pedaled until I got to the dogleg downhill corner. From there, I coasted a mile down into the next valley before I had to pedal again. I pumped my legs, bringing me to another bridge, the last before I'd be in city limits and my first contact with strangers since dealing with Maggie's crew.

Here were two men with fishing poles.

As I made my approach, I patted the pistol to make sure it was still inside my waistband. At fifty yards, the men quickly put down their fishing poles and turned to face me, their own hands on something inside their coats.

"Hey, I'm just passing by!" I yelled out. "I don't want any trouble, okay?!"

They didn't answer, but kept a concentrated gaze on me. I changed lanes opposite theirs, and left my hands on the handlebars, and just kept on pedaling. I have no doubt that they both were armed, and I also have no doubt that their guns would have been tossed into the flowing river below at the first sign of the Washington County People's Commissariat for Internal Affairs.

The men turned with me as I passed and were still eyeballing me as I glanced back, and still stared even after I crossed the bridge a hundred yards on the other side. Only when I was nearly to the next corner did they turn and put their lines back in the rushing waters.

Tensions were already running high and I wasn't even to the city limits sign yet.

As I cruised by the adjacent field, I couldn't help but remember the shootout I'd had with the thugs who followed me back to Black Oak from town last year. Things were so hectic then. The collapse was just being realized and people were going batshit crazy. I still remember the death rattle from one of them. There was no sign of the altercation now except the rotting hay bale I'd used for cover.

I pedaled past and crossed the border line into Fayetteville, a place I'd not set foot in since I'd received word from Rich that I was being hunted with a shoot-on-sight order. I didn't necessarily bug out because I feared for my life; I left out of fear for everyone else's lives. Wherever I went, whoever was with me or associated with me would end up like Rich or worse . . . my aunt and other cousin, if I stayed near them for too long.

Jim didn't know it, and honestly I didn't even want to admit it to myself, but I never intended this to be only a recon mission. The longer I stayed with Jim at the cave, the higher the chances I'd make a mistake and bring the heat down on him, my last surviving family member. With most of the population either starving, under the boot of an out of control government, or just plain dead, I couldn't simply check into a hotel tonight. I'd need to think about finding shelter at some point.

I pedaled past the ruins of Southgate, noticing the rope that once suspended a grisly corpse was still swinging there from the power pole, the corpse long picked away by the birds and the elements. I continued by the gas station just before the tracks. A man sat out front on a stolen park bench and waved a bloody machete as if to say hello.

I pedaled a little faster.

At the tracks, I turned north, bouncing up the railroad ties, and noticed that the actual tracks up ahead had been removed and were stacked on the ground nearby. A government notice was posted on several trees, stating that the Transportation Security Administration had suspended all rail commerce until further notice.

First they stick their hands down your pants without a warrant or probable cause, and now they rip your damn railroad tracks out of the ground. Talk about a slippery slope, mission creep, and all that Thomas Jefferson stuff.

—————

Farther and farther up the tracks I went.

Eventually, I came to the location where I'd first found the train and met Rich. Feelings of nostalgia washed over me and I felt great sorrow for Rich and what he was no doubt enduring as I write this. My resolve was boosted by thoughts of him and I pedaled until I reached the MLK rail overpass. I pulled out my binoculars and began reconnoitering the area.

This place was, for me, the genesis of the resistance. From up here, I first witnessed the unadulterated corruption of the local tendrils of the United States government. College kids were gunned down just up the street on that grassy knoll. Through my binos, I could see wreathes and other items left in commemoration of those lives lost.

The clacking of hooves sent me ducking. I listened as the horse-drawn vehicle approached from the east and transited underneath me. Looking over the tall railing, I watched as a hay filled wagon continued west on MLK until it reached some side street in the distance, turning left where the old sawmill used to be. As I continued my reconnaissance, more wagons and foot traffic passed underneath. The pedestrians seemed to walk aimlessly west on the road, their posture projecting defeat.

I didn't see one overweight traveler in the hour I observed the road traffic. So much for the obese American stereotype. I guess that trope disappeared with all the food.

I knew that the interstate was west from my position, so I decided to follow the others that way for a little while to see what else I could find out. I put on my glasses and walked my bike down the embankment to the road. Ice covered the shaded areas below the bridge, unmolested by the thousands of cars that passed through here every day before the collapse.

That wasn't the only sign of drastic population culling that was evident as I observed my surroundings. I was used to being in remote rural environments over the past several months. I didn't venture into the city unless I had to, so the noted difference in the number of people on the streets was obvious.

Fayetteville was a ghost town.

Where was everyone?

I continued west until reaching a checkpoint near the on-ramp for what I'll always refer to as I-540. There were no feds; just what looked like a local county police officer. He seemed to be concerned with traffic going on and off the interstate and paid no attention to me. I didn't really care about him either, but I did notice the hum of a generator powering the gas station near the checkpoint, so I went towards that, careful not to look directly at the police officer. He no doubt had a mugshot of my face burned into his memory.

As I dismounted, a wagon loaded with people exited 540 via the on-ramp. This seemed to get the officer's attention, as he began to walk over to the vehicle. I took this opportunity to go around the side of the station.

Air pump.

Luckily, the gas station wasn't cheap and didn't make customers pay for air. The station was powered, so that meant that the compressor was as well, so I quickly filled my bike tires and got back on the road, avoiding the checkpoint and the on-ramp.

I pedaled back east and turned down the road where I saw the hay wagon go an hour earlier. I needed to use 540 to get to where Rich was being incarcerated, but didn't want to ruin a good bicycling day by pulling heat on a cop to get there.

There were other ways.

I pedaled for about three miles up the road until I thought I'd found where the wagon must have gone. There were a few heads of cattle with their mouths crunching on hay that looked like it had recently been put down. The sound of jack brakes and revving engines was noticeably absent this close to 540; only the sound of wind and the impact of ice pellets on my hood.

The cattle didn't pay any much attention to me as I lifted my bike over the fence and infiltrated the steep bank leading to 540. Miles of abandoned cars were pulled to the side nearly perpendicular to the road. That must have been a Herculean tow truck effort.

I headed north, beginning my long trip to Bentonville, Arkansas, and the fusion center where Rich was being detained without habeas corpus.

The sun was getting low and so was the temperature, but I wasn't tired. I pulled my NVD from my kit and attached it to my helmet. I looked pretty shady wearing a night vision monocular mounted to a helmet, so I wouldn't be sporting this look during the day. I strapped the NVD and helmet to my pack and kept going until it was dark enough to go night vision capable.

I saw no one on the northbound side of the road after night fell, but some horse drawn traffic moved in the opposite direction.

Progress was slow when I hit the outskirts of Fayetteville. The roads had not been cleared of derelict vehicles and the ice began to refreeze, making cycling a hazardous activity. I needed to find a place to hold up.

Through my NVD, I could see a large bright rectangle about a mile off the interstate on the right. I took the next exit and followed the off-ramp down below the interstate grade, turning right onto an empty road. I looked back over my shoulder at the interstate above; the IR light on my NVD reflected from the dozen or so abandoned cars. Pedaling up a small hill, I turned left at the large but dark neon sign that read 112 DRIVE-IN.

The large white projector screen stood tall and sterile in the distance. Only when I got closer could I see the small imperfections and tears in the screen. Dozens of posts rose up through the gravel dunes, once streaming sounds of drama, horror, and sci-fi into the car radios next to them. I hid my bicycle behind the large screen and walked back to the center of the sound-post forest. For a moment I closed my eyes and imagined all the cars sitting here, windows fogging up in some, smoke wafting out from others. I imagined the children playing on the monkey bars next to the screen and the tinny sounds of movies coming from the speakers mounted to the poles, or from the radios in the cars themselves, tuned to the proper drive-in frequency.

My pack was getting heavy as I approached the concession and projector building. The door was secure, but I made short work of it with the B&E tools I keep handy inside my pack. It's a lot easier when you aren't worried about making noise or being seen.

I was alone out here. Did I know for sure? No, but the feeling you get when you know eyes are watching you was not here, not in this place.

I entered through the steel door and locked it behind me before I began to explore. Keeping my NVD on for the moment, I looked for anything useful. The place was mostly intact, but there was nothing of any significant value remaining, unless you count the bank of popcorn machines and the candy wrappers all over the floor. Empty five-gallon water jugs littered the ground near the cash register. It looked as if someone had holed up here for some time, I guess, until they ran out of candy and water.

Checking all the accesses, I climbed the stairs that led to the projector room. Strangely, at least to me, this door was the most secure one in the whole place. It wasn't locked, but if it had been, I'd have never gotten in without a blow torch and an angle grinder. I swung the steel door opened and stepped inside.

The sound of movement caused me to draw my Glock. Something hit my face and I nearly emptied a mag inside the room before I realize that it was a bird that had been using the room as a nest. It swiftly flew out of the projector opening and was lost to the night.

I raised the NVD and switched on my torch, illuminating the whole room in a burst of warm light. There were film reels sorted neatly on racks against the wall to my left. None of the movies were new, probably because everything had been digital for a few years now. There were some classics among the collection, many of which I recognized.

It was getting close to midnight, so I set up camp in the projector room after securing the door.

Only birds and ex-spies allowed.

At midnight, I tuned my radio to our preset freq and listened to the atmospherics play their random music on the radio. The pops and static yielded no discernible signal that I could tell. I waited until five minutes after midnight, then I gave up and switched off the radio to conserve the battery.

I unlocked the projector's mount and swung it parallel to the opening. Peering out, I didn't think about the bright LED light that spilled through the opening and onto the large screen in the distance. The sound posts cast an eerie shadow, like columns and rows of skinny shadow soldiers, all obediently marching to the screen ahead.

IRREGULAR WARFARE

I awoke to strange noises at around three in the morning. For a split second, I actually believed that I was back at the cabin in Newton County. That feeling quickly went away as I reached for my helmet and NVD, bringing it down, bathing the dark room in a green glow over my right eye. Shaking off the desire to just go back to sleep, I crept up to the projector opening, which I forgot to close before racking out. Peering through, my heart just about stopped.

There were half a dozen armed men on horseback, all wearing NVDs, staring up at me.

"Come out, or we'll light your ass up!" a voice yelled out from horseback.

Be captured or die. Not much of a choice.

I quietly chambered my sub gun and, for a moment, considered opening fire through the projector opening.

Maybe they'd bring me to Rich, I thought.

"I'm coming out the front!" I yelled down.

I quickly stowed my gun in the top of my pack and hid that in the ceiling above the square foam tiles.

Unarmed, I slowly went down the stairs. Rounding the corner to the concession area, I met one of the men, a bearded guy, face-to-face.

"Don't move," he commanded.

I stood there waiting to get shot, but it didn't happen.

"Turn around and pull up your coat."

I complied, showing the man that I wasn't armed.

"Okay, come out. The boss is waiting on you," the bearded man said matter-of-factly.

He signaled for me to walk in front of him, and I reluctantly did what was told. The steel door had been unlocked and now stood halfway open. I stepped through and out into the open area in front of the building.

"Where'd you get that?" said a different voice.

"Where'd I get what?" I responded.

"Well, you got it, might as well use it. Put your NVD down so you can see who you're talking to," the man said, his suggestion accompanied by some chuckles.

Fuck. I'd forgotten to stow my helmet and NVD with the rest of my kit. I swung the device down over my eye again and scanned from left to right, blinded a little by all the IR light blasting from their guns and other kit. They were running IR lasers, bright-ass IR flashlights, and other things I didn't recognize.

"So, where'd you get that? I won't ask again," he said.

"Work. I got it from work before all this happened," I said.

Vague is oftentimes true.

"What kind of work did you do before?"

"I worked for the State Department."

Well, that was mostly a lie, but hey, the truth was complicated.

"Turn on the lights," the voice commanded.

My NVD instantly whited out as the men switched on their visible lights, beaming me with everything from Maglites to 500-lumen tactical lights.

I was blind.

Someone behind me took off my helmet.

Gasps and a few "What the fucks!" could be heard amongst the horsemen.

"My God. It's him," the voice said.

━━━

The trip took two hours on horseback. The leader called himself Mars. I don't know if it was his real name and I didn't care too much while I was bouncing around on the horse, trying not to fall off with a black hood over my head. Mars told me that the hood was for my own protection and that it was best I not know where their NAI cell was located. I didn't really give a damn where the NAI hung their hat and didn't want much from them. I just wanted to find Rich.

Along the way, Mars revealed how the patrol had found me.

"Your IR discipline isn't very good, you know. One of our scouts saw you pedaling down interstate on NODs. He followed on horseback and watched you light up the drive-in screen a few too many times. He called in reinforcements and we showed up. We knew you weren't provisional government. No vehicle, hiding in an abandoned drive-in. This is how we get most of our recruits, by the way. They're hiding out on the run after having survived a year without a supermarket being stocked. Only survivors and government thugs are out here now."

The loud sounds of hooves continued to thump on grass, clack on pavement, and sometimes splash through streams. I had no idea where I was; I just knew that the horses weren't galloping full out. I wasn't tied up or zip-cuffed. I suspect that we made about fifteen miles; we'd been climbing a particularly steep hill when the sounds of the horses' footfalls stopped.

"You can take his hood off," I heard Mars say.

Someone pulled the hood from my head and seated my helmet back down in its place. I readjusted my NVD, bathing the crest of the hill in green. A series of IR lights began to flash from the trees just ahead. After a few moments, Mars returned the signal with one of his own, again only visible in the IR spectrum. After a confirmation flash returned from the tree line, the horses began to move ahead once more. We entered the forest and came to a vast rock overhang, where I could smell some camp smoke and some type of tea.

"Dismount," Mars said.

We all got off our horses and a group of young boys took the reins and tied them off to nearby trees.

The men led me inside the vast overhang of rock and I felt the trickle of water hit my back as I transitioned from trees to rock over my head.

"Please, sit." Mars gestured, pointing to the nearby rock circle that surrounded a large fire.

The blaze heated the cliff wall, reflecting warmth all around the rock circle. I scanned the surroundings, noticing the guards. They carried M4s and faced outward into the darkness from where any threat might come.

Mars stood upon a large boulder like a great statue and spoke.

"NAI, we've found the man responsible for the university prison break, among other very serious crimes."

A series of mocking boos were issued from the crowd. I could see Mars smile as he continued.

"Max, welcome to the mountain complex and the current NAI capital cell."

A chant started with a low whisper, and eventually became loud enough that I could hear it clearly.

Long live the Republic
Long live the Republic
May the traitors pay the price!

Mars quelled the noise so as to not allow it to crescendo into a pep rally.

"What brings you back from the mountains?" he asked.

I was taken aback that he had even a clue as to my whereabouts over the past few months.

Before I could respond, he began to explain. "We've been monitoring transmissions, even decrypting some of the ones that they think are protected. There was a hit out on you a few months back, which is no doubt why you went dark. Now you're back in the area, and I'd like to know why."

I stood and approached Mars and his boulder and the crowd around the fire got quiet, accentuating the silence of the forest around us.

"I'm looking for a friend," I said to Mars, and basically everyone else in the camp.

"At that old drive-in?" Mars asked jokingly.

"No, he's currently a guest at the Bentonville Intelligence Fusion Center," I said.

Mars's demeanor went from jovial to serious in a split second. He jumped from the boulder, hitting the ground flat footed, and sharply asked me to follow him away from the fire and deeper under the overhang.

Safely out of earshot from the fire circle, Mars spoke rapidly. "Listen, this isn't like the university. That place was the temporary holding facility for political dissidents. Bentonville is the final solution. The provisional government changed our Constitution under emergency powers. With martial law in effect everywhere, they'll shoot curfew violators on sight within ten miles of the complex. They've made the center in Bentonville like the Green Zone, get it?"

"Yeah, I get it, but my friend Rich is inside, and he'd come for me, so I'm coming for him," I said, leaving no room for negotiation.

"You're Max! They'll put your head on a goddamned pike in front of that complex! You know this."

"Yeah, but if we leave our guys in there, what does that say about who we are? You talked about *our* Constitution before, or was it just that? Talk?"

Mars was on the ropes, so I did what you do in that situation.

"How many of your people are in Bentonville?" I said, knowing the answer before I even asked.

"Too many."

"So when all those people around that fire realize that you're just talking and that if they end up in that complex, they're in a black hole? No one is coming for them?"

KO.

"Okay, now you've got my attention," Mars said. "Look, why don't you stay for the night. We can talk more after you get some sleep. Sun's coming up soon. The NAI doesn't move during the day. Too dangerous."

"Since you asked me about my kit before, I have one more question: Where did you get all your guns, night vision, and horses?" I said.

"From scumbags that didn't need them anymore."

18 Dec

I awoke to sideways ice pellets hitting me in the face and to the faint smell of cooking meat. I climbed out of my bag and onto a freezing, moss covered boulder to slip on my boots. I quickly rolled my bag up and stuffed it back inside my pack, and then headed for the main fire circle as two boys dropped large logs onto the hot coals. The area near the fire and the overhang face was easily 20 degrees warmer than where I had slept.

Mars was picking his teeth with a whittled twig when I approached. "Good afternoon, Max. What say you and I head out on a little hunt? Horses are saddled up. Follow me."

I followed Mars down a twisting trail consisting of a few switchbacks before getting to the NAIs makeshift horse enclosure. The ice pellet barrage began to lighten up.

"You can take Molly. She can handle a big guy like you," Mars said, handing me the reins.

We set off to the west down an old camp trail, deep into unfamiliar woods. The trees and the terrain still felt like Arkansas, but it seemed that we might be closer to the Oklahoma border. I didn't bother to ask and I didn't really care.

We rode for a good bit until we came upon another cliff that overlooked a river valley. The bend in the valley below looked familiar; perhaps I fished there as a child with my dad, or maybe skinny-dipped with a teenage girlfriend at some point in the past.

"We usually don't ride during the day, but I needed to get away from the camp for a while," said Mars. "Listen, Max, we're into the idea about pushing the feds back across the Mississippi, but half my people aren't trained. What's your play?"

"Well, like I told you, my friend is being held in Bentonville and I'm going to get him. That's about it," I said.

"How do you think you'll get inside the perimeter? Just walk through the control point?"

I could hear the frustration in his voice as he tried to reconcile what he thought might be pure disregard for my own life.

"I don't know exactly how I'm getting inside, but I do know that I will get in, either as a prisoner, an infiltrator, or a corpse."

"Well, we do have some captured equipment I think you might be familiar with. A few of our engineers were able to patch up the ultralight from the liberation of the camp at the university."

"You . . . you have my aircraft?" I asked in disbelief.

Mars went on to explain how his mission in the early days was to acquire as much equipment as he could from the provisional government by any means necessary. This included salvage.

"So, yeah, it's got some carbon-fiber patch tape and some extra wire and wing material, but it works."

"Got any parachutes?" I asked.

"Yeah, we've got a stack of those."

"Wow."

"Paratroopers dropped in from a C-130 a while back. They were deserters. Two of them that were from Arkansas stayed on with us irregulars, and the rest kept moving west on foot to where they were from. The C-130 pilot agreed to do only three drops before he'd need the rest of his fuel to get back to his hometown. He was a deserter too, I suppose. None of those boys wanted a hand in all this bullshit. Pilot made his three drops in three different parts of the country and headed for home. He probably sat the Herc down on empty in a cornfield somewhere."

"Damn."

"Well, Max, let's hunt. I'll introduce you to one of our paratroopers when we get back."

Mars and I then sat quietly, prone atop a thin roll-out ground mattress on the rock that overlooked the valley. His 7.62 AR had some serious glass on it and could probably hit a drinking deer a quarter mile away. My little 9mm sub gun would be lucky to hit a rabbit at fifty meters, so I spotted for Mars and ran security as he glassed the riverbank below. He grumbled about how these woods were picked clean and that it'd be a generation before they'd be full of deer again. Eventually we packed up and started the rocky, narrow trail back to the camp.

After returning to camp, I reorganized my kit and went looking for Mars. The sun was getting low and the activity was starting to pick up here. It was obvious that these guys were the nocturnal type, and for good reason. When going up against a superior force, it's best to lean on the advantage of darkness, especially when you have a night vision capability as robust as these guys do.

Mars was talking to some of his people as I approached the fire. He glanced over and saw me and waved me over as he continued to speak. After giving his perimeter orders, he told me that he had someone he wanted me to meet.

"Savannah, get over here," Mars said over the hum of activity.

A woman about five-foot-nine parted the group and stepped out in front of the fire alongside Mars. She appeared to be about twenty-five and her features were stunning. Her long hair was pulled back in a ponytail, and her golden skin reflected the firelight. The woman stood there stoically when Mars introduced me.

"Savannah, this is—"

"I know who he is; I've seen the posters, sir."

"Max, Savannah was one of the paratroopers that fell from the sky a while back, so save the angel jokes about her falling from heaven, because, well, she did and she's heard all of them."

Savannah wore a camouflage uniform in what looked like a multicam pattern. She had a Fairbairn-Sykes dagger on her hip in a Kydex sheath and a HK handgun beside it. A Remington 700 was slung across her back attached to a buckskin sling. Her eyes were calculating and she seemed to size me up right there in front of the fire. In that second, I was either worthy to hear her words or I wasn't.

"You did good last year, even if half the reports were bullshit."

I responded with only a nod.

I already met my quota of trusting alpha female warriors this decade, no matter how hot they were. I listened to Savannah give Mars a sitrep of the local area, watching her eyes remain locked on to Mars as he responded with new orders. Her body language and demeanor seemed to indicate that she'd follow Mars, but the moment she stopped believing in him, she'd skin him for a raincoat and take over.

She glanced over at me a few times and I didn't dare look away. I just returned her stare with my own, fighting back the dry eyes brought on by the blazing fire. Once her orders were given, she left without a word in the direction of the dying light. I'd hoped I'd get to see Savannah again at some point, but I knew I couldn't count on it in a world like this.

I thought this the best time to tell Mars my plans to leave after sunset.

"Max, wait, I've got a deal for you," Mars said, after realizing that I was serious. "Give it two more days before you leave. It'll give us more time to formulate a better plan."

"I can't afford to lose the days. I don't know what condition my friend is in," I said.

"Yeah, I understand that, but if you leave on foot, it's a twenty-mile hike through enemy territory. It'll take you longer. Listen, stay;

we'll give you Molly two days from now and then you can leave. You can make those twenty miles on her a helluva lot faster than on foot."

The fire licked the large blackened boulders that imprisoned it and the heat blasted the right side of my face to near boiling as the left side froze like the dark side of the moon. I stared at the fire as I weighed both options.

I went with the free horse one.

"Good, that's good. I'm about to go out on a patrol. Savannah will be there. Wanna tag along?" Mars teased. "I saw how you were staring her down. Pretty ballsy. I've seen that go bad real quick."

"Yeah, I'll go. It'll give me more time to get to know Molly. She's the only girl in this camp I think I can trust," I said, firing back at Mars.

Mars gave a huge belly laugh and slapped me on the back with the force of a grizzly bear before heading off into the darkness to where the horses were stabled.

———

It was a bitterly cold night and getting worse as our small patrol headed down the mountain into the deep valley. One of the patrol's horses pulled a small jerry-rigged trailer behind it. I hung back with Mars and kept my eyes peeled for any sign of threats. I could clearly see our own Milky Way galaxy in all its glory, with its hundred-thousand-year-old light somehow reaching through space and time to this little blue planet.

The clouds from my breathing intermittently blocked my sight picture through the NVD. We began to level off at the valley floor and I started to hear water rushing over unseen rocks through the trees to my left. I watched the patrol communicate via hand signals. Molly seemed to stop without prompting when the other horses did. It was obvious that my new horse had already been trained on a patrol or two.

Mars began to let the group open some distance between us. I noticed the large rectangular container lashed onto the side his saddle, but didn't say anything. We hung back a ways so I took the opportunity to whisper.

"Who usually takes Molly?"

"Dicky," Mars responded quietly.

"Where is he?"

"Dead. Raiders got him during recon."

After another two hours of riding, the patrol set up shop inside an old barn at a two-way highway intersection. Its dilapidated condition reminded me of the barn I'd slept in on my way to find Jim. Old hay covered the dirt floor of the barn; the horses sniffed and snorted, but didn't try to eat any.

The patrol whispered in a circle in the center of the barn as I stood near Mars.

"They're on foot from here on out. Can't risk losing the horses," Mars said.

"On foot? Why the hell would they patrol that way?" I asked.

"They ain't patrolling anymore. There's supposed to be a supply truck moving through this area tonight. Got a tip from a reliable CI on the inside. We're taking it. That's why I'm here. The supply truck is due around midnight. We'll be ready."

"What do you want me to do?" I asked.

"We'll hang back and let Savannah's team do what they do, unless you want in on the action."

I didn't respond and waited for the team circle to break up.

"We're ready," said Savannah.

"Roger that. Execute," Mars commanded.

I watched two men pull explosives from saddlebags along with a familiar weapon I'd used last year. A drum-shaped explosively formed penetrator. The concave circle of the hammered copper projectile plate shimmered in my NVD. I still remember Rich sending the plans out last year over HF radio so that people could build their own and take down armor; it appeared that it worked.

Teach a man to fish.

The assaulters pulled down their masks and readied their guns and stepped through the barn doors into the darkness, owning the night.

I followed Mars behind them.

The team set up a kill box at the intersection. I watched one of the assaulters construct a tripod from sticks and 100-mph tape before placing the EFP on top. He then proceeded to wire it up and take his position behind a massive dead oak tree fifty yards behind the explosive, opposite its intended blast cone.

I wasn't part of the assault team. Mars and I stood back a ways on the crest of a rolling hill overlooking the action. It was two hours till midnight and the waiting game would begin.

I extended the side folding stock on my MP5K and screwed on the silencer. My reload mag was taped to the mag inside the gun using a dead NVD battery as a spacer. Sixty rounds of food for my roller lock sub gun to eat through. I checked my selector switch, making sure I had it in single shot instead of burst or auto. The gun could empty a full thirty round mag in about three seconds.

We waited.

And waited.

And waited.

Finally, at about an hour till midnight, I saw something coming through the brush in front of Mars and me.

A skinny winter rabbit.

I pulled the HK up to my shoulder and put the rabbit on top of the front sight. Depressing the trigger, I sent the animal tumbling. I ran over to the small creature with my fixed blade already out to make sure it didn't suffer. I did a partial field dress and tied the rabbit off on the outside of my pack. My bloody hands were stained and frozen against the cold metal of my sub gun, but at least I had some meat for stew later.

Worth it.

Through all the action with the rabbit, Mars said nothing, and aside from some IR light sweeping in my direction, there was no other reaction from the assaulters below.

Midnight came and went, and at about 0015 I caught an IR flash below. Mars quickly responded and the rest of the team didn't move.

At 0030, things got interesting. A motorcycle engine revved and got louder, coming from the east. I began to see a bright beam of light coming down the hill, but I couldn't see the light with my unassisted eye. The rider was using night vision like everyone else. As the engine noise increased, I could see real headlights appear on the hill behind the rider.

The rider was a scout for the supply truck, and if the rider was using NVD technology, it could see us if we didn't secure any IR sources of light. Mars yelled "Douse!" down the hill and the small light sources went dark, just as the scout buzzed around the corner before the intersection.

I broke off from the group, nodding to Mars. He acknowledged right back.

Leaving my pack behind, I sprinted down the hill to the west and took position behind an abandoned tractor that lay flipped over on the side of the road. The motorcycle would be on the intersection at any moment, a minute or so ahead of the supply truck.

As the motorcycle approached, I stepped out of cover with

my sub gun bearing down on the biker. The man skidded sideways, simultaneously pulling a sawed-off from the leather scabbard attached to his bike. I instinctively switched the gun from single- to three-round burst and squeezed the trigger. The silencer did what it was designed to do, and so did the heavy subsonic 9mm rounds. All three shots impacted the rider, sending the bike to the asphalt skidding and arcing sparks in circles like fireworks. The bike sailed off into the ditch with a loud crash.

The supply truck was at the intersection when I saw the bright flash. Instantly, I cupped my ears and got flat on the ground just before the sound and concussion wave hit. Bits of talcum-fine dust launched up into the air and slowly settled. The biker corpse remained still, as I expected, but I waited some time for him to bleed out. Gunfire erupted from the assaulters and the sounds of steel-core ammo punching through thin metal were eerie to listen to in the darkness. I caught a glimpse of a couple tracer shots coming from somewhere and hoped it was ours.

While the others were busy, I flipped over the biker, removed his NVD, and looked at his blank, lifeless face. I really shouldn't have. You only get so many times to do that before you're lifeless yourself. I closed the poor bastard's eyes and scavenged what kit I deemed useful.

I didn't bother checking the outlaw's saddlebags, for reasons too messed up to go into here. Kinda funny—this guy working for the government; two years ago he would have been on their watch list. Now I'm on their kill list, when a couple years ago I was on their hire list. Just like Afghanistan, Iran, Iraq, and Syria—just wait a regime or two to find a friend where once there was only the enemy.

The NVDs that the biker wore were scratched up, but still worked fine. I snagged his radio and turned it up as I walked back to the intersection where the assaulters were pulling cargo. My walkie let loose a split-second modem noise and screeched a frantic message.

"This is Supply Run Echo Tail, cargo under attack, send support, now!"

"Echo Tail, Talon One Six with two hours till bingo, state your posit, over."

"Oh fuck, here we go," I said aloud as our coordinates were being sent over the radio.

The pilot's voice held a heavy Asian accent.

I began to run to the assault team, waving my IR light and trying to get their attention.

"What's the fucking problem?" Savannah asked, somewhat annoyed.

Out of breath, I began to explain to her what I'd heard on the radio and how we'd likely have air support on top of our position soon.

"Roger that. Go get your ass up that hill and tell Mars!" Savannah barked as she and the others began to rapidly load the horse cart.

I hoofed it up the hill to tell Mars what I'd heard.

"Okay," Mars responded.

"Okay? That's it? A helicopter pilot with a GAU on NVDs will really fuck up our night, Mars," I snapped.

Mars got up off the ground and calmly walked over to his horse. I heard the sounds of buckles and straps being loosened before Mars appeared from behind the animal, grunting as he carried the large rectangular container I'd noticed before.

He slowly flipped open the buckles on the container and opened the clamshell lid, revealing a Stinger antiaircraft missile. Mars configured the weapon efficiently, stopping just shy of inserting the battery coolant unit. He'd been saving that portion of the weapon configuration for aircraft targeting and engagement.

He then sat there atop the Stinger container chewing on some deer jerky.

"Okay, then. How many of those do you have?" I asked.

"A lot. More than enough to make these fuckers think twice every time they send air support. We don't go on patrol without Stingers."

I immediately felt better about our odds. I watched from our vantage point as the assault team loaded the cart full and sent the horse away. After ten minutes or so, the cart would return empty. They must be off-loading the supplies and hiding them for later recovery. While the team stacked the second load, I could hear an engine, but this time it wasn't a motorcycle or a helicopter.

Mars gave a quick IR flash sequence and the team below began to scatter like cockroaches.

"Hit the tree line—now!" Mars screamed. I grabbed my kit and rode Molly fast, galloping to the adjacent wooded area farther up the hill.

I knew jet noise well enough. Two low, hot engines should be an easy enough target for the Stinger to lock onto. I made sure I wasn't leaking any IR light and stared up at the sky, looking to find what I knew was no doubt up there.

The Flanker came into view, breaking from the cover of tall trees and banking sharply out over the field. I held the radio up to my ear.

"Echo, Talon, remain clear, going hot," the accented voice said firmly.

BRRRT!

The Flanker let loose a half-second burst from its gun, but it was too late. I could see the Stinger's rocket light as the warhead began to break the sound barrier twice over. The missile hit the empennage of the aircraft, shooting shrapnel into the fuselage, avionics, engines, and human flesh. Numerous loud backfire sounds were heard just before a large explosion and then an even larger one as the plane hit the earth with massive amounts of highly flammable jet fuel remaining.

With the air threat neutralized, I dug my heels into Molly, sending her shooting down the hill to where I'd left Mars. As I approached the site, I could see the marks in the earth where the Flanker rounds had impacted and plowed the ground with several deep gouges. The oak tree nearby had holes blown out big enough to put a fist inside. I searched for Mars galloping back and forth until my eyes picked up some movement farther down the hill.

As I approached, I recognized the outline and clothing. It was Mars, stumbling, cussing, and waving an empty Stinger canister around like a battle-axe.

"You okay, Mars?!" I yelled down at him.

He turned to face me. Although everything was green through the NVD, his face was covered in something darker.

Blood.

I jumped off the horse and ran over to him, checking his limbs first. Aircraft guns had a way of knocking off body parts. With all his limbs intact, I began to examine his head. I don't know how anyone could be so lucky, but it appears that one of the aircraft's rounds had nicked him there.

"You are one lucky bastard. You got hit in the head with a . . ." I said just before Mars hit the ground, unconscious. I quickly removed the med kit from my pack and began applying first aid. Scalp cuts always bled pretty badly and his was no different. I broke out a pack of clotting agent and applied it to Mars's head with some pressure, wrapping it over with a bandage. I elevated his torso until the rest of the team began to trickle in from the hills.

"What happened to him?" Savannah asked.

"He got hit with one of those rounds. Just grazed. He'll be okay as long as the concussion isn't too bad," I said.

"Can we move him?" she asked.

"I don't think we have a choice, unless you guys brought more ammo and Stingers."

After the bleeding stopped, we strapped Mars onto his horse and tied it off to another, making way back to the camp.

"Was whatever that was in the truck worth it?" I asked Savannah.

"Yeah, you could say that."

0400

We got Mars back to camp about an hour ago. The doctor in the group informed Savannah that it was a concussion, and too early to tell how bad it might be. Mars would be on light duty for at least a week, and knowing what kind of guy he is, I doubted he'd be very happy to hear that. He's passed out on some painkillers, but I'd be feeling pretty shitty too if I'd just got shot by a burst from a jet fighter gun and lived to tell about it.

The sun is coming up soon. I've set up a cold camp away from the fire circle. After watching that Flanker go to work, I don't want to sleep anywhere near a heat or light signature. When I wake up, I'm going to see about getting some intel, perhaps some maps of the best routes into Bentonville.

After operating with these guys, I will say one thing: they're not afraid to get it on.

BLUE YONDER

I rode with Savannah this afternoon. She woke me up with a kick to my sleeping bag. I nearly drew down on her until I realized with a freezing start where I was. Frozen pellets of ice covered my bag and peppered my hair. After shaking those off, I slowly crawled out of my cocoon, wincing with the aches and pains of running, gunning, and sleeping on the ground for extended periods.

Savannah saw my face and said, "Getting old sucks, huh?"

"It's not the years, it's the mileage," I said, quoting one of the classics. After shaking off my bag and stuffing it damp back inside my pack, Savannah shoved a thermos into my face.

"Drink up. Instant coffee. We don't have sugar."

I twisted the lid open on the thermos and sipped, enjoying the heat. The coffee, not so much. I watched the steam rise from the thermos, swirling into the cold air.

Savannah said nothing for a few minutes. She seemed to be

fixated on something in the distance, something I could not see or hear.

"We better get moving. Good cloud cover," she said.

"Going where?"

"Before the mission, Mars said that you might want your hang glider back," she said.

"You mean the ultralight."

"Whatever. Kit up, get your horse. We ride in five."

I kept the thermos, grabbed my kit, and headed for the fire circle to warm up a minute or two before heading out into the snowstorm that was maturing overhead. The large flakes fell, covering the trails and other areas, leaving the ground under the large cliff overhang clear of snow.

The fire circle raged, blasting heat like a furnace in all directions, melting any snow that fell within five feet of its perimeter. I soaked in the warmth and checked my watch. It was just after 1300, and the sun that was concealed behind the snow clouds had only about three hours before it went away. I was about to take my last sip of bad coffee and get on my horse when I heard the children begin to sing. I remembered some of them from when I first arrived at the NAI camp.

It was soft at first, but they soon began to gather around the fire circle and sing Christmas songs.

They had a pretty good "Jingle Bells" going before they forgot the words and went on to "Rudolph" and beyond. I smiled for the first time in a long while and hoped that these children would one day get the country that I and others enjoyed at their age.

I turned to see who was tapping my shoulder and was met with Savannah's impatient glare. She nodded in the direction of Molly, who was already saddled up and ready.

"Thanks," I told her, before jumping on the horse and following her down the trail.

"One more day," she said, pacing beside me as we journeyed farther down the trail.

"Until?"

She pushed her horse ahead. "Until you leave."

"That's right," I said.

We rode, neither speaking to the other until we reached a waterfall and she commanded her horse up the steep trail obscured by leaves, branches, and snow. I pushed Molly to follow and she obeyed, bringing me swiftly up the hill and beside another cliff face. We passed some cow ponds and meadows and reached a large fence that blocked off the path of a power transmission line.

Savannah dismounted and approached the fence with slow caution. Even though it was still snowing pretty heavily, I could see a hundred yards in both directions up and down the transmission line clearing. I noticed burn marks on the power transformers that hung high on two of the nearby poles.

After cutting through the fence with her master key (bolt cutters), we crossed into the woods and eventually reached an NAI cache hidden under some radar netting.

"This is where we kept the stuff we salvaged from the university prison. We got it just before the feds sent reinforcements to the area."

Underneath a brown tarp, I recognized the wheels of my flying machine. I disconnected the bungee and pulled off the tarp. The machine looked to be repaired with fiberglass wrap holding the frame together. Since the frame was the battery, I could see where the NAI engineers connected severed circuits from where the frame snapped upon impact. My dried blood remained splattered on the wing, but some decent patch jobs covered up most of the bullet holes and small tears from the crash and after.

I checked the battery sequence and noted it at fifty percent charge. Opening the fuel reservoir, I shined my light inside seeing about a quarter tank of fuel remaining.

"Does it still fly?" I asked Savannah.

"Yeah, our engineers tested it. They flew it here, but it won't hold the same charge it used to. Something about the battery cells being damaged."

I began to calculate all options. Did I take the chance on riding Molly twenty miles north through countless checkpoints and hope that luck remained on my side?

Or should I attempt to take this old dragonfly under the cover of darkness and hope it didn't crash or fall apart at a thousand-foot altitude?

If hungry raiders didn't kill my horse for food and murder me, whatever was left of the government would shoot on sight. There was also that foreign troop and air support problem.

We spent some time organizing the cache and gassing up the ultralight. Savannah lashed some of the items from the cache onto her horse and I did the same.

"Can you get her back for me?" I asked, handing Savannah Molly's reins.

"Yeah, I figured that's what you'd want. The weather is pretty bad—might want to wait until it clears up. I'll head back at nightfall."

I made a quick camp, digging a shallow hole for a small fire to stay warm until sundown. Savannah remained until an hour after dark before she handed me a black hood.

"You'll need to fly with this on, you know, for your own protection."

I'll be damned. The woman was no stick in the mud; she actually possessed a sense of humor. We both laughed and she wished me good luck on the flight back, giving me tips on where best to land near the camp.

I shook her hand, enjoying the warmth of it, and told her that I'd probably beat her back. We shared a silent gaze before she released my hand and spoke.

"Don't count on it."

After Savannah left, I pulled the ultralight out from under the camo net and out to the transmission line clearing. Snow and ice covered the ground on my take-off strip, and the left main gear tire was a little low, but not enough to cause any significant problems. I placed the tarp back over the plane and went back to the netting to wait on the visibility to get better. I then stoked the small stealth fire I'd made, adding more dead twigs. The warmth was welcome as the temperature plummeted to about twenty degrees, according to the solar powered smart watch I wore on the outside of my jacket.

I monitored the air pressure every so often, looking for indicators of weather change. I nodded off and woke up after midnight. The small fire had gone out and I was shivering, even through all the layers I wore to fight off the Arkansas winter chill.

I gathered my belongings and made way to the power line airport. I pulled the tarp from the machine and stowed it under the weight of a large rock behind a tree. The ground had a few inches of frozen ice and snow on top, but it shouldn't have made a difference to the large balloon tires on the ultralight. They were designed for landing and taking off on the sand dunes of Syria, after all.

After folding out the wings and checking all the repair sections via flashlight, I put on my helmet and clicked my NVD over my eye. Energizing the system, the glass instruments came to life. Sensing the darkness, they auto-adjusted brightness so that they could be read clearly via the optic I was wearing. The aircraft was configured, so I hit the electric starter on the motor. After a few attempts, the engine spun to life, puffing out black smoke before the auto choke adjusted the mixture and the engine began to rapidly build RPMs. Even at idle, the carbon-fiber propeller began to nudge the aircraft forward.

I stowed my pack on the airframe and got in the pilot's seat. Harrowing memories of nearly freezing to death while flying this thing over Fayetteville last year returned as soon as I began to buckle my harness.

I hit the throttles, putting them halfway from firewall, and the aircraft began to roll faster. Gaining speed down the transmission line–clearing hill, I increased the throttles even more until I could feel the mains taking long skips on the snow-covered ground. At a good rotate speed, I pulled the light aircraft up and banked right into the darkness, just missing the overhead lines—a good thing to remember.

I retraced my path back to the cliffs using my NVD to pick out the light from the fire. Before I got too close, I kicked the propulsion over to electric to both monitor how much the damaged batteries could take, and also to make a quiet landing so as to not attract any undesirables to the cliff operating base.

I picked a hillside with a gentle grade and sat the aircraft down in much the way I took off, gently skipping until my speed was slow enough to let gravity pull me down and let the brakes do the rest. I skidded to a stop and secured the power to the avionics. Just before my instruments went dark, I saw the frame battery level holding at forty-five percent. Not too shabby.

After folding the wings back, I slowly pulled the aircraft to the tree line and concealed it enough to make it until tomorrow. Designed for stealth, it would be difficult to pick it out on radar or IR camera. The repairs made to the wing material and battery were probably not IR tested, but those only covered about ten percent of the aircraft.

I took my kit and made way in the direction of the fire circle that must have been about a half mile away from what I saw in the air. As I approached, the hair on the back of my neck began to stand up. Getting closer, I could see not just one fire but several. The fire circle that once stood as the heartbeat to the camp lay strewn in ruins.

I dared not venture closer; I pulled back to observe.

It didn't take long. I could hear gunshots and other sounds of skirmish being muffled by the snow and dense trees surrounding the camp. I saw movement through the trees pushing me to close the distance. Visibility wasn't great, but I managed to get near enough to see a line of three soldiers taking cover behind a fallen tree. They didn't lay down suppressive fire, only taking shots after carefully aiming at a target I could not see. I didn't bother unfolding my sub gun stock as I crept closer.

One of the soldiers said something. I recognized that it was Chinese, but that's about it; it wasn't my language.

At about fifteen yards, I leveled my suppressed gun on the most active rifleman and put his lights out. The other two reacted with expected panic; I took their lives before they could swing their AK-47s around to chop me in half.

I liberated the best AK of the three as well as all the magazines the soldiers had. My suppressed 9mm sub gun had its place, but that 7.62x39 AK punch was a league of its own. I flashed my IR light in the same pattern I saw Mars flash his, waiting a few moments before my challenge signal was returned with a valid reply. After a few tense minutes, Savannah appeared from the darkness covered in blood.

Through her gasps, she began to recount what had happened at the camp.

Upon her return on horseback, the whole camp was under siege by Chinese shock troops. A vicious fight ensued between the NAI and the Chinese, with both sides taking heavy losses. Savannah stayed back and set up a sniper's hide, picking off as many soldiers as she could. With everyone killed or captured, she waited until the Chinese troops departed the camp before returning. As she looked for survivors, three Chinese soldiers—the ones I took out—appeared and began shooting at her. Her NVD enabled her to sink back into the edge of camp without being killed. She was engaging those troops when I outflanked them.

"Mars?" I asked.

"I don't know . . . I doubt he made it," she responded sadly.

We searched the entire camp for survivors. The only signs that anyone might have made it were the groups of fresh boot tracks leading down the hill away from the camp. After covering the dead and scavenging for supplies, we fell back to the ultralight with our horses. Savannah pointed out key areas on my map where the NAI kept supplies. Any camp survivors would probably rendezvous at one of the caches. She was the only NAI soldier that knew the locations of all the weapons and supply caches the NAI had in the area. I picked a rally point ten miles to the north of our position. We only had two hours of daylight left. I could make it well before sunup in the ultralight but she wouldn't, not in this weather and with the potential for troops to be lurking around every boulder and tree.

The ultralight would be too heavy to pull very far, and too loud to fly. It was a good thing we had two horsepower with us. We dragged the aircraft deeper into the woods and covered it with more foliage. It wouldn't be safe to remain this close to the now defunct camp, so we mounted up and headed into the valley.

As the horses took us away from the camp, I looked behind,

observing the smoke rising up through my NVD and the tracks we were making behind us.

"We'll lead them right to us," I said, gesturing at the horse tracks behind us.

Savannah said nothing—she just pulled the reins and led her horse to the left to the tree line where the snow wasn't as heavy. I followed. After trailing her course, I couldn't really make out the tracks behind us very well and the snow was still falling.

I followed her for a mile before she led her horse out of the clearing and deeper into the woods. She stopped the horse near a creek and got off. She pulled some branches off a small fire pit and began to break them up and stack them inside. Soon a small fire was crackling and popping, warming up the area.

I pulled out my mess kit and scooped a pan of water from the near freezing creek and placed it on the rocks near the small fire. As it began to boil, I poured two pouches of instant coffee inside and sloshed it around, offering Savannah a cup. She didn't answer.

I unrolled my sleeping bag and set up my bed before heading out into the woods to gather firewood. You always need three times as much as you think. After provisioning up for the rest of the fleeting morning, I crawled inside my pack with my boots still on. Not very comfortable.

Right now, Savannah is still up and I can see the first subtle signs of morning to the east. I hope this fire is small enough not to be noticed from above, but something told me Savannah wasn't worried. She has a long rectangular container strapped to her horse, just like Mars.

We've discovered more data using the latest digital forensic techniques on the archives we've recovered. By taking quarter angstrom imagery of recovered HDD storage media, we are able to feed the damaged drives into quantum state analyzers, reconstructing the data by brute force.

The first documented foreign attack on United States soil occurred at the cliff overhang NAI camp on the early morning of December 20, 2023. Records indicate that the provisional government located the camp by lacing intercepted supplies with micro RFID tags. The spaced-based systems active at that time were able to track the stolen supplies in real time, enabling the geolocation of the NAI cell and subsequent attack. This attack acted as a jumpstart to a larger resistance movement based on the post-attack propaganda we've analyzed. We've only extracted about seven percent of possible data from the hardware we recovered at the sites of interest.

Very respectfully, ▇▇▇▇▇▇▇▇▇▇

Lead Tech, Big Iron

▇▇▇▇▇▇

20 Dec
Noon

Savannah was still awake when I woke up, staring at the fire. She had fed the thing all night, keeping us warm. It was nice not having to rise and handle that for once.

It wasn't until mid-morning that she spoke. "Take me with you to Bentonville," she said, finally breaking her stare with the fire.

"I can't," I said flatly.

"I can handle myself, you bastard!" she said, near tears.

"It's not about that. You're too fat," I said in a rare moment of bold gallows humor.

"What?!" She looked for something to throw at me.

"Wait, wait, relax! The ultralight only has a 275-pound payload. I weigh 200 pounds, and I need fifty pounds of gear. You're about a hundred pounds too heavy," I said, smiling.

She returned my smile and then began to cry, reaching out. I embraced her, pulling her close. I wasn't very good at this sort of thing, but it felt like the right thing to do. She wept heavily and deeply for a long time before pulling away, looking at me with her red, teary eyes.

"You're not going to be able to land that thing near where they're holding your friend," said Savannah. "Definitely not inside the perimeter where you need to be. If you land outside, you'll be shot on sight trying to infiltrate."

I expressed to her that I had to try to get my friend out of there and that if I died doing that, well, it would be better than living the rest of my life in regret.

She nodded like she understood, but I still think she thought I was crazy.

2300

After breaking camp at sundown, Savannah brought me to another cache. I took some fuel and other things that could come in handy before we both headed back to where the ultralight was stored. It was about 1900 when we got close enough to see the lights. There was movement in the darkness of the camp site. I told Savannah to hang back with the horses while I checked it out and she reluctantly agreed.

"If I start that engine, you go back to where we camped and wait for me," I told her.

I crunched through the top layer of frozen snow, trying not to make too much noise as I began to climb the grade to the ultralight. I could see the darker area where I'd concealed the plane with natural camouflage. Eventually, I made it to the plane undetected and began pulling the branches off the top and brushing the snow from the wing fabric. As I tugged and pulled the aircraft out of the edge of the trees, I could hear voices echoing from the camp.

The Chinese.

My legs strained and my muscles burned as I pulled the aircraft out into the clearing. I was unfolding the ultralight wings when a soldier walked into the clearing and looked right at me. The AK was slung across my back, making the MP5K the fastest draw. I brought the gun up and pulled down hard on the selector. Not knowing what position it ended up landing in, I squeezed the trigger, spraying a burst of 9mm at the soldier as he was leveling his AK. At least one round hit him, causing him to scream out in pain. I watched him as I worked, unfolding the wing and placing the lock pins in place. Through my NVD, I saw his AK come up off the snow, so I hit him with another burst, stopping his movement cold. My rounds were suppressed, but his screams from the first machine gun burst were not. I put my kit in the plane and strapped in before engaging the startup sequence.

The engine turned over on the first attempt. I could see flashlights beaming through the woods in my direction and some dark figures spilling out into the opening behind me. I went to firewall on the gas mixture, jerking the aircraft forward and down the hill. I pulled back the controls, waiting for enough speed to pick up my nosewheel, and found it at about forty knots. Not long after, my main wheels came off the snow and I was airborne once more.

It didn't register at the time, but I was being shot at from the ground. Nothing that I could see hit the aircraft, but I could hear the distinct sound of automatic AK fire below. Looking over my shoulder, bright muzzle flashes peppered the darkness as the AK spit rounds at me.

It was all about the holdover, and I'm glad those soldiers didn't seem to understand that.

I flew only about twenty minutes before starting my corkscrew descent to the valley floor. Landing was uneventful and I again strained my legs to pull the aircraft into cover, waiting on Savannah to show.

I didn't stay at the rally point camp, choosing to set up an observation post a hundred yards up the hill so that I could look down from above and make sure she didn't arrive with company.

She showed up at about 2200 with both horses. We are not sleeping.

Tonight we plan.

Tomorrow night, I fly.

FUSION CENTER

The past twenty-four hours went by in a flash. We relocated camp farther away near another NAI cache and planned for most of our time. Savannah expressed to me that she'd hope we'd run into a few of the cliff camp survivors here before we'd arrived. The children. We didn't talk about them, but we both had grave concerns. After heavily gearing up, I began making calculations on exactly what I'd be bringing with me on the flight north into the occupied zone of Arkansas. I took my Glock, MP5K, and AK-47 along with spare mags for all. I also brought a few other things that might be needed.

Savannah had a bag full of IR firefly markers. If she wanted to mark something for me, all she'd need to do was connect a 9v battery to the IR firefly and drop it on the ground. The number of fireflies on the ground meant different things. The small devices would strobe for a couple days before dying.

She left several hours ago to gather intel. I'm taking off soon.

I left under the light of a mostly full moon, hours after Savannah, speeding north high enough to not be detected from the ground. I flew slowly at near stall speed, conserving fuel. The landscape below could easily be some rural mountainscape somewhere until the lunar light bounced from abandoned buildings hit my NVD just right. Up ahead, I noticed an IR flash and a large pavilion covered with a bright tent structure came into view off the nose. It had to be the Amp. The firefly signal was strobing west of the Amp in the center of a large field. I temporarily kicked over to electric motor, killing the loud internal combustion engine. The quiet brushless electric motor allowed me to hear the rush of the propeller through the cold dense air behind me.

Looking at my display, I began to see the battery countdown percentages at the rate of about one percent every thirty seconds. I had about twenty minutes on battery reserves before the electrics couldn't sustain altitude. Good to know.

I orbited overhead the signal for two minutes, losing 5 percent, when I saw a second firefly turn on near the first. The signal worked out with Savannah meant that it was now safe to land. When I dropped two thousand feet in altitude I could finally make the outline of two horses in the field below standing near the IR fireflies. After one more orbit overhead, I brought the aircraft down in the field and cut the engine as I flared, hit the ground, and came rolling to a stop about a hundred yards from the horses. Twisting the five-point buckle, I stepped out of the aircraft to Savannah's dark silhouette.

"That thing was ghost quiet when you landed," she said.

She helped me pull the aircraft out of plain view and handed me the gas can that was strapped to Molly on the trip north. I filled the aircraft's fuel reservoir, then handed Savannah the empty plastic jug as I tossed over the plane some camo netting scavenged from the last NAI cache.

"I contacted a friend," Savannah said as we began to walk away from the aircraft to gather the horses.

"Who?"

"Someone that's heard of you; he'll be here in an hour."

"How'd you contact him?"

"Dead-drop chalk mark. NAI has allies, and our allies know our marks. Radio communications are completely compromised. SneakerNET is the only way to exchange information without being exploited and targeted. There's a huge signal intercept vacuum cleaner apparatus still operating despite the grid being down and the GDP being reduced to zero."

The bastards just couldn't let go of their precious total surveillance state.

We set up a camp under a canopy of trees and began constructing the small, stealthy fire that Rich taught me how to build. Using my small latrine shovel, I laboriously dug an eight-inch hole in the ground, crushing through frozen earth and pulling rocks. Savannah gathered the small kindling and some inch thick branches. I used the last few drops of gasoline in the can to quickly start the fire. We built a small lean-to over the top so the flame couldn't be observed from overhead. We warmed up and cooked some dehydrated food over the meager fire.

Finishing up, I was about to get up to find a tree when I heard the rumble of a diesel engine approaching from the road that ran east and west adjacent the field we were in.

I began to sprint to the edge of the field as Savannah yelled out, "It's probably NAI, Max!"

"I don't operate on probably!" I shouted back, hoping she'd follow me to concealment.

She didn't.

I stayed there at the field's edge with my AK pointed at the road, ready for the source of the engine noise to come into view. It was very odd, seeing Savannah standing out there in the open with her arms crossed, waiting on the vehicle to arrive. I felt as if I needed to do something, but she was her own person.

There were no headlights as the vehicle came into view. The foliage that lined the fence that followed the road covered everything but the top half of the vehicle.

MRAP.

A gunner manned the crew-served machine gun atop the machine, scanning it back and forth until Savannah picked up one of the fireflies and held it high. The gunner reacted, slewing his machine gun to Savannah.

It was at that moment I thought that the last surviving member of the Cliff Camp Cell of the NAI was about to be chewed to pieces.

That was until the MRAP lurched farther forward, into a break in the fence foliage.

I could see the white spray-painted letters as they appeared through the chain link fence.

#FIGHT

We were being visited by a ghost.

———

I crept from cover, moving slowly to the MRAP. Seeing the #FIGHT painted on the side calmed my nerves somewhat, but anyone could be inside of that thing and the gunner on top could easily handle anything short of an EFP, something I was short on at the moment. My AK rounds would just chip the paint and windows of the beast.

I watched Savannah fearlessly approach the fence, and couldn't help but ponder on whether or not that cavalier attitude among the NAI was what led to the fall of their cliff cell at the hands of the Chinese security forces. No. I shouldn't think that way. More than likely it's my own guilt talking.

Savannah scaled the fence and approached the driver side door. I heard the gunner greet her from up top at the same time. A man stepped out of the vehicle and walked around to the back. I recognized the gait from before.

Inky.

The former marine and OEF vet. He walked with a distinct limp from taking shrapnel somewhere in RC East back in the day. I dropped my gun, allowing it to hang on its sling as I ran to the fence and began to climb.

"Inky!" I shouted, forgetting to whisper.

He stopped in his tracks and just stood there for a moment before spinning around.

"Max . . . ? Holy shit, you're alive! Where the hell have you been, man?!"

After embracing him and telling him how happy I was to see him, I told Inky that out in the open on the road wasn't the best place to catch up. He agreed, opening the rear door and gesturing me and Savannah inside. It was warm in the vehicle, inviting. I could see the gunner's torso as he turned left to right, scanning the area for any threats. Inky secured the aft door and climbed up into the rig.

We executed a turn and the MRAP began to travel back the way it had come for a few miles until turning onto a dirt road and through a rusted gate sitting ajar, which was probably used to keep trespassers from hunting out here.

After rolling through the gate, the MRAP's brakes squeaked the giant to a stop. I saw Inky click a garage door opener and the old gate behind us began to slowly close. Covered in vines and weeds, it looked as if no one had been through in some time. The MRAP moved ahead as the metal gate met in the middle. I moved up closer to the front, asking Inky how he kept the wrong kind of people out of where we were headed.

"We keep wireless sensors under the ground on this road, and some pre-staged explosives. Anyone but us comes down and they get smoked and cleaned up by the people that are no doubt watching us from the edge of the road right now. We've got enough firepower to defend this place from ground assault. Hell, eventually, we'll have enough to go on a limited offensive."

After another mile, the MRAP pulled under another canopy of trees and into a large area covered by familiar surplus camo netting, placed there to fool any overhead sensors that might be watching. As soon as the big diesel engine shut down, I swung the aft door open, stepping back out into the cold, feeling a harsh, icy slap to my face.

Crates of Stinger missiles, fuel, and other interesting and useful items were neatly stacked, forming a sort of garage bay around the large armored vehicle. Fifty-five-gallon drums of diesel fuel were placed dozens of drums deep behind crates of ammunition. A makeshift sign carved into a pallet hung over the supplies.

LITTLE REDSTONE

I took a visual inventory of all the supplies, hoping that this wasn't all the NAI had. One five hundred pound bomb and all this was gone via secondaries. I'd probably think about spreading this stuff out a little better if I were the supply guy.

After a few moments, Inky gestured me to follow and I did so, back into the woods, down a small deer path, and into the side of a hill.

Another damn cave, I thought as I ducked into the hole behind Inky.

As I began to take in my surroundings, I realized that it was really a man-made dugout structure that more resembled a mine, or one of those drug tunnels you'd see on the news at night coming from Mexico into the U.S. Two-by-four studs framed the tunnel, keeping the earth at bay all around us. LED lights were strung overhead, providing just enough light so you didn't run into the person in front of you.

Inky turned left, left, right, and then I lost track until we parted some canvas curtains and entered what looked like a very expedient command center. Computers, maps, and even a small library adorned the eight-hundred-square-foot space. A large planning table made from plywood and more two-by-fours sat in the center, surrounded by people poring over plans and even copying things down from headphones connected to what looked like HAM radios.

One of those signal interceptors tore off a piece of paper from her notepad and handed it to someone who looked like a supervisor.

"Drone sighted over 540, Springdale," she called out, passing the intel over to someone else who left the room with it.

Inky used that example to expound on the function of this small but effective command center. This node was capable of reception only, as transmitting here would soon bring down the full force of the provisional government and their henchmen. If there was a piece of actionable intelligence collected, it would be sent via horseback courier to a transmit post, where a designated field radioman would send the intel via low power signal relay to one of many hidden high-powered transmitters. The radioman was trained in guerrilla warfare, as the job was hazardous to say the least. This network of radiomen reported that every week they'd lose a hidden high-powered transmitter to provisional government SIGINT strike forces, but they still managed to place enough in the field to offset the losses.

So far, signal intercept to transmit was averaging about an hour because the horseback courier had to locate their radioman somewhere out in enemy-controlled areas. The notes that the courier carried were in code only known by the original interceptor and the radioman, meaning if they were captured, any messages they had on hand would be unreadable, by even the courier.

This was how to communicate under hostile government surveillance. Encrypted handwritten notes and digital radio dead drops. The government owned any and all cellular and data networks as they were hardwired into the towers they powered and brought online. As another security measure, the radiomen carried dice so that random high-powered transmitter choices could be made in the field. When a transmission order was made, only the field radioman would know the tower to use based on the random role of the dice. Also, any government SIGINT operator would need to be on the right channel during the right few seconds to intercept the code worded communications meant for the receiving NAI cells.

Even then, the near unlimited power of the intelligence apparatus was still able to find and fix our people sometimes. This is why this station's radiomen were trained in the arts of guerrilla combat. Inky has a few special operators on the team that defected from various bases, eventually making their way back to their home state of Arkansas. These pipe hitters had no problems training the radiomen on how to strike back hard if they were intercepted and attacked. Each radioman carried an M4 and two hundred rounds with a medium range optic, and some that operated in particularly hostile environments carried Stingers on horseback.

You can't stop the signal.

I asked about the Chinese troops I'd seen. I needed answers.

"Oh, you mean the UN troops?" Inky responded.

UN troops? I thought to myself, shaking my head.

Seeing the confused look on my face, Inky went on to explain that the currency and subsequent economic collapse of the United States disintegrated our national and domestic security apparatus. Aircraft carriers were docked and scuttled when the good faith and confidence in the American dollar was lost. When military credit lines started declining, jet fuel procurement and canal passages were canceled, stranding our navy in every sea worldwide. Whole Army divisions were left to fend for themselves and find their own way home. Squadron after squadron of Air Force jets were abandoned in the desert, left there to erode in the winds as no one could afford to fly them.

America could no longer pay for the endless wars for which it continued to engage; until the very end, we persisted with the deadly economic Russian roulette attempt to jumpstart systemic poor economic performance through outrageous Keynesian war spending.

With echoes of Soviet fleets left abandoned after Moscow's collapse, our unpaid military was forced to follow in Communist footsteps.

But what happened to our military in the beginning was nothing like the gutting of our domestic security.

Police officers were off the force in droves, replaced by the worst of the worst federal law enforcement officers—those loyal to the state and seeing anything that stood in its way as a barrier to progress. The good local and federal police resigned, most of them joining their local resistance, leaving only statists behind to man the helm of domestic security. Formerly disgruntled TSA agents were promoted to positions of power within the new Federal Police

Force (FPF) and given the authority to stop travelers on any road or thoroughfare in the United States—for any reason.

Papers, please, I thought.

The new War Powers Act, passed by a quisling traitor provisional government, gave the FPF the powers of a judge during times of crisis, meaning that they could kill on the spot for what the state deemed as egregious violations of enacted national emergency laws. Laws such as the banning of all semi-auto firearms and some curfew violations, especially those inside prohibited areas. The list of executable offenses was too long to summarize.

This was where the United Nations came into play. Angst fueled from decades of American exceptionalism opened the gates to outside intervention. The provisional government, in a bid to leverage power from our debt status, called upon China for help with domestic security . . . actually promising land as payment for past debts. As in U.S. soil.

Being reliant on technological infrastructure, urban China was hit just as hard as the rest of the world when the grid was attacked, but their massive rural farmscape and mining infrastructure allowed them to revert back to preindustrial supply lines faster than most first world countries. Their place behind us in industrial development actually helped them weather the storm faster than the technologically crippled United States.

With supply lines running back and forth with Russia, China was able to trade raw materials for military hardware. It turns out that starving Russians preferred food and diesel over their own fleet of idle naval troop transports. Intel from ex-pats overseas via HAM radio reported that in the months after the initial collapse, Chinese shipyards were buzzing with activity, returning former Russian troop transports to conditions of readiness for a transpacific voyage.

The United States possessed thirty trillion in debt when I left for Syria last year. Yes, most of it was owned by the American people, but a huge chunk of that money was owed to the People's Republic of China. A country that in past decades had constructed islands and claimed hundreds of miles of territorial waters above and beyond Law of the Sea Convention constraints. A country whose thousand year plan was to extend their empire east to Guam, and eventually to the west coast of the United States. The cyberattack that brought down the world seemed to accelerate that plan, as there were already quite a number of Chinese security personnel in the major population centers of the United States.

It was rumored that self-sufficient ranches out west, rich in oil, natural gas, and cattle, had already been seized for debt payment, a move endorsed by the current government representing United States interests. Millions of acres have already been signed over in lieu of the promise of order from the Chinese. There have also been reports of Tiananmen Square–style enforcement.

Inky had managed to become the resistance intelligence hub in this region. His communications apparatus sucked up information like a Dyson, sifting through it daily and forming accurate and actionable intelligence. He'd managed to tell me more about what had transpired since I escaped to Newton County than anyone else I'd encountered since meeting the NAI.

After going into a lot of detail on this underground rebel base and its function, Inky brought me over to the table.

We sat down, and his first words were "I know they have Rich, and that's probably why you're here."

I nodded and began to tell the details of what had happened since I disappeared, melting into the hills of Newton County, and how I came about the information of Rich's subsequent incarceration.

Inky knew Rich. Rich, me, and the ghosts were the goddamned resistance before it grew to what it was today. There was no one else in those early dark days of chaos and confusion. Inky could see the rage and pain in my eyes as I told him the information that Maggie had revealed to me.

Slapping me on the shoulder, Inky said, "Fear not. The building they're using is well known. We recovered the schematics from county paper records, and we have people here that used to work there; they know the layout of the floor where they're keeping Rich. The only issue is getting inside the building perimeter fence. Once you do that, security is a lot more manageable."

Inky called one of his adjutants over, asking for the ex–retail giant HQ blueprints. He scurried off, returning in less than a minute with ten scrolls of paper tucked inside cardboard tubes.

"If you can get inside the perimeter, we can get you to Rich with these," the former marine said with confidence.

"I can get inside, but ex-fil with an injured sixtysomething-year-old man is a different matter altogether," I said.

"Max, have faith. I'm sending for the three people we have nearby that used to work there before the government nationalized it. They know the things that we can't see in these blueprints. But, please, tell me how the hell you intend on getting inside the wire?"

I told Inky precisely what I was going to do. He just laughed and called me a crazy bastard.

Twelve-hour Planning Session—FML

I never thought all the joint planning courses I'd slogged through would ever be of any use until today. Well, they're still a load of shit, but there was something to be said about the techniques one used to strategize a complex paramilitary operation. I started off as a one-man mission going in to get Rich, alone and unafraid; that has changed. Yes, I'm still going in alone, but I've also gained the advantage of power, cyber, and explosives support.

Inky wanted Rich out of that place just as bad as I did and his actions verified that in spades.

12 Minutes

I took off just before midnight, flying into a slightly waning moon. Using the full tank I had, I pushed the engine to max safe RPM as the small craft began to climb high into the dark Arkansas sky. After function checking the trim settings on the aircraft, I was more confident that my plan might actually work, at least the first part of it. As the aircraft approached ten thousand feet, I twisted the valve on the oxygen bottle I'd brought with me and placed the clear plastic mask over my mouth and nose. The aircraft continued its climb.

The snow-covered landscape below looked as if it could be a scene taken from the skies of some Siberian forest. I decided to turn the aircraft 180 degrees to give me more time to hit my target altitude. The aircraft's battery charge held steady at fifty-two percent as it trickle charged from the small alternator being spun by the gas engine.

As I ascended, I began to shiver from the extreme cold. My wrist altimeter read twenty thousand feet as I leveled off and kept flying north. An instrument had been retrofitted to the aircraft before the mission, which allowed me to fly over the fusion center by following a needle pointing to a transmitter placed just outside the security zone that led inside. I needed to be five hundred meters north of the beacon to be on top of the facility at 20,000. Using mental math calculations, I estimate that I had about fifteen minutes before go-time.

I placed the O_2 sensor on my freezing index finger to make sure I was getting air from the green bottle I was sharing the seat with. Satisfied with an upper 90s percentile on O_2 saturation, I set a timer for two minutes so that I could check my readings again. I knew it would be cold at that altitude, but I didn't expect it to be ten-below-zero cold. I flew with my knees for a bit, letting my hands defrost until the O_2 reading reminder went off again.

I repeated this cycle of cold torture what seemed like dozens of times but it could only really have been about seven based on the countdown to the facility in front of me on the iPad multifunction display running the ultralight aircraft systems.

My face was completely numb when I cut the internal combustion, replacing propulsion with the battery. The cold must have had a negative effect on the battery's performance, as the charge percentages began to plummet by the second. The beacon needle swung 180 degrees and I started another chronograph. I'd need to be out of the aircraft in forty-five seconds.

My kit was prestaged. I attached the heavy pack via carabiners and straps and set the trim controls on the ultralight in a very slight climb.

Ten seconds to go.

I strapped my long gun across my chest, unbuckled my harness, and clutched the O_2 bottle like it was my own life. When the timer began to blink wildly, I rolled out of the seat, over the safety bars, and down, down, down into the frigid air below.

I began to flail, trying to angle my legs to stabilize my tumble. Unfortunately, I'd forgotten since training that I really needed my arms to do that. Reluctantly, I shuffled the small O_2 bottle over to one arm and began to stabilize. At about 12,000 feet, I regained control of my body.

At ten thousand feet, I removed the O_2 mask and began to scan the fast-approaching earth as well as my altimeter as it spun like a ceiling fan. The winds were light and variable on the flight up, so I decided to pull the chute a little early at 9,000 feet. Unfortunately, after I did that the chute yanked so hard that I dropped the O_2 bottle, sending it shooting down to the ground below, the mask and O_2 line fluttering behind it like a drogue chute.

I wasn't yet low enough to make out any details besides the massive fusion center building, so I didn't know where the metal bottle would land. I released my pack on a twelve-foot strap so that it would hit the ground a second before I did.

With newfound mobility, I began to work the risers on the chute, flying to the target as I descended. There was a helicopter on the roof, but through my NVD, I could see no IR signature or signs of preflight activity. As the building got bigger, I began to wonder where my trusty ultralight might end up when the battery ran out.

I made final course adjustments on the parachute risers, steering myself to an area of the roof a good distance behind the helo pad so that I could quickly land and stow my chute. The lack of any searchlights or activity below indicated that my O_2 bottle hadn't drawn much attention when it shot into the ground at a couple hundred knots.

So far so good.

The building approached at breakneck speed. A few seconds before a hard touchdown, I flared the chute, significantly slowing my descent. My pack hit first and began to drag when I landed just in front of it. Thankfully, I didn't break anything. As soon as I hit, I deflected the impact energy, rolling from my feet to my knees, to my buttocks and up my back. The first thing I thought of was the chute. I frantically reached for the risers and began to pull the large silk half sphere down to me, crumpling it up, making it smaller so the breeze wouldn't catch it and pull me over the side of the building.

As soon as I got the chute to low vis, I released my Koch fittings and wrapped the shoot around one of the many roof vents, tying it off with the risers.

It was time to go to work.

I made weapons ready and adjusted my NVD, giving a knock to my front XSAPI plate if for nothing more than extra peace of mind.

I moved forward to the roof access door positioned twenty-five meters ahead. With no movement or lights on the roof that I could see, I was beginning to feel confident. At the monolith-like roof access structure, I checked my watch.

Twelve minutes to go.

I planned for six minutes of extra time, not twelve. I had no clue as to how I'd made up those extra minutes. Maybe I flew too fast, or I didn't calculate my drop speed correctly after my chute opened. It didn't matter. I knew at that moment that all I needed to do was survive on the roof for twelve more minutes.

I stood there hunched over in the shadows of the small access structure, calculating my plan and working out possible contingencies to things that hadn't happened yet.

I had five minutes remaining when the roof access door went flying open, spilling bright light into my face, whiting out my optics. The steel door behind the two unsuspecting men closed behind them with a thunk. As it did, I brought up my sub gun, instinctively firing at center mass.

Four pops from my suppressed 9mm rang out in quick succession, punching through the chest cavities of both men, sending them stumbling out of breath to the asphalt roof, where they died in short order.

They were armed and would have wasted me if given the chance. If you worked in this building, you were a traitor in my book—at least, that's what I kept telling myself.

The two men were dressed like Maggie and the goon that tried to smoke me back at my father's cabin, the same clothes I now wore. They had sidearms, but I was already covered in that department.

I dragged them into the moon shadow and away from the door. As I did so, a pack of cigarettes and a lighter fell from a dead hand. They were only coming outside for a cigarette break. It's all about timing, I guess. Everything is.

Three minutes left until go-time.

That was when I remembered why I needed the extra minutes. I needed to work the lock that had just closed behind the guards. Quickly, I tried to bump it first, rake it second, and with only a minute remaining I had to go OG and pick the individual tumblers. My watch gave a single beep when the time came and went. The lock wasn't letting me in.

At one minute past go-time, things got really quiet, telling me that Inky's people had held up their end of the deal.

The generators that powered the building were down. Inky and his people had induced a massive charge into the local micro-grid, frying the generators from a power line that ran outside the wire to a security checkpoint two miles away that they'd likely just hit. Inky assessed that he could keep the power down for thirty minutes.

I began to sweat as my fingers became numb from trying to get through the roof door lock. I was about to give up when the last tumbler was pushed into place, calling me to torsion the cylinder over and free the internal mechanisms that were keeping me from my objective.

I brought my gun up and opened the door. The fact that no light spilled from the door frame brought a sinister grin to my face. The power was down, and I seriously doubted that many people inside the building had NVDs, or were near enough to them that it mattered. How many times did I have them on me in the halls of the intelligence community?

Never.

I had a series of cards encased in a clear plastic sleeve that I wore on my left forearm.

Simplified and miniaturized building schematics.

I knew where the holding cells were located. Moles that worked as contractors on the inside told the NAI where they were paid to install the bars and reinforced holding units.

I had two hundred rounds of subsonic 9mm. My trilug can checked tight on my MP5K, giving me the confidence to go kinetic at will in the halls of the fusion center.

As I descended the stairs into the bowels of the building, I checked my schematics and headed for the nearest elevator shaft.

Using the small titanium pry bar I'd jumped with, I forced the elevator door open, revealing, you guessed it, an elevator. Cursing, I left the open door and headed for the stairwell.

I had about another ten minutes before the NAI rained down mortars on my position; I had to hurry.

I hit the door open, seeing movement at the bottom of the stairs. Raising my gun, I began to descend. Red emergency lighting cast the shadow of someone approaching. As soon as the guard rounded the corner, I blasted, but not before he let loose a round from his pistol, hitting me in the chest, hard.

I doubled over, feeling the skin behind my bulletproof armor plates. It hurt like hell, but there was no blood. I spent the next couple of minutes recovering on the stairs, hoping that the guard was a fluke and that I still possessed the element of surprise.

After catching my breath and fighting through the pain of being shot, I kept moving forward, down the stairs and around the landing to the floor below. At the door, I opened it slowly, creeping onto the next floor.

Confusion abounded. Battery-powered emergency lighting was removed from the wall; people on the floor were using them to move around. I tried to act like I belonged and kept going. The clothing I wore seemed to be familiar to some, and so they went past me without even really acknowledging that I was there . . . until someone in a suit and tie began to question me.

"What's going on? Do you know anything?" the man in the fancy clothing asked.

"Sir, it looks like it's only a power disruption. Should be cleared up in a few minutes," I responded, trying to put him at ease, so that perhaps he might do the same for the rest of the people on this floor. They were all bad guys as far as I was concerned, but I only had so many rounds and my objective was Rich. The suit scurried away wearing a bewildered look. I'd let these compartmentalized traitors live for now.

At the elevator door, I waited for a group of workers to pass before I put the crowbar to the door again. This time I knew it'd be clear, as the elevator car was one floor above. The door budged open about two feet and I climbed through, gripping the greased cables for my descent to the basement. With only ten floors to go, the trip only took a minute. I was of course covered in thick cable grease, but I wasn't in this mother for a fashion show.

At the bottom of the shaft, I took off my gloves, tossing the spent rags to the grease-covered floor. The door to the basement level was about hip height, giving me perfect leverage on the center of the closed door. In a few seconds, I had the elevator door open just enough for me to squeeze through into the detention area of the fusion center.

There was no movement in the hallways, but I did hear voices at the end of the hall. I homed in on those and started moving, gun up to my cheek.

Rounding the corner, I heard two confused guards asking one another what they thought the problem might be and when it might be fixed. I immediately shot one of them in the head, sending him to the ground, putting the other guard in a state of terror.

He raised his hands up, begging me not to shoot him.

"Rich ▄▄▄▄▄▄▄▄▄▄. Take me to his cell, right the fuck now!" I demanded.

"Y-yes . . . okay," the man said, turning slowly and walking down the hall with his hands up.

We went to the end of the hall and made a left, where I was forced to shoot two more guards. This only reinforced the resolve of the guard under my control to do exactly what I told him.

At the door marked C3, the man gestured to the nameplate that displayed only one single word.

TOURIST

"This is him. I've done what you asked. Please."

"Open it! Open it now!"

The man reached for a key ring on his belt as I touched the end of my silencer to his chest. Nervously, he flipped the rings around in the red emergency lighting until he found the one he was looking for, inserting it into the lock.

As soon as I heard the lock disengage on the cell door, I squeezed the trigger, sending a 147-grain round into his chest, his body hitting the tile floor with a thud.

The door sat there, partially open. I stepped forward and opened it the rest of the way, revealing a semi-dark room with a chair in the middle. Emergency lights in the cell flickered revealing someone balled up in a fetal position in the corner of the room. I placed my gun on safe and brought it up, pointing it to the body on the floor. Just because the traitor I'd killed said this was Rich didn't mean it was true.

I sidestepped the chair, noticing the thick leather straps and the empty jugs of water that sat arranged in rows next to it.

They'd been waterboarding him.

My blood pressure shot up, thinking of how painful and frightening that must have been for Rich. I reached the body and nudged it with my foot.

"Rich, it's me. It's Max," I said quietly to the motionless body on the floor.

At the sound of my voice, the body stirred, throwing off an old wool blanket. The man lying on the cold floor was definitely Rich, but a much more gaunt version. Instead of the hobo Santa Claus I was used to seeing, I found a Bin Laden look-alike. Rich looked up at me but I realized that he couldn't see me. The power was still cut; Rich was squinting at me, trying to make me out through the dim red light.

"Max . . . ? Is it really you?" he asked, reaching for my hand in the darkness.

I offered mine, gripping his hand tightly before responding.

"Yeah. I'm here to get you out of here. Take this."

I pulled a squeeze package of caffeine-infused energy gel and gave it to Rich. He downed the whole package in just a few seconds.

"Got any more?"

I gave him another without saying a word and told him to get on his feet.

"Things are about to get sporty—you get my meaning?"

Rich nodded and asked for a weapon. I quickly recovered the AK-47 from across my back and handed it over to him along with an extra mag. Rich stuffed the extra down his scrub pant waistband and donned his paper slippers.

"I'm ready to move. Let's roll," he said, checking the condition of his Combloc weapon. "Where'd you get this?"

"Chinese soldier. He didn't need it anymore," I responded with a chuckle.

"Thought so. Feels Chinese."

With that, we stepped out into the open. I told Rich to let me take the shots, as I was running the silencer. If I needed help, I'd yell out and hit the deck. He'd need to spray the fuck out of whatever was in front of him.

"Just don't shoot lower than knee level, okay?" I said.

We turned right out of his cell and headed for the stairwell.

As I passed the cell marked ▬▬▬▬▬▬▬, I heard a familiar voice. "I know those were gunshots—what the hell is going on out there?"

Maggie?!

So, it looked like getting into bed with these fuckers came back to bite her. Wonder what she did to piss them off?

I hesitated for a moment before taking the keys from the dead guard's hand. Sliding the viewport over, I took a look inside and was instantly met with Maggie's bruised and beaten face, obvious even through the green optics of my NVD and the flickering emergency lights. For a moment I thought back to when I'd first met her, deep inside a strange building that also happened to be an unacknowledged classified direct action support facility.

She just stood there in her dirty scrubs, her arms hanging down at her sides as if standing at the position of attention.

"Step back," I said through the viewport.

"Max?!"

Saying nothing, I began to cycle through the keys to open the door.

"I've heard her screams, Max," Rich whispered over my shoulder. "They've hurt her pretty bad over the past few weeks."

The power flickered on for a second before cutting out again. It was time to move. The lock relented on the third key. I opened the door, telling Maggie to come out.

"I don't owe you a goddamn thing," I said to her coldly as I kept moving to the stairwell access.

I have no idea why I chose to let her go.

Before going in, I broke the nearby glass pane and pulled down hard on the switch marked FIRE. All hell broke loose as Klaxons and emergency strobes began to fire, causing confusion and disorientation, hopefully enough to get us to the first floor and outside. Rich moved slow, a side effect of sleep and calorie depravation. I was really happy to find him vertical and mobile, but at his current weight, which I estimated to be about a hundred and sixty pounds, carrying him was doable.

We hit the stairs and were met by people in normal civilian clothing. They weren't armed.

"Hurry, go back upstairs—there's a fire raging in the holding areas!" I yelled, hoping I got the terminology correct enough.

It seemed to work, as the civilians turned around and began to run back up to the first floor. I followed them up and through the access door to the floor.

I heard someone say, "Why aren't the sprinklers on?" and someone else respond with something about the lack of water pressure. This played to our favor as panic and fear began to spread.

"Hurry, it's spreading—it's all over the basement!" I screamed, trying to use a different voice than the one I'd used on the civilians in the stairwell.

That was it.

Another voice of authority that I didn't recognize began to give instructions, "Everyone, follow me to the exit. There is nothing here worth saving—just grab your phones and follow me."

Cell phone flashlights began to wave back and forth, resembling digital lighthouses inside my NVD. There were enough of them on the floor that I raised my optic up and stepped back into the shadows, waiting for the floor to clear. As the workers began to leave the floor for the fire exit, I filed behind them.

The lights flickered once more, this time staying on for nearly five seconds. Luckily, no one noticed the "prisoners" I had with me during the brief moment the lights were on. I moved with a little more speed as I looked over my shoulder, gesturing Rich to catch up when the lights went out again.

Maggie was following behind Rich.

I didn't know where she thought she was going, but it was a pretty bold move.

Ignoring her for the moment, I reached the door that led to the outside and stepped through, blending in with all the evacuees in the darkness. I grabbed Rich's clothing, keeping him concealed by the moon shadow behind me. One of the evacuees started to ask a question, but I cut her off, telling her that I'd received a radio call about restoring the power and that I'd answer all her questions when I got back. She nodded in acceptance, and Rich and I made for the back side of the building towards a space of fence between two tall guard towers.

The tower on our left was empty, or at least no one was standing up in it. The one on the right had a guard, but he seemed focused on outside threats, not inside.

With careful deliberation, I pulled my handheld radio and quickly removed the tape that prevented the power source from contacting to it.

Depressing the transmit button, I said, "Fire in the hole."

Two minutes.

I headed toward the tower to the right, knowing that if I got close enough, I'd be in its blind spot and could do what I needed to do. I pulled the small master key strapped to my pack and began to cut the fence wires.

An explosion hit the building somewhere behind me; the blast wave nearly blew the NVD off my head.

The NAI mortars were beginning to fly.

As soon as I'd finished cutting a 3x3 section from the fence, I sent Rich through, knowing that the guard's attention would by now be shifted 180 degrees toward the building. After Rich was on the other side, I looked back one more time.

A dark figure moved toward me from a dozen yards away, gaining the attention of the tower guard. Goddammit, fucking Maggie.

"Halt!" the guard commanded.

I stepped out away from the base of the tower and took aim at the guard. I squeezed the trigger as another mortar detonated; the man doubled over and fell from the tower, slamming to the ground with a thud.

Moving quickly through the opening I'd cut, I took the lead and checked my wrist compass before moving south and west, dissolving into the winter landscape as if I was never there. As I moved farther away, my NVD lit up with a new light source. Power had been restored at the fusion center, illuminating the ongoing NAI mortar strike in vivid incandescent color.

I adjusted my speed to go faster until Rich began to lag behind. Letting up a little to allow his beaten and tired body some reprieve, I noticed Maggie's shadowy figure pacing us from a distance. I decided to address this once and for all.

As I approached, I caught a flash of steel, instantly bringing my gun up to meet her. She was carrying an M4 carbine and wore combat boots with her prisoner garb.

"From the guard?" I asked.

"Yeah," she responded. "Kill me or let me come with you. I only want one thing. Just one."

"And what's that?"

"Payback. For what they did to my child . . . what they did to me," Maggie replied through clenched teeth.

Knowing that she could have killed me at any time from the fence line until now, I just turned away and began to trek southwest once again. Maggie followed—not because I told her that she could, but because she knew that she should.

Rich was in poor shape and shaking with exposure and hunger by the time we arrived at the rally point, ten miles away. As we approached, I heard the massive diesel engine from Inky's MRAP fire up. The familiar IR challenge signal was sent from the crewserved operator on the machine gun on top, and I responded in kind, using the signal of the day as briefed.

Rich was back in the fight, but so was Maggie. To what end, I didn't know or comprehend. I placed a canvas sack over her head as soon as she entered the MRAP and we were on our way.

ARKANSAS UNDERGROUND

I ripped the hood from Maggie's head after getting her back to the camp. She was checked head to toe for any electronic surveillance devices on the way in. For someone as strong as she was, for all of her training, I was slightly perplexed as to why she wouldn't stop crying. After a series of questions, she finally let go and told me what I needed to know.

When she was repatriated by the provisional government after I left her at the helicopter, she was interrogated. Heavily. They didn't believe the story she told them, and promptly arrested her on charges of abetting a known terrorist. The interrogation turned extreme. They then brought Maggie's daughter into the chamber and went to work on her. Maggie finally gave in and admitted to providing false information as to my whereabouts to her interrogators.

Do I believe her?

Yes.

The interrogators *accidentally* killed Maggie's daughter on a water-board, right in front of her, days before I showed up to extract Rich.

She was only twelve.

For people that think torture doesn't work, they're wrong. It definitely fucking works, but once you do it, you're a piece of garbage forever. If there's a God, he's coming for all the torturers, murderers, and belligerents, and the ones that give them orders. And the only thing worse than garden-variety torture is hurting a child, and that's a line I'll never cross—the same line that will make Maggie forever question her notions of reality.

Inky reports that the fusion center has been heavily damaged, and that it'll take them a good while to get back up online. The word has been dispatched to the radiomen and should soon be in the hands of every NAI cell.

Rich gorged on food the rest of the morning after our return, and is now sleeping somewhere in the tunnels below. Maggie sat wrapped in a blanket near a small fire, drinking coffee and soaking her feet in some warm water.

I'm not done with these tyrants. Through my own mistakes in Syria, I tipped the first domino that eventually caused this entire collapse.

I'm going to spend the rest of my life fighting, to somehow right these wrongs, any way that I can.

━━━

I awoke to bustling activity in the passage underground, near where I slept. Sliding my curtain open, my bare feet touched earth, and I felt like some caveman about to pick up his spear and go to work, hunting and gathering in the saber-tooth-tiger-dense hills of Arkansas. Instead of a spear, I reached for my machine gun, a cold, harsh German tool of war that hasn't failed me yet. Rich was still sawing logs in a bed that was dug into the earth waist-high like some ancient grave one might find underneath some church in Europe.

Stepping groggily out into the passageway with my boots in my hand, I shuffled to the war room atop a line of wooden pallets that meandered through the tunnel to the lights up ahead. Inky sat at the table scanning over charts, passing what appeared to be important notes to the radiomen-bound couriers near and far.

"Hey, Max. We really shook things up. The system is requesting more UN troops to augment the security forces in Northwest Arkansas. That ain't necessarily a good thing." Inky slid photographs over in front of me.

Three grainy black-and-white photos that looked as if they were Normandy invasion archive pictures depicted dozens of large ships sitting in a harbor. A giant star could be seen on the superstructure of the closest vessel in the photo.

"What am I looking at, Inky?" I asked.

"The harbor at 32nd Street Naval Base, San Diego. Yesterday," Inky responded.

"How did you get these from California in a day?" I asked, incredulous.

"We have a digital network setup with the coasts. It's not even close to 56k speed, but we can receive low-resolution images via digital shortwave radio network from our radioman out there. Bottom line is that the troop transports from China keep showing up, dumping military personnel on our shores."

Inky analyzed the intel just like he did when I first showed up. The more troops that arrived on the coast, the harder our job would be to take the country back and restore our own brand of order.

The influx of UN peacekeepers isn't our only problem as I write this. Most of the military deserted, leaving for their families when all of this shit went down. The rest left their posts when they stopped getting paid and fed, electing to strike out alone and survive with whatever military hardware they could bring with them. Some of them were a threat in the uncontrolled areas. Some of them might be a friend to the NAI, and some of them may not. The whole country was torn in hundreds of pieces, shards, and factions all vying for survival by any means necessary.

Savannah walked into the operations center, brightening the room, and skimmed the table's intel for a few moments before speaking.

"Good work out there—I hope the old man was worth it," she said.

"Anyone they take from us is worth it," I said flatly.

"What about the woman who was with you? She's not allowed in here. We've got a couple guards posted on the surface, keeping an eye on her."

"I'll talk to her," I said.

"Make it soon. We don't like her here," Savannah said on her way out.

---

23 Dec
Noon

After enduring Savannah's concerns about Maggie, I thought it a good idea to check in on her to see what she was up to, or maybe how big her testicle necklace was getting from all the guards she'd killed. I approached her fire cautiously, waving the guards away so that I could speak in private. She looked better today, her face less swollen and her eyes less bloodshot. Maybe it was my imagination, but I could see the burning desire for revenge swirling in the dark circles of her eyes.

I didn't say anything, letting her adjust to my presence. The fire popped and cracked.

"Got any food?" was the first thing Maggie said to me.

I ripped off a layer of beef jerky from my cargo pocket and handed it to her.

Chewing the jerky, she asked, "They took my gun. I'd like that back. We're going to need it."

"What do you mean 'we,' Maggie?"

" 'We' means a collective group, two or more persons; in this case, the latter," she said. "There's a small chance we can fix this mess. Turn off what we turned on. They sent me after you to kill you, but that wasn't my plan."

And down the rabbit hole I went. I had to send the guards away twice while listening to Maggie's story, which is what I'm going to call it for now.

Maggie explained that the virus we hardwired into the Syrian telecom network could be neutralized if we could get back to Alexandria, back to Delmay Glass. The secure storage facility there would have a duplicate telecom interface unit. Against orders, she had two constructed. One went to Syria and one was hidden away in a vault under Delmay.

"Why the hell didn't you just go back there and wire it up yourself?" I asked.

"Because I need the six digit fucking code you entered in Syria. I only have one of the codes; I need the other one to control the worm and tell it to die. The weapon, which is what this thing is, was designed so that no single person could let it out, Max."

Taking a deep breath, I nodded in acknowledgment.

When I asked how we could reverse the grid collapse by attaching the hardware to a box inside a powerless grid, she revealed that we'd need to activate the box in an urban area that still had power to allow the kill switch to spread. As nearby communities brought their grids online, the command signal would spread, just as it had to bring down the grid before.

After letting Maggie's story sink in a bit, I came to the realization that I had no choice. Stay here and fight endless waves of Chinese invaders was an option, but not a logical one. Bringing down the virtual barrier that seemed to handicap all computer networks and controls seemed like a better goal than playing guerrilla warrior in the hills of Arkansas for the rest of my life. Both choices would probably lead to an early death, but at least I had a shot at turning the country's course in a better direction than the one it was on now.

I had to ask her: "Why didn't you tell me at the cabin after I shot you?"

"Because you wouldn't have believed me then, and also, I needed you captured to save my . . . my daughter. I could have gotten the codes from you under the waterboard, maybe saved her and then used them to bring the grid back up."

She began to bawl; her words became barely discernible.

"Seeing the way they killed her. The fear in her eyes. I couldn't do that to you. To anyone, but those worthless demon bastards."

Looks like I'll be working with Maggie again.

_____

Christmas Eve

I entered the operations center enjoying the decorations that adorned the radios, chart table, and other areas of the room. A small plastic tree with battery powered LED lights sat in the center of the table, blinking. Last night, I'd revealed to Inky some of the details that Maggie told me about the device she'd cached in Alexandria and how we might be able to eventually reverse the weapon's effect.

It would have been too complicated to explain my involvement in this mess. Although the NAI followed a generally noble cause, I mostly trusted no one, and that's kept me alive throughout all this.

I approached the table and sat down next to Inky, grabbing a cookie from the tray in front of me. It didn't taste too bad, as it was made from grain harvested locally and probably hand-milled.

As I chewed on the ultimate all-natural certified non-GMO Christmas cookie, Inky scooted his chair in closer to the table and began to whisper. I could barely hear him under the chirping of the radios and the bustle of the operations center.

"I have a plan, Max. Follow me . . . we can't talk here. I can't even trust my own people with this information."

We then went through the intricate passageways of what I'd recently been calling "Shire Base." Eventually, we reached the entry control point and passed guards carrying 12-gauge shotguns to keep the riffraff out. As we exited into the bright sunlight, three runners with slung messenger bags ran past me from the tunnel. They mounted nearby horses and all went different directions to find their radiomen.

"This way," Inky said, picking up the pace.

At the main stable, we got our horses. Molly snorted with happiness at the sight of me. I thought that was pretty cool, and I gave her nose a good rub to let her know I appreciated it.

We saddled up and were gone within a few minutes. We rode two miles in a direction I'd never gone, not stopping until we reached a waterfall. Rocks smoothed by thousands of years of PR: water rushing over their surface was forming the water as it fell, abating the splash with Olympic diver efficiency. Inky dismounted, so I did the same and followed him up to the edge of the water. He began to scan our surroundings as if to check if anyone had followed us here. This made me nervous, as it was something I'd probably do right before I killed Inky.

Uneasy, I put my palm over my sub gun, feeling its curves and mentally preparing to draw and shoot it with the stock still folded.

Inky began to speak. "Okay. There will be a summit in just over a month in Washington, DC. In attendance will be the President, the entire cabinet, the director of the Department of Homeland Security, the attorney general, and creditor heads of state. We've received the intel on what they're planning and it's not good."

Inky reached into his vest pocket and pulled out a printout from one of the digital HAM radio images he'd received from resistance agents imbedded in DC. The image depicted a map of the United States broken up into several sectors. Within these sectors, other flags were represented. I could see dozens of Chinese and Indian flags spread out just off the coast in the oil-rich fields of the Gulf of Mexico.

"They're slicing us up and giving us away, Max."

We talked at great length. I questioned the vetting of his sources and contacts on the inside and he responded with what I needed to hear.

He'd been receiving intel from his contacts in DC for some time now. Eventually the intelligence provided panned out and was verified. This intel would be no different. The meeting being held in DC next month was like the one held after World War II that decided the fate of Germany in that post-war era.

After going over the summit guest list, dates, and times, I asked the obvious question.

"So, what are we going to do about a summit being held a month from now over a thousand miles away?"

Inky stood there and looked me in the eyes for a long while, deciding whether or not he should speak.

"Max, the NAI wants you to execute a terrorist attack on the summit," Inky said.

"You want me to do what?!" I responded in disbelief.

The NAI had cracked government communications methods.

Inky wouldn't tell me how or from whom the encryption keys were given, but did reveal a few details.

"The source is someone you've heard of, seen on the news before all this, maybe," he said.

The plan would be to head east to a weapons cache location where some explosives and other nasties were stored, recover them, and continue to DC in time for fireworks at the summit.

"So you want me to dig up some C4, take it a thousand miles to DC, and use it on the President and the cabinet?" I said, nearly floored at the prospect of this.

Ever since last year, I've been deemed an enemy of the state, a domestic terrorist, but at my heart I still have some respect left for the office, for what it stands for, and for what it means to be elected by the people. I've shot a few unlucky men in the face since all this began, but most of them deserved it. What Inky was talking about here was pure guerrilla rebellion against elected civilian leadership. I wasn't sure how I could start to reconcile an action of that magnitude.

"The President ordered the shredding of the Constitution and suspension of habeas corpus. That's high treason and flies in the face of liberty. Millions are dead, Max. A lot of them at the barrels of government guns. Everyone that will be at the summit is implicated, culpable. Listen, Max, you don't have to do this . . . but if you want to really make a difference in the world, for future generations . . . now's your chance."

I sat for a moment, listening to the water and the snorts of horses before answering. I could in no way really agree to this right now. Killing an elected sitting president went against everything I stood for. The accusations Inky laid out were compelling, but I needed time to make a decision like this. There was still a modicum of respect for the office remaining, at least to me.

"I'll go east," I said, changing my future forever.

Inky nodded, retrieved a telescoping fishing pole from his saddle, and started negotiating the uneven terrain that led up to the flowing water. Extending the fishing pole, he reached behind the waterfall, retrieving a rice bag. He quickly opened the bag and pulled out something wrapped in plastic. Placing the item in his back pocket, he returned the bag to its hiding spot behind the waterfall.

Back down the hill, he took the item from his pocket and handed it to me.

Glancing at the paper through the clear plastic bag, I could clearly make out coordinates.

"What else is behind the waterfall?"

"More cache locations. Many more," he responded flatly. "Let's go back and pick your team."

I stopped walking, prompting Inky to do the same. He looked at me quizzically.

"I already have my partner picked out," I said without hesitation.

"Rich? Shit, he needs a month of food and water before I'd even take him a mile on horseback."

"I'm not talking about Rich, man. I'm talking about Maggie. The NAI doesn't trust her hanging around, and I don't either, but I know what she's capable of and I can keep an eye on her. It's a gamble but something tells me she'd be an asset more than a liability."

Inky shook his head. He could tell that my mind was made up, but he obviously didn't agree with my decision. Going a thousand miles on horseback was going to be rough as it stood, but going with half a dozen people I'd never operated beside would be even worse. I'd love to take Rich, but Inky was right: he was too weak to go much of anywhere at the moment and we were on a timeline.

One month until the summit. One month to decide.

PART THREE

EASTWARD

<u>On Person:</u>
Helmet mounted NVD
Electronic Ear pro w/ comms integration
Soft body armor
Plates
Med kit (human & horse)
Filtered drinking straw
Encrypted HAVE QUICK radio
.300BLK M4 select fire SBR w/ silencer, w/ torch, w/ 1-4x glass, w/ four mags
Integrally silenced .22LR pistol w/ holosight, w/ five mags

<u>In/On Molly's Saddlebags:</u>
500 rounds of sub and super .300BLK
Two bricks of CCI standard velocity .22LR

Four grenades
Two small EFPs
Stinger missile
Food stores
Water container w/ filter & pump
Hygiene (human & horse)
Sleeping bag w/ Goretex cover
Concealment netting

Christmas

I enjoyed a meal of mostly canned goods complemented with venison and other local wildlife, washed down with one of the local microbrews some ex-frat boy conjured up for the rest of us; the beer was damn better than I thought it would be.

The only gifts I saw given were from the adults to the children, and the gifts I saw would have been tossed over shoulders like new socks or underwear on Christmas morning a few years ago. Instead, stockings filled with fruit and candy brought huge smiles to young faces, ones even bigger than if they'd opened up a box containing the latest gaming system or VR headset. Our situation, our waking lives, were horrible and nearly unbearable, but there were moments like this. Moments of pure happiness and thankfulness that reminded me that we're not all demons.

Like me.

As Christmas dinner came to a close, I thanked Inky for the Shire's hospitality and said my good-byes to Savannah, who, in her typical fashion said only, "Don't die out there." Inky and Rich were standing nearby.

I reached to shake Inky's hand and was instead presented with a parting Christmas gift.

"Portable shortwave radio with long wire, Morse key, contact and freq schedule, and codebook. Eat the first and the third sheet if you think you're about to be compromised. They're the ones with perforations, in case you're in the dark when the time comes. Good luck and godspeed."

I thanked Inky for the trust and hospitality and told him that I'd be in touch when I was near the first objective.

Saying good-bye to Rich sucked the most. I'd been to hell and back to save him and it was worth every chance it took to get him back. We'd been through a lot together, and it was like leaving a close uncle. Rich reassured me that he'd be just a Morse click away if need be. His parting instructions were explicit: *Avoid transmitting shortwave more than one message per stop with minimum of twenty miles between transmissions.* Shortwave was difficult to geolocate, but too many transmissions in the same area wasn't a best practice for comsec, persec, or keeping your brain inside your skullsec. I laughed at the former NSA spook's joke before giving him a man hug and saying my throat-lumped good-bye.

"By the time I see you again, you'll have gained a hundred pounds! Merry Christmas, Rich." I said, trying to laugh back any water-based signs of sadness.

Maggie saddled up Molly (it's only a matter of time before I screw those names up) and was waiting for me at the edge of the Shire control point, which led down the road to a derelict-looking electronic gate that would be triggered open by a hidden overwatch sniper once we got close enough.

Mounting Molly, I could hear the children singing Christmas songs, the sounds drifting from the tunnels and out into the winter night and cutting through the dense air like angel's voices.

Maggie's horse, Elvis, snorted in short protest about his new master, thumping his front hooves on the ground. The sound of singing got louder as the carolers emerged from the tunnel entrance holding candles. The guards tried to quiet the children, but couldn't. The music was a good send-off into the cold winter evening.

Maggie didn't say anything as the horses walked down the heavily rutted dirt drive to the fence. As we approached, I heard the creak of metal as the battery powered gate motor slowly cranked the exit open.

The highway to hell was in front of us.

I was the only one with the map to the explosives. Maggie knew that we're stopping by an NAI cache and also about the summit, but not the exact date. As we moved farther and farther east, I would assess her loyalty and go from there. It was going to be a long trip.

The final brief I'd received from Inky was tucked inside my saddlebags. It wasn't too sensitive—just several pages of useful information like friends and foes strongholds, and who might be sympathetic to the NAI's overall cause. There were a few militia organizations from here to the East Coast . . . not all of them redneck survivalists that cable TV used to demonize via creative editing to drive ratings before all of this. Some of the so-called militias were composed of police, military, farmers, and some other groups that unfortunately delved into the fanatic realm of racists of all colors and creeds.

The most sobering aspect of the report was the estimated casualty rate. At this point, eighty-five percent of the population of the United States was either dead or dying. All due to the grid going down. I didn't want to fathom what the rest of the world might look like.

I had to really try not to think about that too long. How many millions of children had Maggie and I inadvertently (at least for me) killed? It took Jedi concentration not to let this get to the core of my mind and cause me to walk down a self-destructive path. The only thing that drove me forward in the saddle was the possibility of somehow, at least in some way, making things whole again. Maggie and I were a huge part of why things were the way they were. I'm not going to lie, or gloss over the fact that I've pondered suicide at the thought of what I've inadvertently caused.

What would it solve? I'd be getting off too easy. The option in some dark way is still on the table in the back of my mind, but I want to try to reverse this, even if only in some small way.

Recovery from losing millions of people to famine, civil war, disease, and other atrocities was going to take at least a century, and would forever be a horrific chapter in the history books, eclipsing the Dark Ages and the genocide of World War II many times over.

With the population being down to mid 1800s levels, we'd potentially travel days without seeing a living soul if we stuck to the areas outside federal control. The feds simply didn't have the resources to even get close to controlling the rural dark zones that spanned the hundreds of miles between the urban centers. I knew which cities were provisional government strongholds and fully intended to avoid all of them until I reached Alexandria, where the surveillance grid remained alive and well, the hearts of the worm we had unleashed last year still digitally beating, restricting thousands of once-automated processes.

The worm had strange effects. The feds had to be careful where and how they brought digital cellular networks back online. If the newly established network brushed even briefly with a mistakenly powered infected node, the new network would have to be wiped and the infected node quarantined before the network could be re-imaged and brought online.

Some of the intelligence I'd read outlined examples of the worm jumping networks via infrared ports into devices that were not RF wireless capable. Devices once thought to be "dumb" would start showing the effects of the worm. Generator control panels, smart meters, vehicles, and other devices that the government was utilizing in the urban centers were getting infected and shut down. The only technology that could be utilized had to be truly dumb, with no programmable interface or anything that could come into contact with the worm. The NSA really engineered some lethal zeros and ones.

After initially reading this, I found myself mentally going over my equipment list, looking for anything that might be vulnerable to the digital hunter-killer that buzzed invisibly around every powered infected device in the world. Even the watch I wore on my wrist had the capability to receive RF time updates from transmitting sites, which hopefully remained down or somehow uninfected. Disturbing beyond belief.

████████

We rode for an hour until we finally reached the last observation post controlled by the Shire. The guard flashed IR and gestured a friendly wave from his hidden spot. And then, just like leaving earth's orbit, we were in the chaotic by-product of a grid down world.

The ice and snow wasn't falling, but the cutting wind forced us to go slower than the horses wanted to as we made our path east. We had Springdale to cross through and then we'd take one of the lesser traveled roads that skirted Huntsville. Before Huntsville, we'd need to make a stop to pick up the NAI explosives cache. Reports suggested that we'd see few people on the road between there and the eastern border of Arkansas, and I was just fine with that.

Molly was loaded down heavy with dehydrated food, maybe enough to last a month if we stayed on horseback and let the animals burn the calories. Could be a tough prospect if we couldn't find enough grazing for the horses along the way.

Midnight came and went, and the road just came. Maggie's horse, Elvis, was eyeballing a nearby pond and began to snort and pull in the direction of the water. We took a horse break and I drank deeply from my canteen and immediately broke some of the edge ice to filter and replace. Best stay in the habit to keep the canteens full.

I saw lights and in a flash we were on horseback galloping to a nearby line of trees. An old pickup truck with only the parking lights illuminated stuttered past the field and kept going.

We made it through Springdale without incident. The city collapsed a year ago, its population mostly gone. Springdale was in an unfortunate position; it was a forgotten city, stuck between the federally controlled Bentonville, and civil war stricken Fayetteville. Although we didn't go right through the middle of the city, we saw no lights flickering in the windows as we skirted along the outside of what was once a beautiful southern town with the only passenger train depot in the area.

With Springdale behind us, the road narrowed and the first mountains guarding the distance between here and eastern Arkansas stood like dark sentinels up ahead. We'd be back in Newton County in another night or two.

At about three in the morning, we rode past something that caught my eye. I wouldn't have noticed it, but I saw the IR reflection from my NVD coming from the edge of a field. At first I thought it was a sign or maybe a tractor reflector, but after riding in a bit closer I could see the very top of a large RV positioned behind shrubbery about three or four hundred yards across a field off the road. The fence was damaged and large black skid marks were clearly rubbed into the road pointing to the downed fence.

I cautiously approached and Maggie followed. When close enough, I dismounted and handed the reins to Maggie and moved in for some recon. The door was open on the side, telling me that the RV was probably abandoned. No one would sleep with the door open in this weather. Upon closer inspection, I saw that the rear tires were flat and noticed a series of bullet holes all across the back end, penetrating the spare tire and at least ten other places.

I knocked on the side of the RV and called out, with no answer. At the door, I opened it a bit more and took a look inside, expecting to see bodies. Although I saw a fair amount of dried blood, there were no corpses or people inside slumbering. The RV was just another story told via visual cues. Skid marks, damaged fence, bullet holes, blood. Whoever was inside this thing didn't make it. Probably a victim of the raiders or bikers I'd seen dominating the roads in the beginning.

I whistled to Maggie that it was clear and continued my inspection of the inside, if only out of morbid curiosity. Anything useful was gone from the RV, from hand soap to food and water. There was a roll of duct tape sitting on the counter, which was a pretty good find, considering I didn't bring any.

The place was a mess, but the bullet holes were only in the walls, not the roof of the RV, meaning we could at least stay dry until tomorrow night, when we'd head out again. I've decided to only move at night until we get deeper into rural Arkansas. Turning, I saw Maggie standing silently in the doorway. She hadn't said ten words since we departed the Shire, and I suppose I can understand why. I'm not going to push it, and to be honest, I'm not sure I care. Yeah, she'd been through a lot and seen her whole life ripped from her. She's not the only one, though, and she knowingly had a hand in all this. Can't forgive or forget so easily. In some ways, I hate her. I was naive in Syria. I trusted the Agency and all it stood for.

I stepped aside and Maggie walked in, rolled out her bag on the bed in the far corner, and crawled inside.

"I guess you're not taking the first watch?" I asked. No response.

I checked on the horses and grabbed my compressed sleeping bag, tossing it inside the RV onto the other bed. The trees covered all but the top third of the RV from view of the two-lane road. Without NVDs, I'd never have seen the RV at night and I doubted it was much easier to see during the day, unless you were looking and noticed the road and fence. With the inside of the abandoned RV secured, I surveilled the immediate area, making sure that we weren't right next door to another fusion center or rival road gang. Satisfied we were truly remote, I went back to the RV, checking the outside cargo areas. Within the first compartment, I found a wakeboard and a bunch of folding chairs. Not helpful.

The next compartment contained the RVs generator, and my God, it had fuel inside!

I messed around with it for twenty minutes before I got it to turn over and start. Loud static boomed from the RV, and I heard Maggie rustle out of her bag to turn it off. Lights were on inside. I rushed around to the door and saw Maggie in the cab of the RV, frantically flipping switches to get the static to stop. I reached past her and turned off the CB radio, killing the static. Overhead, I could feel the cool air coming from the air conditioner. I selected the heating mode and the cold air turned much warmer, which was the reason I'd powered on the generator in the first place.

I took the roll of duct tape and went outside, placing strips over the bullet holes to catch all the light that spilled from them. I then went up to the road to see if I could see or hear the RV. If I concentrated, I could barely make out a hum, but the way the hill was situated, it was difficult to tell where the noise was coming from.

Satisfied, I made way back down the hill through the field to the RV. Elvis met me about half way so I decided to ride the rest of the way back. I hid my kit in the woods, as I didn't want the explosives coordinates compromised, and headed back to the RV for some sleep. Yeah, we should probably have kept one of us awake, but I was too damn tired.

—————

The small generator ran out of gas at about 0700, which was fine, as the sun was already peeking over the tops of the trees. The heater had kept the interior of the RV warm until it stopped working. In a way, I was happy, as the noise was gone and there'd be little chance of anyone wandering around on the nearby road to find us sleeping out here. After getting used to the lack of generator humming, I fell back asleep and woke up a little after noon.

Grabbing my rifle, I stepped outside into another damned snowstorm, watered a nearby bush, and went looking for Molly and Elvis. I found them standing close to each other next to a tree, so I decided to build a fire. I dragged several downed branches into a pile and dipped an old rag down into the generator tank to soak up the last ounces of fuel that couldn't make it into the carburetor. After breaking my kindling and arranging everything, I started the fire in a flash, burning through the small stuff and using that energy to ignite the larger pieces of fallen branches that I'd piled up. The horses moved over to the fire and began to snort and swish their tails in approval. I could've sworn I saw Elvis smile, but I think he was just positioning himself to nip my tricep.

The snow was coming down pretty good, but I had a four-leg drive vehicle that didn't care too much about snow and ice, so I wasn't too worried about it. Rounding the corner of the RV, I caught a glimpse of movement in the tree above. A squirrel jumped from branch to branch, probably on its way to its home inside one of the trees. I quickly ran back into the RV, grabbed my Ruger .22LR pistol, and checked the can for tightness before I barreled outside again. I raised the gun up, simultaneously twisting the red dot switch to the on position. I took a shot but pulled it, knocking off a chunk of branch the tree rat was occupying. The second suppressed shot hit the animal in the side of its chest, dropping it from the high branch with a tragically soft thud on the snow-covered ground. I ran over with my knife and quickly made sure the creature wasn't suffering before I immediately began to field dress the small animal. It wasn't a lot, but the meat would complement a small handful of dried food, water, and bouillon cubes to make a pretty damn good stew. My mouth watered as I sliced every good bit of meat from the animal, tossing it in one of the pots that remained unscavenged inside the RV.

I emptied my canteen into the pot along with some snow I'd scooped from the ground. I mixed in some dehydrated noodles and two bouillon cubes and covered the food, placing it in the fire, eventually bringing it to a nice boil. I allowed it to boil multiple times, dropping in handfuls of snow before it began to boil over. I repeated this for ten minutes until I was sure that whatever nasty diseases that squirrel might be carrying were dead, dead, dead. Satisfied I wasn't going to die from a parasite, I sipped some of the stew. It was damn good considering our current situation.

I didn't need to shake Maggie to wake her up. All I had to do was bring the food inside the RV and wait thirty seconds. As soon as the smell hit her nostrils, her eyes sprung open and locked onto the steaming pot of squirrel stew.

After eating our fill, we looked over the maps, deciding the best way east, eventually agreeing on 412 due to the lack of traffic and general activity we'd seen on the road since we'd stopped at the RV. Secretly, I steered us on this road so that I could make a pickup at the easternmost boundary of the NAI's border. I remained torn, conflicted on what I'd be doing with the explosives.

I bagged another squirrel after a few hours of hunting—tomorrow's meal. With only a few hours until dark, it was time for a nap. Had to stay frosty.

Night fell and Maggie and I continued east. She was quiet. Too quiet. I still thought I might have been a little crazy for letting her have a gun and allowing myself to sleep within her proximity, but I had an unexplainable feeling about her. The leverage that controlled her before made her crazy. She'd have killed me and then worn my skin if it meant saving her child, and I couldn't blame her. I couldn't pretend to know what that was like, to have kids you'd die for. But, with that leverage now gone forever, she was transformed. I was just her guide east, to a place where she could let loose the rage buried inside, just below the surface of her failing sanity.

Hours went by and we stopped just outside of Huntsville, Arkansas, at a sawmill marked on the NAI map I was given by Inky. The mill had the unfortunate name Love Logs, Inc., and was massive in scope, covering at least five acres. It looked as if it had been in operation before the economy collapsed, based on the condition of the equipment and the piles of good lumber still sitting banded up in stacks beside the mill's green chain. The cache was hidden here after passing through several hands from the defunct government arsenal it used to call home. The exact location wasn't marked; that information was given in secrecy to me by Inky's NAI head of intelligence. All in all, they'd revealed that the NAI controlled at least half a dozen well-stocked explosive caches stolen from government custody when the shit hit the fan and the guards all went home to keep their own families from being raped and murdered by the bands of thugs roaming the cities and countryside.

"Maggie, wait here and watch the horses. You hear shots, meet me here." I said, pointing to a cafe downtown I'd circled earlier, before we'd left the RV.

Two green dots nodded up and down, indicating that she acknowledged. It was nice not having her question what I was about to do.

I dismounted and brought my suppressed carbine to the high ready before moving deeper into the sawmill. Mammoth piles of sawdust and scrap lumber were spaced evenly under machinery designed to turn hundred-year-old living organisms into homes, furniture, and paper. I moved to the pile that sat underneath a great red piece of equipment with the words RED EASY stenciled on a steel beam ten feet across. Grabbing a scrap two-by-four, I began to search, confident that Maggie would watch my back as I did so.

The pile was larger than a two-story house, but my instructions were clear: find the black toolbox and dig underneath. I scraped my silencer over the pile of sawdust and debris until I heard the loud clank of metal two-thirds from the top of the inverted cone, where a large rusted blade sat like a sentinel in the darkness, waiting to cut more trees to shape, to boost our GDP through production of what people used to demand before government intervention had its way via the naive actions of one agent who shall remain nameless.

As I began to dig into the sawdust, I heard the far off sounds of barking and howling. At first I thought it was coyotes, but I'd spent many a night in Newton County, and that wasn't it. I needed to hurry it up here.

Found it. Unearthing the toolbox, I opened it up. A simple handwritten note sat inside with a few words written in black ink.

REMEMBER WACO, RUBY RIDGE, FAYETTEVILLE

I took the note and put it in my vest pocket before tossing the toolbox to the base of the sawdust pile. The barking and howling was louder and closer. Now I heard the sounds of small bells, and chains being dragged across concrete just before the piston sounds of suppressed gunfire and horses crying out.

Maggie was engaging whatever they were. Molly ran past the dirt pile with something chasing her. I drew down on it and took a shot, hitting it in the gut.

It was a dog, once domesticated.

The dog struggled to yelp as I ran down off the pile to put it out of its misery. Spooked, Molly kept running into the mill, making scared horse noises. I pulled my sidearm and put a .22 round into the wild dog's skull. Even as I pulled the trigger, I felt sorry for the thing; it had to do what it needed to survive.

But so did I.

Forgetting Molly for the moment, I ran back to where I'd left Maggie and Elvis. Maggie was dismounted, her gun held high as she kept circling around Elvis in a protective posture. Her green electric eyes and black gun made her look sinister and lethal, which she absolutely was. I knew from experience.

"Any injuries?"

Her green eyes swung back and forth horizontally. I went back into the mill to look for Molly, as she was kind of a big deal if I wanted to reach the East Coast before I was eligible for social security.

I went back into the mills, underneath the metal building that housed some of the planar machinery and other rain sensitive and expensive equipment. Looking at the steel beams above, I saw white pinpricks of light. Bats, hanging by their feet. Most of them didn't even bother to look back at me, but some of them did, craning their heads to follow me as I searched for my trusty steed.

I found her huffing and puffing next to the pallet-making machine. I approached the scared animal slowly and carefully with my open hands out, calling her name in a soothing voice. This seemed to calm her a bit, which enabled me to get a hand on her nose, rubbing her face until she relaxed.

"That's a good girl," I said to her, adjusting her saddle and guiding her out of the sawmill.

Outside, I regrouped with Maggie, who was still gun up, watching for more wild dogs. She'd stacked a few up on the ground near where we were, one of them wearing a short chain attached to its dirty leather collar. Sad. These animals had no chance without their master, but still somehow survived, only to be ended here, now. They'd have eaten us and our horses if we hadn't fought back. Having said that, I wasn't very impressed with Molly's response to nearby gunfire. I filed that little factoid away before returning to the X on the NAI map to finish my digging.

Going deeper, I finally came to a plastic case wrapped in a thick contractor quality trash bag. Tugging, I managed to get the case out from under the damp sawdust and down the side of the mound. I took the instructions from their protective plastic in my cargo pocket and pulled the case out of the trash bag.

The case itself was Pelican style, weighing about thirty pounds, mostly explosives with some det cord and other items. It would need to ride on Elvis, as Molly was already tapped out with all my kit and a Stinger missile. I estimated Maggie weighed a hundred pounds less than me, if my ability to guess such things was still accurate.

Clicking open the clasps on the composite case, I raised the lid, revealing neat stacks of plastic-wrapped, white cakelike explosives. I pushed the dense explosives aside, taking inventory of the other items in the box.

I closed the clamshell on the explosives and placed a thick zip tie through the metal tabs where a padlock should go. I didn't want the case flying open if we had to haul ass, but I was pretty sure the explosives would be just fine being transported a thousand miles on horseback over mountainous and unforgiving terrain.

I returned to Maggie with the black case, strapping it to her horse, nicely counterbalancing the weight that hung from the other side. Elvis was a brute and probably wouldn't even notice the extra thirty pounds. There was still a lot of night left and I didn't want to spend it in the creepy, bat-infested, wild dog hunting ground that was this old sawmill.

We mounted up, got back on the road, and kept moving east until we reached the small, one-intersection empty town of Osage. We took sanctuary for the night a good distance away from 412 in an abandoned home.

Although Maggie wasn't talking, neither of us were used to the chilling silence we'd experienced ever since leaving NAI territory. I just wanted to hear another human talk for a while, and wished I'd brought something to listen to, a book on tape, perhaps, anything to get my mind off the crushing quiet. I'd even settle for killer dogs, something. The winter cold even silenced the bug symphony that could be heard outside in these parts during the warmer months.

The very walls of the abandoned home we found ourselves in seemed to close in with the tragic memories of those who lived here when society collapsed. From the empty cupboards to the half-eaten leather belt I found, all told the same story. Famine, desperation, and death. Bullet holes riddled the front and back doors, possibly indicating coordinated and simultaneous forced entry. A stuffed bear lay on the floor with scattered crayons and a shattered jewelry box. Some poor children had to watch their parents get torn apart by machine gun fire, or worse.

INTO THE DOGPATCH

Dogpatch, USA

More silence. Maggie was still sleeping when I woke up to the sight of my own breath. The house was stone cold. We'd slept most of the day. I tossed a couple logs into the fireplace to bring the temperature out of the teens and knock the chill off. After she woke, we climbed back on the horses for our long trek east.

By my calculations, we'd be reaching our next stop, Marble Falls, a couple hours before sunup. The population was less than a thousand before all this; I doubt it's even single digits now, counting the possums.

Even though we were on NVDs and sticking to the two-lane paved road, the grade was punishing. We both either leaned forward in the saddle going up hill, or leaned back, hoping that our horses would not lose footing, sending us down craggy cliffs or hollers. After navigating a switchback up the mountain and back down again, the ground began to level out some, but this was Arkansas. Unforgiving and gray most of the winter.

The night seemed to last forever with no sign of fading stars. I kept playing a game every hour or so, trying to guess the time to see how close I was to my digital watch.

Still Maggie said nothing.

We pulled over to give the horses a water break and I noticed a sign, heavily grown over with leafless vines and moss. If it had been summer, the sign would have been a near invisible rectangle shaped green mass. As it was, the paint and letters were heavily faded from days, seasons, and years gone by.

DOGPATCH, USA
TROUT FISHING–RIDES–SHOWS

A spark of memory passed through some long dormant synapse in my mind. Dogpatch.

Had I been here as a child?

Either way, the time I'd most recently guessed was 0438; when I checked it was closer to 0450, and I could see a hint of light on the eastern horizon fighting back the night and pushing back the cloudy darkness. After the horses drank their fill and grazed a few minutes on snow-buried grass, we mounted up and followed the DOGPATCH, USA sign, turning at the next right, as indicated on the ancient billboard.

We carefully went around the rusted and chained barricade meant to keep cars from coming to the park after hours. Judging by the condition of the parking lot, it looked like we'd missed our chance to do that by a few decades. We trotted over to the office marked TICKETS AND TRAM, where I dismounted, handing Maggie the reins.

"Don't let her go this time. I don't care how many rabid dogs show up," I said half-jokingly to Maggie, trying to get a rise out of her. Anything at this point. I was growing more than a little weary of talking to myself and playing the guess the time game, I'll admit.

She grabbed the reins without so much as a nod, and I turned to face the decrepit and abandoned ticket office and tram station.

Apparently we'd stumbled onto an ancient Arkansas theme park nestled in these hills. I still felt there was something familiar about it, maybe an old picture I'd seen of my mother holding me as a child here, perhaps? All the memories that were resurfacing seemed to be of photos, not of my own memories of this place. I saw the cloudy image of a picture in my mind, but couldn't quite pull it out of the chemical switches located somewhere beyond a million turns of wormlike tissue.

The ticket office was clear inside and stood shoddily beside a set of tracks that led steeply down the mountain to more structures below. A rusting blue passenger tram sat fused to the ground via hundreds of vines. I got back on Molly and gestured for Maggie and Elvis to follow. We proceeded slowly past the abandoned tram car and down the track to the theme park itself.

It was almost getting to the point that I didn't need a NVD to see. Careful to avoid the half-buried rails and railroad ties, I followed the tracks and a lone black cable that ran between both sets. The tracks terminated at the bottom of the hill at the uphill's sister tram station where another twin tram car sat gripped by the vined tendrils of Mother Nature.

A padlock lay shattered on the ground next to the metal door behind a turnstile that counted visitors to the park. We rode the horses around the side of the station and jumped over a downed section of three-log fence before spilling out onto the cracked and uneven pavement.

Moving out into a more open area, I saw two *Indiana Jones*– killer-sized boulders sitting side by side in the tall overgrowth. I approached out of curiosity, discovering the park's first quirky display and bringing back the memory my mind had been searching for ever since we arrived here at Dogpatch.

Two large rocks in the shape of a face, their lips puckered as if about to kiss each other. It was hard to tell rock gender, but one appeared to be a girl.

The memory was now clear, but not of me being here. It was from my mother's photo albums. She was holding me as a child in front of these kissing rocks. People were smiling and laughing all around her. I remember the photo well. It was a sunny day and my mother was squinting as she held me, posing for the camera. She looked happy in the photo—perhaps that's why I always remembered it. I don't think I ever recalled her that happy in the years before her untimely death.

This was that place in the photo.

I put my back to the kissing rocks. The abandoned park was at the halfway stage of nature's reclamation. This was what the rest of the country might look like in thirty years. Thick vines overtaking and topping buildings, cracking concrete, and starting the process of removing all evidence that man broke ground here long before I was born.

My mind wandered, clicking and replacing images in my head like my uncle's old 3-D viewer he showed me when I was young. I began to see scenes of Fayetteville in my head overtaken by nature like Dogpatch, through extreme neglect.

A gentle touch on my shoulder got my attention. Maggie swung her NVD up and made eye contact, gesturing up ahead beyond the overgrown foliage to a tall structure made up of mostly stairs. It reminded me of some twisted Emerald City spire that glimmered in the distance across a field of thorns.

Maggie led with Elvis and I followed behind to the structure.

As we approached, it became obvious that we were looking at an ancient water toboggan slide of some type. The sun was probably fully up somewhere behind the clouds and mountains, but it was still dark enough to break cover and risk the ascent.

We both dismounted and tied our horses off to a nearby post and began to summit the several flights of stairs leading to the top of the ancient theme park ride. The structure was in horrible disrepair. As the heaviest, I went first. If the damp boards held me, it would hold Maggie's birdlike frame. I threw my carbine over my back so that I'd have both hands to stop my fall through the boards to the flight below. Although they were old and covered in moss and mildew, and they creaked, the steps held. It only took a few minutes to get to the top, fighting brutal sticker bushes along the first flight.

At the top, we had a commanding view of the park. A large lake stood between most of the park and the back road highway beyond. I could see a couple of cars abandoned on the highway through the trees, but no movement. Although we were at the highest point in the park, we were still in a valley. The mountains towered all around us, enclosing us in this rotting time capsule, a place that society had abandoned and forgotten years ago. I scanned the area with my binoculars, seeing no signs of recent human activity.

"We're not making camp here," I said to Maggie before starting my way down.

The tower would give us a clear view of our surroundings, but it would be cold, and there was only one way down. At the bottom of the stairs, I made for a set of small railroad tracks and followed them to a dam. The miniature dam was also in extreme disrepair, and the reservoir it held back was littered with branches and other debris. A waterfall fell over the face of it, feeding a stream that supplied the lake. I followed the tracks to a span of bridge that overlooked the waterfall.

A cracking sound sent my carbine to the high ready, searching the tree line like radar scanning for a confirmed target. Continuing forward, I heard the splash of hooves as Maggie rode across the stream, leading Molly across by the reins. We needed to take the saddles off the horses and give them a break soon or risk having issues.

We rounded a bend and discovered the train that seemed to belong to these tracks. It was a small model replica of an old steam engine pulling several passenger cars behind it. Most of the cars were full of debris from where animals had made nests, and were probably run off: rinse, repeat. Approaching the caboose train, I nearly shot a static display coiled around a nearby tree. A large fiberglass python replica was poised to strike Dogpatch train passengers.

We passed the broken-down locomotive and continued on what was very likely a train loop around the theme park. Eventually we came to a small cabin that sat right off the tracks. It was no bigger than a one car garage and had moonshine jugs sitting on the front porch adorned with XXX. Rounding out the hillbilly stereotype were hanging deerskins and rocking chairs on the front porch. I bet that the theme park actors used to have fun with the passengers as they rode on by the old cabin.

I approached the small wraparound porch and stepped up onto its old planks before shoving the front door. I didn't notice the large, tarnished brass lock attached to a rusted metal clasp until I was up close.

I went back to Molly's bags and pulled out my small master key. With two quick snips, the brass lock fell to the damp wooden porch, giving us access to a place long abandoned. The roof was still intact, but leaking in a few places. Three chairs and a table sat positioned in the center of the cabin and an air conditioner was in the window to the back, not visible to train passengers. On the middle of the table was a small CB radio, probably used to communicate with the train conductor so that the actors knew when to come outside to start their show. Jugs of water lined a wall and cans of bug spray and a first-aid kit were on the shelves at the back wall, along with a small propane camp heater with three small green propane tanks. I also noticed a binder on the shelf, so I pulled it off and gave it a look.

[TRAIN 10 SECONDS OUT: LEAVE CABIN IN CHARACTER]

Ma: "Look Pa! It's more of them city folk!"

Pa: "Quick Junior, grab yer gun, them look like bandits!"

[JUNIOR RUSHES INSIDE FOR HIS RIFLE]

The binder went on to outline four different scripts so that train passengers might have variety if they rode the train more than once. It was pretty cool to read the scripts and imagine what it might be like to go back in time to this park's heyday.

We rolled out our sleeping bags and made preparations to bed down for the day. The water in the cabin jugs was still clear and drinkable, having been sheltered in the containers away from sunlight. I poured some into my mess kit pan and boiled up some dinner. Maggie supplied some of her dried food to supplement mine. Food might eventually be an issue, but not today.

Havin' a Heckuva Day

Dogs. It was the damn dogs again. They tracked us to the cabin just as the sun was about to set. We heard the horses act up, so I went outside. I could see headlights beaming through the trees, coming from somewhere down the tracks beyond the small locomotive. Maggie had already packed her kit, but mine was still in disarray. I shoved my shit in my pack and the rest in Molly's bags. I put on my helmet and put my M4 at the ready and began to follow the tracks clockwise just as we'd done from the entrance to the park.

The dogs were yelping and barking from somewhere behind us and motorcycle engines were revving, bringing back some memories from last year I'd rather not have dredged to the surface. Eventually the tracks turned right and seemed to meander back in the direction of the park. I hoped that the oil and other residue from the train's countless trips might throw off our scent. I mean, they'd likely track me to the cabin because I was on foot from the waterfall, but they'd lose the scent there, and hopefully not find us as we made our loop back to the tram station.

We galloped faster, seemingly outpacing the dogs as their noises became quieter, muffled by the thick branches and evergreens that split the trails between our pursuers and us.

Nearly rounding the next bend, I jumped off Molly, passing the reins over to my silent partner. I gave her the signal to disappear into the woods and I stalked forward to the tram station under the cover of the nearby tree line.

At the tram, I saw about a half a dozen men standing next to their motorcycles. These weren't your average Harley cruisers; they'd been retrofitted with additional external fuel tanks, rifle scabbards, and knobby tires for gripping backroads and godforsaken places like Dogpatch, USA.

These men weren't just standing around bullshitting. They were paying attention to their surroundings. I heard the loud beep from one of their handheld radios and watched one of them, who must have been six and a half feet tall, approaching his motorcycle to take the call.

I couldn't hear what he'd said, but he swung his leg over his bike and started the engine, sending the growl of his tuned up and modified Harley echoing back and forth between the hills, temporarily drowning out the sounds of the dogs that were no doubt sniffing up the tracks behind me. The biker turned toward me, and I got low into the cold and snow-frosted grass. What I saw attached to his bike made my blood turn cold.

A human head was attached to the bike's handlebars with bailing wire; its mouth looked to be wired open in a grotesque grimace and a knife was stuck straight down into its skull.

The biker only came in my direction long enough to give himself room to turn around. He zoomed past the tram station into the park and down into the creek bed where Maggie had led the horses earlier this morning. I followed the bike until it disappeared. Just as the sun disappeared behind the mountain, I noticed movement on the tower we'd explored.

The sound of dogs grew louder and the motorcycle engine revved again, probably speeding down the tracks to the cabin we'd spent the day sleeping in. I felt the heavy lump in my cargo pocket, reassured by its presence. The other three grenades were in Molly's saddlebags. Most problems can be solved with grenades, I was certain. I brought my NVD down and gave the IR signal to Maggie—exfiltrate.

I brought my gun to the high ready and got within a good throwing distance of the five bikers that were guarding the tram station, or the only clear trail back up the mountain to the road. Looking over, Maggie walked out of cover and began going up the hill adjacent to the tram clearing.

Just as I figured, I heard one of the five bikers break the chatter.

"Shhhhh! Listen!" someone said, silencing the group.

I instinctively pulled the pin; I don't remember if I intended to, but my hands seemed to work autonomously. I waited, live grenade in hand, gripping the spoon firmly. I saw the flash of a weapons light begin to search the clearing when my body again began to act without me telling it to. I reached back and lobbed the grenade hard, listening as the spoon hit the gravel. A few seconds later the grenade hit the ground at the bikers' feet with a thud.

This time I had to force my legs to move; force my eyes not to watch the carnage that was about to be the rest of their lives. My M4 began to beat my back mercilessly as I pumped my legs past the tram station and up the hill. A loud crack signified the grenade's underwhelming detonation. Shrapnel tore through flesh and motorcycles, some of it hitting the metal tram station structure beside me, and the screams ensued. Grenades only kill everyone instantly in the movies. In real life, there are soul shuddering screams and howls of pain and agony. I learned to tune those out, my privilege of being a normal human being long gone, never to return.

I ran faster, opening the distance between the twisted hunter-killers and myself. I grabbed the M4 from my beaten back and turned on my IR laser. I hoped the bikers didn't have NVD capability as I began to lasso the sky above me with the bright IR laser beam. A few seconds passed before I saw Maggie's IR lasso response. I adjusted course to her position and kept running. I needed to be on Molly right now, riding fast away from the savagery that would no doubt be pursuing us in a short time.

My lungs felt as if they would burst as I summited the hill atop the tram track. Looking back over my shoulder through my NVD, I could see beams of motorcycle lights flash wildly in the valley below. Nearly puking, I forced myself back into a trot in the direction of Maggie's IR signal. My legs burned and my back was bruised from my gun. I should have put on my body armor when I woke up, body armor that was currently in one of Molly's saddlebags.

Up ahead, I saw Maggie emerge from the trees, leading the horses onto the weather damaged two-lane road.

"We gotta move!" I said dramatically in a low whisper.

We began to push the horses harder down the mountain road away from the old theme park and deeper into the dark mountains that guarded the way to the Mississippi River. Leaving the revving motorcycle engines behind for the time being, we carefully negotiated sections of washed-out road, hoping that they'd slow any pursuing bikers down. I used every opportunity to tie off a section of rope in order for them to abandon vehicles, put them in neutral, and pull them across the road to further complicate any night motorcycle riders. I didn't have time to do it more than once, but I removed the oil drain plug from one of the vehicles and covered a section of road with oil just in front of a turn, hoping it would make one of the bastards lay down their bike.

We rode for three hours before stopping to let the horses rest and drink at a spring that trickled from a cliff face next to the road. Maggie was calm and cool, not seeming to care about the level of hate and murder that was following. After about twenty minutes of sitting still, I began to hear the familiar sound of motorcycle noise bouncing between cliff faces and mountainsides like pinballs.

Jesus, they weren't giving up.

We rode through the mountain pass for another hour before we finally stopped to make a stand.

The noises were louder and our pursuers were gaining on us. If we kept riding, they'd just run us down like dogs and put our heads on their handlebars as ornaments. I don't even ask myself why people become like this anymore. I already know. We're goddamned animals, all of us. If we miss more than a few meals, we become the road, we become the people that ride all night to kill another human being for whatever they're carrying . . . or even the very meat on their bones.

We chose to stop near a low-water bridge, letting our horses cross, stepping through the three inches of icy flowing water to the other side. The bikers would be funneled here, unable to fan out to avoid any ambush.

Maggie and I pulled our encrypted radios out of our packs and connected them to our helmet/electronic ear pro combo. I'd set up one EFP at the crossing, just out of view, aimed down the middle of the low-water pass. I'd run the wire safely into the tree line behind the business end of the EFP. Maggie would set up shop about a couple hundred meters up the road, setting up a pincer attack on the approaching bikers. She'd tie up the horses, keeping the explosives payload safe along with our crucial supplies.

I'd lay in wait to detonate the EFP after Maggie gave me the advanced warning. Post-KABOOM, we'd pick off the survivors, separating our targets via IR laser designation so we wouldn't be working the same target at the same time. Deadly efficiency, just like we were taught by the very government we were now trying to fight.

We waited until the stars began to fade, listening to motorcycle engines get louder and then softer as the bikers negotiated the countless turns, peaks, and valleys on their way to our position. The first lights flashed through a bend up ahead simultaneous to Maggie's transmission.

"Strength one, moving fast. Probably a scout," Maggie said.

Wow. It was so weird hearing her finally speak; she'd been dead quiet up until this point in the trip. Maybe this was the juice she needed.

I watched the lone biker accelerate until just before the bridge, where he slowed down before pushing through the shallow flowing water. The biker rode a large enduro motorcycle with saddlebags and extra gas cans. On the other side of the creek, he cranked the gas and shot off down the road until his engine faded out of earshot.

Ten minutes later, the real target began to approach. This time, a lot more headlights broke through the trees at the bend where Maggie sat watching them approach.

"Strength twelve, main body. EFP worthy, I think."

I clicked the mic in acknowledgment, wanting to limit my transmission from space-based sensor detection, even though our advanced radios were frequency hopping a hundred times per second.

The biker's headlights swept over the shallow rushing water of the bridge. I saw some brake lights, but some of the bikers must have disabled theirs. As the first one crossed into the water I squeezed the EFP detonator like a nutcracker.

The explosion was loud enough to cause ringing in my ears, even though I wore over-ear electronic sound attenuators. The flash temporarily disabled my NVD and blinded my unassisted left eye. The NVD returned a picture in half a second, revealing chaos on the bridge. One of the bikers was on fire from an exploded gas tank; he fell into the creek and began to float, with the part of his body that wasn't underwater smoking as he slowly drifted downstream.

The bikes were now a mangled mess of chrome and rubber, burning from the intense impact of the hypersonic copper projectile. I wasted no time shaking the concussion of the explosion from my mind. I sprang from cover with my carbine pointed downrange at the bridge. Switching on my IR laser, I began picking out my first target. A man sat screaming and in flames from a gasoline explosion who didn't think it smart to follow his dead friend into the creek. My laser met his chest and I squeezed two rounds of .300 Blackout into him, dropping his corpse to the concrete as Maggie's IR laser came to life on another target. I saw her laser and deconflicted my shot, neutralizing it in tandem with her medium distance shots.

All in all, every biker had lead in them within about five seconds.

"All tangos down," I said on our secure channel.

A single key on the net told me that Maggie understood.

As I began to walk down to the bridge to get a closer look at the carnage, I saw Maggie's laser illuminate and pass over my head. It began to lasso, so I hit the ditch.

"His lights are off—he's coasting down the hill to you," she said ominously.

I lay in the ditch as a dark figure opened fire. The rounds whizzed over my head and up the hill to Maggie's position. Her IR laser went dark. I made sure mine was off when I brought my gun up from the edge of the ditch.

I was cold and covered with mud when the motorcycle came into view. The scout was coasting in neutral with his engine off, wearing an NVD. He'd seen Maggie's IR and taken shots at her.

He didn't know I was right there and about to put the hurt on him.

He slowed the enduro motorcycle as he approached the situation of all his hardcore biker buddies in pieces on the ground and in the water. Confused, he looked around, trying to find the source of what could have caused all that mayhem.

That's when his single ocular NVD met mine and he nervously reached for the pistol inside his shoulder holster. I took the shot, this time to his head, sending the last one into the ditch under his heavy motorcycle. I waited to make sure the target was neutralized. Approaching the bike, I could smell burning leather, or flesh; I couldn't tell. The hot exhaust was pressing against one of them. I painstakingly righted the motorbike and pushed it back to the road and dropped the kickstand. The guy in the ditch was dead, and his NVD was smoked, too.

Good. Most of the groups that might scavenge that device were probably not the type of people I'd want running around in the dark with a rifle.

With the threat neutralized, Maggie came bouncing down the hill. I could see enhanced light reflecting off her smile. I wasn't smiling at all but Maggie seemed to be having fun with this. I didn't even ask, as I didn't want to hear her response.

"Interview with a Sociopath" would be the title of that article.

"Let's check the saddlebags," she said to me, walking over to the low-water bridge where the corpses and mangled bikes sat spilled over.

"Wow. You're actually talking," I said. "But, no. I don't think I can check their bags right now. Would you mind?"

She cocked her head sideways at me for a moment before turning away to check the cargo that the bikers were carrying before we ended them.

I went over to a nearby guardrail and leaned up against the frozen metal as Maggie rummaged through the disaster area. I winced every time I saw her open a flap on a saddlebag, hoping she wouldn't find inside the horror I'd discovered when I was operating in Fayetteville, just after the shit hit the fan.

Some things you just can't unsee.

She came back with a box full of energy bars and some iodine tablets. Better than nothing, I suppose.

"Bikes were wired with human body parts," Maggie said nonchalantly.

"Yeah, they were road warriors. Probably not working for the provisional government. Most likely a pack of feral bikers moving like locusts."

We recovered our horses and walked them down to the stream to water them up before it was time to leave again. I stared at the enduro bike for a few moments, trying to talk myself into taking it instead of Molly. Yes, it would be faster, and yes, I could cover a lot of ground and scout ahead for Maggie, but it'd be loud as hell and the gas can strapped to the back wouldn't get me all the way to the East Coast. Adding a motorcycle to the mix would only mean more problems.

With the theme park behind us, we rode on, leaving the twisted pile of chrome and flesh behind for eastern horizons once again.

THE BIG MUDDY

Happy New Year

We didn't see another soul on our way across eastern Arkansas other than an old mountain man early one morning. He didn't say much as we rode past, just tipping his hat as he set snares in the field adjacent to the road we traveled. I didn't know for sure, but something told me that he didn't much care for the troubles of his fellow man. He looked as if he'd been setting snares and running trotlines since before all this went down anyway. I waved, and the man just ignored me and we kept on moving.

We are currently camped out in an old warehouse about ten miles from the Missouri-Tennessee border. We'd thought briefly about crossing the Mississippi River on I-40 into Memphis, but the report we'd received via shortwave from Rich warned against getting anywhere near the city. It was under the control of a group even more vicious that the provisional government, and now resembled Somalia more than an American city.

Rich was sending out intel, trying to time his report with where he thought we might be on our trip. Every few days, I planned to send a Morse signal to update our position based on the secret kill box grid he gave me before leaving the Shire.

The only other crossing besides the I-40 that I knew might still be intact would be the 155, which is where we're going tonight.

We made our approach to the bridge that spanned the widest river in the once great United States. Abandoned cars were everywhere; some of them blocked access to the bridge, unless you were on foot, motorcycle, or horseback. At the mouth of the bridge, we stayed back for a moment, observing any signs of activity. I watched for nearly an hour in the darkness through my NVD, trying to pick out cigarettes being smoked, or any other lapses in light discipline that a would-be ambusher might let slip as they waited on a couple of suckers to try to make their way across.

"You ready?" I asked Maggie.

She nodded and led the way ahead, unafraid of anything that would be on the bridge. The four-lane giant appeared to be in decent shape, with none of the wire supports frayed or snapped yet. Give it a decade and this whole span would be in the bottom of the mighty Mississippi.

We moved farther across the bridge until we came to a giant hole in the span. I looked down through the opening beyond the frayed rebar and crumbling concrete. The water rushed rapidly below. The hole covered both lanes on our side and a truck was leaning halfway inside. We backed the horses up, as combined we weighed as much as a small car.

"What the hell could have caused that?" I said aloud.

We backtracked a hundred yards or so until we found a way

that the horses could negotiate to the other lane and resumed our crossing.

The bridge was long and the details on the other side were still too dark to make out. We continued to move forward, slowly, moving around abandoned vehicles. I could hear the water forty feet or so below the bridge. We kept going, eventually making it to the last third of the bridge. After going around an ambulance Swiss cheesed with large caliber bullet holes, the far end of the bridge lit up.

A flare had been fired into the night sky, illuminating the area all around us with eerie incendiary glow. Maggie and I slinked down like vampires exposed to sunlight and turned our horses around in slow retreat. The next sound was faint, unmistakable.

Incoming mortar.

Why wouldn't one of the only passages across the Mississippi be guarded? What the hell was I thinking?

Those were just some of the thoughts going through my head as the mortar came down somewhere in front of us, blasting concrete and steel into the bullet riddled ambulance we'd just passed.

"You hit?!" I yelled.

"No, but they're not gonna launch just one!" Maggie said.

Just as those words left Maggie's mouth, another round came whistling, then slamming down from above into about the same spot as the last, again rocking the ambulance, this time turning it over. I watched in slow motion as the ambulance flipped in an awkward direction, a way in which didn't seem quite natural considering the blast from the explosives.

It was too late when I realized what was happening.

The ambulance was falling into a hole in the bridge, just blasted open from the high order detonations being fired from the eastern end. The emergency vehicle lurched in over the side and the concrete below us caved, sending us down into the deep brown, murky waters of the Mississippi. The last thing I remember before going over was screaming to Maggie, "The explosives!"

Then impact.

I went under with Molly. She flailed and kicked to get to the surface and the current tore me from the saddle sometime after we hit. The cold water impacted like a planet strike, evacuating the air from my lungs. My foot was still caught in the stirrups, dragging me awkwardly behind the swimming animal, and I was having trouble reaching the surface, especially after the horse kicked me in the stomach (accidentally of course).

Eventually, I wrestled my foot loose from the saddle and took in a deep breath of cold air. I began to shake uncontrollably as I gripped the saddle horn for dear life. I knew Molly was cold too, but she had a much higher probability of resisting hypothermia than I did.

I forced myself to stay lucid, concentrating on the pain, letting the continued mortar strikes serve as alarm bells to my senses.

I craned my head over my shoulder and watched as part of the bridge came apart from the violent attack that continued from the eastern shore. Nearly passing out, I just held on, not daring to call out to Maggie for fear of getting mortars redirected as a result of my voice carrying too far over the water. My hands began to lose their grip, so I climbed up higher onto Molly, causing her to whinny in protest. She was pushing as hard as she could to get across to the eastern shore. The river kept rushing us downstream and away from the stricken bridge and I hoped that Maggie was somewhere out there, in front or behind, awake and commanding Elvis to carry on, somehow.

I blacked out as I felt my body get even colder.

I woke up to a campfire on the banks of the Mississippi somewhere far downstream. I couldn't see the bridge or a sign of anyone other than our small camp. At first I was concerned about the fire, cautious that we'd be seen and killed, but as I got warmer, logic prevailed. We'd have died without the fire, no doubt about that. I still shook from hypothermia, but the fire began to cut through my icy skin and muscle and eventually reached my core, meeting the warm water Maggie made me drink somewhere in the middle.

"How?" I asked, barely able to speak.

"Elvis is a much better swimmer than Molly. It was cold at first, but after the initial plunge, I was out of the water the rest of the way to the bank. Granted, I had to come in after your dumb ass as you fell off Molly about fifty yards out."

"I see you enjoy talking again," I said, cracking a thin, hypothermic smile.

"Don't get used to it, Max."

Maggie had all our gear spread out around the fire suspended on paracord clotheslines to speed up the drying. I make a quick visual check and saw that everything seemed to be fine. Fatigue began to rob my consciousness, and before I drifted out, I swore I could hear the click of a weapon's latch. I tried to force myself awake, but my body would have none of it. I went down for a hard reboot to the crackling of fire.

Maggie woke me up at about 0600, just before daybreak.

"Let's move," she said after pouring river water on the fire. "Don't worry, I made another."

I was still cold from the plunge from the bridge, but I reluctantly crawled out of my bag that I'd luckily stored in a dry compress and began to ball it up and follow Maggie. I was half naked, my clothes strung out over branches to dry, but they were missing. It all became clear to me as I walked into the tree line from the banks of the

Big Muddy. The glow of another fire beckoned me back into the open arms of the riverside forest. At the fire, I dropped my bag near and crawled back inside, still shaking from exposure.

Maggie allowed me to sleep until about noon, when she smacked me on the back.

"Suit up and follow. You need to see," she said.

I quickly got dressed, glanced at the horses, and followed Maggie onto the bank. She didn't venture too far out, skirting the tree line that the Mississippi River had carved out, the polished stones relenting to softer dirt where the trees grew from fertile soils brought downriver.

We passed our camp from before, charred black driftwood being the only evidence left behind, to be erased the next time it rained somewhere upstream, somewhere uphill. Rounding two more bends, the bridge was revealed, the same one from which we plummeted last night. Maggie pulled out her binoculars and glassed the eastern side before handing them to me, gesturing that I do the same.

I cleaned the lenses with my dirty T-shirt and brought them up to have a look. Clearly, I could see white armored vehicles covering the eastern side and could make out black UN letters painted on the side. A few years ago, I'd have been called a conspiracy kook for even talking about UN vehicles at a checkpoint, let alone a UN force firing mortars to close off passage across the river.

"That's weird," I said, handing the binoculars back to Maggie.

"Chinese, all of them," she commented.

"How do you know that?"

"I got close this morning. They're not wearing blue helmets. Straight up People's Liberation Army. Listen, Max. I think they were guarding the bridge because I think they're laying claim to this side of the river."

Damn, that really stung to hear. I chastised Maggie for getting so close to the action, but couldn't fault her success. We didn't know for certain, but it appeared at least from here on the riverbed that her assessment of the situation could be true, especially knowing what I'd learned from the intel reports at the Shire. The Chinese wanted their share of what they were owed from the thirty-two trillion dollars in national debt, backed up by sovereign U.S. territory.

After getting back to camp just off the river, we tended to our horses and checked their hooves and coats, brushed them good, and made sure they had enough to eat for the night's journey away from here, away from the Chinese threat.

Enemy of My Enemy

We were prepared to leave camp on the Big Muddy and continue our journey east, when the explosions commenced, again. It wasn't long after nightfall and we were about to mount up when light flickered over the trees. A few seconds later, the sound of an explosion. We poured some silty water onto the concealed campfire, got on our horses, and moved towards the bridge held by the UN armored vehicles and Chinese troops. Rounding the last bend before the bridge became visible, I saw the arc of tracer fire through my NVD. A high order detonation rocked the middle of the bridge and more abandoned cars fell into the river.

An RPG returned fire from somewhere near the middle of the bridge, impacting a jackknifed semitruck near the UN vehicles. Before it detonated I watched the large projectile travel fast between the steel beams that held the bridge up. The Chinese responded with another volley of mortars, but whoever they were attacking were not giving up without a helluva fight.

I heard the revving of motorcycles and saw a few of them weaving through the cars, rushing the checkpoint position.

Bikers.

The suicidal and feral bikers navigated through the abandoned cars and appeared in front of the eastern blockade of armored vehicles. Both sides opened up with fully automatic machine guns, inflicting what looked like losses on both ends. I was too far away to see detail through my NVD, but I saw multiple grenade detonations behind the white UN vehicle blockade and heard screams carried by the wind down to the riverbank where we watched. The skirmished raged on for twenty minutes before the Chinese were able to kill every last biker that didn't fall into the water like Maggie and I did.

We disappeared into the trees and down a small deer path for a few miles before it led to a clearing where we could see a road. I checked my maps and we decided to follow the pavement east, keeping our eyes and ears tuned to our surroundings so that we could disappear into the forest at the first sign of trouble.

I thought back to the bridge and how viciously the bikers attacked the Chinese checkpoint, no self-preservation. Rage. Hatred. From now on, it was shoot on sight for anyone on a motorcycle. No hesitation.

We rode mostly east until the road branched off to the north. We followed it until reaching a crossroads, where we had to make a decision on whether or not to risk skirting a small city. Nothing like Memphis or Nashville, but still big enough to show up on my map. Besides the bikers and the checkpoint, we'd seen no significant threats, so we decided to take the shorter route and avoid Nashville, but travel south near Clarksville. With any luck, we'd reach the Blue Ridge Mountains in a week.

MOONSHINE AND TREASON

I sort of lost count of how many days have passed since we left the Mississippi. We travel at night and sleep during the day, so things sort of bleed together. My watch says it's the seventh of January; it's cold in these higher elevations. I don't think we've hit the Blue Ridge Mountains, but we're close. We had to detour a few nights ago when Rich transmitted that one of the nuclear power plants along the route he'd estimated (correctly) we were on had been left abandoned; the neutron rods were dropped during the SCRAM, but the area could still be dangerous. Better to avoid. Eastern Tennessee was nearly as quiet as Arkansas, but there was some military activity near the interstates we observed and also in the skies above.

Two days ago, as we slept under a tree canopy, I woke to the sound of jet engines. I jumped out of my bag and slipped on my coat to have a look as Maggie slept. Funny how she would wake up if I looked at her while she slept, but not to the noise of low flying fighters.

Leaving the cover of the trees for the nearby field, I brought my binoculars up. Two Flanker aircraft adorned with red stars on their vertical stabilizers were conducting low passes. Configuration dirty, with numerous bombs and fuel tanks hanging from the hard points on the wings.

I mean, it made perfect sense if you think about it.

What U.S. military pilot would conduct armed patrol on American soil, ready to bomb their fellow Americans into oblivion when ordered?

None, I'd wager. If any were alive, they were all home with their families, trying to get them through all this.

When you want cold and calculating military power on your soil, you need foreign muscle to do the dirty work, muscle that wouldn't think twice about dropping a bomb on someone like me, or strafing me with the machine gun that was no doubt cleared hot on the Flankers that patrolled overhead.

━━

We'd been on a red clay road for most of the night. I haven't seen any sign of Chinese troops or air support in a stretch, which was fine by me. Even though we had a Stinger missile, by the time we armed it and got it ready to fire, any Flanker might have us cut to pieces before we could go up against them. The Stinger would be used to prosecute targets of opportunity; to have a chance at a fighter, we'd need to get lucky and know where it was going to patrol beforehand.

Elvis acted up half the night, picking on Molly a little bit whenever he'd walk past with a snort and a nip. Molly wasn't taking any shit from him, though. Good for her. She'd check him, knocking him and Maggie over to the other side of the road when she'd had enough. Elvis was an ornery horse, but he was the only explosive capable horse that I currently knew of.

Maggie asked me about the case. She finally admitted to examining it when I was unconscious from hypothermia back at Big Muddy. We were approaching the halfway point to DC, so I didn't see any reason to keep it from her any longer.

"There's going to be a meeting of the minds in Washington. Our creditors and our so-called provisional government are going to get together and decide who gets what part of the United States," I told her.

"That's what the NAI said to you?" asked Maggie.

"Yes, they did. That's why we have the explosives and that's why we're currently headed to Washington," I said.

"You don't sound very enthusiastic about going," said Maggie. "I mean, you should know that it wasn't supposed to be a significant amount of land in the beginning; it was originally negotiated as a fifty-year lease. They agreed to give the land back after the time was up."

"Maggie, get the fuck out with that," I said.

"I know. I didn't say anything back before they locked me up. Maybe I should have. And maybe I should have done something," Maggie said, sounding like a lump was developing in her throat. "Max, if what you're saying is true, you need to wipe any doubt from your mind. Those bastards deserve more than a few pounds of NAI C4 shoved up their asses."

I wasn't so sure. What positive difference might another pile of bodies make, besides pushing me over the edge?

We kept riding, down the red clay road, under old light that beamed from long-collapsed stars.

After finally reaching an end to the red clay road last night, we hitched up an old logging trail that was supposed to find a two-lane road in thirty miles or so. A couple hours before sunup, we came across an old, mossy stone dam built a long time before Maggie and I were even a twinkle in anyone's eyes. We decided to make camp for the night near a wooden shack that sat next to the old dam. The sun was peeking up and the lock on the door to the shack wasn't something I wanted to mess with before I'd had a couple hours of sleep, so we just built a small fire and unrolled our bags while the horses drank and sniffed round for food.

After falling asleep to the sound of trickling water, I awoke at about 1400. Maggie was already boiling water for food, and I tried my hand with a fishing pole I'd made from a straight stick and the handful of hooks I'd brought. Luckily, I caught a bass after half an hour of struggling and quickly cleaned it for the fire. I had been looking for a catfish when I caught the bass, which is a fine indicator of how bad a fisherman I am.

After we had our small meal of fish and rice, I tried to get lucky again, but just ended up losing one of my hooks. I went over to check the dam shack and gave the lock a go with the master key. Their large brass lock marked "U.S." fell to the ground, reminding me of Dogpatch for a moment. Inside I found a simple breaker box with a series of labels made with old school label-maker ribbons.

I flipped on the one marked TURBINE 1.

Nothing.

TURBINE 2, nothing.

TURBINE 4, a light over my head began to flicker and then go steady, and a radio began to play static. I turned the radio off and checked the shack for anything that might transmit, giving away our location. I saw no electronic threats inside the old shack. I flipped the turbine breaker off again, dousing the lights, and went outside to survey the area. There were no visible power lines, so I began to look for any conduits that might be buried and eventually found one at the back of the shack.

I pulled the shallowly buried conduit up from the ground to at least find out the direction it might be going so I'd know where to even start looking. Maggie paid little attention, glancing over at me from time to time, just sipping warm broth by the fire, picking her teeth with a fishbone. I began to walk in the direction the conduit was going, into the trees and up a hill. Eventually I spotted another small building resembling the shack at the dam, maybe a little bit larger, but definitely the same design and workmanship down to the roof, walls, and door.

I went back to camp for the master key; this time Maggie took interest and followed. The horses remained by the fire, not giving a care about the musings of humans.

At the second shack, I walked around the outside, noticing that the door wasn't padlocked so I didn't need the bolt cutters. Figures. The same type of conduit sprouted out of the ground and up to a breaker box on the side of the shack. I twisted the doorknob and pushed. The door didn't budge. I gave it a good kick.

Nope.

I searched around the building and grabbed a nearby log that had been cut down and used it as a battering ram to finally get the door open. Splintered up and nearly defeated, I walked inside the dark windowless shack.

The smell of a corpse slapped us both in the face. The door we'd breached was solid and about three inches thick. Two cross-beams kept the door closed, put there by whoever lay decaying on the ground nearby a large moonshine still. Coiled copper line arced at a constant angle around the shiny metallic still and stacks of yeast bags sat waist high in the corner. Milk jugs full of clear liquid sat stacked deep on a shelf against the wall opposite the still. A bushel of some sort of long-rotted fruit was sitting on top of the corpse's torso. I used a coat that hung on a peg near the door to cover up the body.

"Well, we're making good time. Let's have a snort or two, what do ya say?" I asked Maggie.

She nodded and said simply, "Definitely."

We took a gallon of the clear liquid back to our small camp next to the dam and had ourselves a few sips of untaxed liquor.

The shine was a little stronger than I'd expected. I woke up at sunset to cottonmouth, feeling dehydrated. We had a good time during the day, playing poker under hydroelectric light inside the shack. We were missing a couple cards but it was fine; we made it work. After getting up and around, I pumped the empty moonshine jug full of water through my filter. I sat for a while and drank it slowly in the time before we mounted up for the logging trail once more. I flipped the breaker in the shack off for the last time, saddled up the horses, and checked their hooves for any problems. They were holding up pretty well, all things considered, but I think that Elvis might have lost a few pounds since we left Arkansas.

The trail was dark and devoid of old growth. Smaller Christmas tree–sized pines sprinkled the hills as we headed up the mountain, meandering on a small switchback. The cold was biting down to the bone with the wind coming off the hills, but Maggie and I were used to it by now and the horses didn't seem to mind as long as we kept them full of water and let them graze.

As we found the peak of the hill we'd been negotiating via switchback for the past few hours, I saw a light in the valley below. I gave the silent signal to halt and we both stopped at the same time.

I couldn't use my binoculars effectively with my helmet mounted NVD so I sat still, concentrating on the light.

It was well after midnight. After a long stare, I determined that the light was a campfire of some sort, but it was too far out to tell. I asked Maggie to hang back so that I could scout ahead while she kept the payload safe with Elvis.

I took Molly down the pass to within about two hundred yards of the fire. I led her off into the woods a little distance and slung her reins around a low branch that had been broken off. I made sure my carbine and my silenced Ruger pistol problem solver were loaded and chambered and approached the fire.

At first, I thought I'd go through the woods and approach from cover of the trees, but I'd make too much noise in the dark. I decided to stick to the logging trail and stay low.

I moved slowly, but found myself just outside the firelight before I knew it. I stepped back away from the fire and observed. I saw nothing but two sleeping bags with lumps in them and the fire. Whoever was here was fast asleep and didn't give a shit. I didn't see motorcycles or armored vehicles, so my plan was to just leave them alone and sneak on by. I backtracked to Molly and called Maggie via secure HAVE QUICK radio, letting her know to come quietly down the mountain.

After two minutes, I met her and we both continued down the trail past the fire. I glanced over and saw that one of the sleeping bags was empty.

I threw my reins to Maggie and jumped off the horse, carbine at high ready only to discover a man standing in the darkness just outside the fire, pissing on a tree. He didn't see me but the branches that I'd broke jumping off the horse alerted him pretty fast. He ran back to the fire and pulled a long gun out of his sleeping bag.

I gestured for Maggie to get the hell out as I tried to talk the man down.

"Hey, I'm just passing by, no need for the weapon!" I yelled to the man.

He obviously couldn't see me as he leveled his deer rifle, sweeping it left to right blindly in the darkness.

An IR laser clicked on, beaming over the top of my head at about horseback height. The powerful beam came to rest on the man's chest and hardly moved. Maggie's steady aim.

"Don't," I said, whispering into the radio.

The IR beam remained.

"Listen, I'm going to keep going. I don't want anything to do with you," I said, trying to throw my voice so the man wouldn't point his muzzle in my direction. Not because I was afraid he'd shoot me, but that Maggie would ice his ass if he flagged me with his gun again. By this time the other sleeping bag opened up like a chrysalis, revealing the second camper, a woman with matted hair and a very skinny frame.

Incredibly, the man lowered his gun, placing it on the ground. It must be because of the woman and his desire not to get into a gunfight in the middle of the cold night with someone he couldn't see. When the gun hit the deck, Maggie's IR switched off.

"Okay, I'm leaving," I said.

"Wait, wait . . . can we trade before you go?" the man said.

"Hold on a second," I responded.

"Maggie, what do you think?" I asked discreetly over the radio.

"Well, she's skinny as hell from where I'm sitting. I doubt they have food, and what else would we need?" Maggie replied.

Damn her and her Spock logic.

"What do you have to trade?" I asked, this time from a different position outside the fire so that the man wouldn't triangulate my voice.

"We have maps. We know where all the checkpoints are all around this place. We've mapped them ourselves. What's that worth to you?" the man said. "You're damn lucky to be here. This is a dead zone, but go a few miles in a certain direction and it's not."

"I stand corrected," Maggie's voice said over the radio.

"Okay, what do you want?" I said from a different location.

"The usual: food, medicine, anything you have that you're willing to trade."

After shouting back and forth a few times, I agreed to step into the light to meet the man. I was comforted by Maggie's IR beam, lasing the chest of whoever was speaking to me inside the glowing light of the fire. My bearded face, NVD, and helmet concealed most of my recognizable facial features. After a short story about how the man and woman came to be in these hills, he went back to his pack and pulled out a ratty worn road atlas.

"What have you got for us?" the man asked.

I told him to wait and I returned to Maggie to retrieve the gallon of white lightning we took from the shack and our own maps. I gave the man the alcohol and told him that it was strong enough to have medicinal application. He handed over his maps and I began to copy all the checkpoint information over, checking every few seconds to make sure the laser was on the man's chest.

"Hey, my name—"

"I don't want to know you, mister," I said, cutting him off.

I marked the hydroelectric shack on his maps and returned them to him.

"Go there, and you'll find a dozen more gallons of this stuff and a still," I told him before stepping back into the darkness. "Bye."

The man waved and Maggie and I rode away, letting a mile open between us and the fire before letting our guard down enough to sling our rifles.

Maggie commented that she hoped the trade was worth losing the shine. Based on the direction we needed to go, I thought it just might be.

We rode on through the rest of the early morning until our NVDs let us see the reflectors from the road signs up ahead.

"We found the highway," I said to Maggie. "Sun's up soon. Let's find camp."

We took a turn off the logging trail into the forest to hole up for the night before heading out on the pavement we'd been moving to for days now.

A Spartan lean-to was all we could manage. We slept on the ground next to yet another stealth fire and didn't have the luxury of playing cards under hydroelectric light, but hey, the sun was coming up anyway. Feast, famine, rinse, repeat, and hope you didn't get smoked. That was life out here.

Most recent encoded transmission from Rich:

> "Best bet, use [decoded to Appalachian Trail]. Fallout and troop concentrations are [decoded to thin] there. Had to use [decoded to Stingers] here. Sukhois getting thick. Stay on target and godspeed."

FOUR-LEGGED FRIENDS

24 Jan

Rich's advice was sound. Using the intel we'd gathered from the people we'd run into after the dam, we were able to avoid two security areas on the highway and make it to the Appalachian Trail. We'd have probably predicted the checkpoints, as they were all on the eastern or northern sides of large bridges, but it was nice to have it marked on our maps to help us make route decisions ahead of time.

The trail was abandoned, with no signs of recent human activity. Every so often we'd come across a snow-covered cache box where wealthy hikers would have their supplies prepositioned to facilitate their midlife crisis hike along the AT. No luck inside any of the caches unless you count the nearly empty roll of toilet paper, which I did.

If we thought the road from Arkansas was lonely, the AT was even more maddeningly silent.

January 19, 0100 GMT

OPERATION HAYSTACK
DIRECTOR'S EYES ONLY

We managed to bring two of our older KEYHOLE SIGINT birds online after reconfiguring a ground station back to analog function. We put a team of NSA operators on the console after we managed to squeeze out satellite orbital adjustment fuel to tweak the HEO of both birds to work in tandem. The team was able to receive a SIGINT hit on a suspected HAVE QUICK transmission on the western side of the Blue Ridge Mountains in east Tennessee. Likely source of transmissions are from captured radios. The geolocation major/minor covers a wide area due to the older equipment and antiquated techniques utilized. The team is working around the clock to exploit the spectrum to ensure we catch the next instance of unauthorized HAVE QUICK radio utilization. Recommend a QRF be on standby near last intercept to conduct rapid direct action when the next SIGINT tipper is received.

▬▬▬▬▬▬▬▬ sends.

▬▬▬▬▬

We continued north for two days until we were forced to make early morning camp where a rockslide had blocked the trail some time before. Thick moss covered the north faces of the jagged boulders and the bones of a dead animal lay strewn about the rubble.

With GPS being hard down, I've had to rely on Molly's pace to figure out how far up the AT we'd gone. There were surprisingly few trail markers, or at least not many we'd seen along the trail. Our packs were a lot lighter than when we'd left and my belt was about to need another hole to keep my pants up. It wasn't that we weren't eating—it's that we were burning a lot more calories than we were consuming.

That very thought was on my mind as I set out with my carbine and NVDs to poach the king's game. Before Maggie and I left the camp, we tied the horses so that we wouldn't accidentally shoot them. When you were hungry, everything that moved looked like cheeseburgers. Hunting on night vision was the only way to fly. Things you couldn't notice during the day jumped out when you wore seven thousand dollars of technology on your head. The compound eyes of insects shone on the leaves of branches as we stalked our prey.

We moved through the frosted grass and trees for an hour in a concentric circle around the rockslide camp. At high ground, we could see the glow of the fire like a great beacon, and the eyes of the horses as they scanned their surroundings flashed in our NVDs. I was watching the camp, thinking about our next move, when Maggie's IR laser flashed in front of me and a shot snapped from her muzzle.

The frantic gobble of evading turkeys told me that breakfast was going to be a good one. Maggie sprinted into a turkey fight, the glint of her blade flashing moonlight from the mirror-honed edge. With one swat, the head of the turkey lay snapping on the grass. Maggie waited for a few moments so that the turkey's sharp talons would stop jerking in defiance of its own demise. Maggie could switch into predator mode quickly, and was an efficient killer.

We built a real fire, not worrying about being seen in this remote area of the AT. The heat reflected back off the avalanche rocks, making me warmer than I'd felt in weeks. It didn't take us long to prep the turkey, and soon we were eating like tourists at a Renaissance

faire. We ate half the turkey and put the rest of the cooked meat inside a plastic bag surrounded by ice and suspended it in a tree away
from camp. Ain't no way I'd keep it in the camp with us. I knew for
a fact that the cats and bears were bigger and meaner here. This
wasn't Arkansas, and I had no desire for a Newton County repeat.
When the weather is just right, or I've had a particularly long day, I
can still feel the scars.

We both slept well, knocked out on the turkey drug I hadn't
experienced in so very long.

———

Shortwave intercepts—transcribed from Max's recording device
onto paper in the field.

Real State of the Union

0700: "It's all over, at first it was the government we had to fear . . .
you know . . . their brand of order and restoring justice. They've
all burned out. Most of 'em gone home to their families, unless
you're unlucky enough to be living nearby one of their intel centers. Might as well be a Dark Ages castle. Lords and barons living
inside the heavily guarded fusion center forcing their will on the
region they are charged to occupy. The provisional government
is on its knees, it's true. That's why Chinese and Russian troops
are on our goddamn soil! The Russians? They are in no better
shape than we are, but a helluva lot less dependent on the grid.
Besides, who's going to maintain the Sukhois? I never thought I'd
see Flankers on patrol in U.S. airspace. Never."

0923: "The President has given authorization for the UN to operate in all fifty states to facilitate the restoration of order. Citizens

are reminded that the UN troops are only here to help quell the lawlessness occurring along the major roadways and that their presence here is only temporary."

1202: "Max, whoever you are, wherever you are, we need you now more than ever [jamming phases in and out from unknown source] . . . you did in Arkansas spread more than [jamming]. Everyone listening to this, you are Ma [more jamming]. Flip the script! Long live the Re[some interference]."

1319: "UN troops boarding large helicopters for unknown regions on a regular basis. Government media calling them QRF. Rumors swirl that their sole function is to double down on "unlawful transmissions" and to find and eliminate pirate radio stations like the one you are listening to right now. They can't stop all of us. Bastards."

1600: "Hey, America, what's left of you; the UN is just the enforcement arm of the World Bank. Funny how most of the troops wearing UN helmets come from the countries we owed money! Here is the real kicker: the biggest debtor was the American people! Stop listening to this, get out there, and start shooting anyone in a foreign uniform!"

1822: "Hello, my name is Harold, I worked for the DHS before all this. I resigned last year when things started getting . . . ungentlemanly. I saw the writing on the wall before, stocked up like most of you out there. If you didn't, you're dead and most likely not listening to this and are probably inside someone's stomach . . . well, sorry for that, but it was modeled out. People knew. I'm here to tell you that upwards of <u>90 percent of the U.S. population is</u>

<u>dead</u>. This outcome was briefed to the highest levels as far back as the turn of the millennium. They knew the consequences of a nationwide grid down event and did nothing! They . . ."

Well, it's been a shitty night, to say the least. Maggie has been shot in the arm—just a graze, but still going to be a problem. Molly was hit in the flank, but seems to be okay enough to still move without too much trouble. Elvis and me made it out with only minor surface injuries.

Bastards.

12 Hours Ago

We started with a hunt as we'd run out of our turkey meat. We decided to spread out a little farther apart, as seeing Maggie's laser cross over my shoulder right before she took her shot was a little spooky last time. She was a beast when it came to killing, no hesitation. Yeah, I can swing a pipe too, but not the same way Maggie does. Females are the alpha killers in many species, and Maggie certainly was a lioness when it came to hunting.

We spread out and moved into the forest from the main artery of the AT. After half an hour, Maggie sent me a message on the HAVE QUICK.

"Tracking something," she said.

I clicked the radio in acknowledgment and began to move faster. As a point of pride, I wanted to kill the next meat instead of letting her go two for two. That all went out the window a few minutes later when her HAVE QUICK phased back into sync with my radio.

"Rabbit down," she said.

Before I could answer, I heard the sounds of rotor blades beating the cold air over one of the adjacent hills.

"Go dark," I transmitted before switching off my radio.

I began to head for our distress point, a place we'd worked out nightly before bedding down. Normally we'd pick a spot two hundred paces off a compass direction from the campfire; this time the direction was northeast and the spot was a large boulder with graffiti on it from the people hiking the AT, which I thought was uncharacteristic for the types of folks that hiked the trail, but whatever. I moved to the boulder looking for the glow spilling from Maggie's NVD.

I ran quickly, fighting off the urge to go back to the camp to secure the weapon and let the horses free. Nearly to the boulder, I looked over my shoulder and saw a large twin rotor helicopter in a hover atop a cliff. IR glow sticks attached to assaulters' webbing shined brightly in contrast with the darker sky. The twin rotor tips formed twin arcs while the large machine hovered, dropping off its pax.

I counted four.

Based on their landing zone, I had time. I sprinted down to the camp and grabbed the horses and supplies, leading them back into the cover of the trees. Quickly, Maggie and I donned our body armor. I grabbed the three remaining grenades, giving her one of them. The helicopter was already gone, probably headed somewhere to wait on the call for pick up, a call that would occur after Maggie and I were ventilated in these hills. Attaching the grenades to my plate carrier, we mounted up and drove deeper into the cover of the forest in case a drone was loitering overhead, providing a real-time video feed to the team that pursued. I knew the game. I used to play it.

Maggie and I rode hard for an hour until stopping at a natural choke point. Two high cliffs stood face to face twenty feet apart; if we were being pursued, they'd need to come through here. Maggie and I hid the horses and began to set up a trap. We had one EFP remaining and Maggie and I agreed that this would be a damn good reason to drop twenty pounds from our load out.

I set the explosive device up to shoot down the corridor between the cliffs and rigged an expedient tripwire using copper snare and paracord. After checking and double-checking the trap, Maggie and I retrograded back to the horses and found some high ground a safe distance from the pass so that we could pick off any survivors after the blast.

We waited for half an hour until the trap was sprung without warning. The explosion rocked the pass, sending boulders down into the gap. The flash of suppressed muzzles began to pop off like camera flashes, but not in the area behind the blast, to our right, coming from the direction we were now hiding.

They were planning to pincer us!

The blast probably killed one of them, but judging by the chunks of rock that hit my face, they knew that we were out here somewhere. I signaled to Maggie to check her radio as I checked mine. It was off.

Maggie mouthed the word "Sorry" as she pointed to her radio.

They were likely tracking the RF leakage from her powered on radio. They found us with our transmissions, but refined our position off Maggie's goddamned radio. I thought we were dead until I remembered the one thing that tended to solve most problems.

Grenades.

I signaled to Maggie that I was about to send a frag in the direction of the muzzle flashes. Instead of taking cover behind a tree, she tossed her frag out with mine and we both hit the deck. Explosions once again echoed back and forth between the hills, but there was now less shooting.

Maggie's IR laser came to life, prompting me to click mine on, too. Our beams crossed like flashlights in an old *X Files* rerun as we scanned for remaining shooters. One rifle kept barking from a nearby tree, the rounds exploding on the face of a nearby boulder. Glancing at Maggie, I could see that she was bleeding. Her arm was black from the dark blood that covered it and half her gun.

If I fired, it could give away my position, so I decided to lob my last grenade at the base of the tree. I gave Maggie the signal to dive and as soon as she did so, the pineapple left my hands. I heard it hit just before the explosion sent the last shooter to the ground; the shrapnel from the point blank grenade to the torso seemed as if it nearly cut the soldier in half.

Maggie and I waited behind cover for anyone left alive to bleed out. What would be the point to walk up on one of them only to get shot by an AK-wielding possum?

The wait was forever, time marked by our breath shooting into the air from underneath our NVDs back and forth in tandem. After an hour of shivering, our adrenaline wore off and we broke cover to check the bodies.

Chinese. All of them. Their bodies were covered in holes and lacerations from grenade damage.

Their NVDs were of an older generation. We removed and smashed them. We took their AKs and magazines and concealed them inside a plastic trash bag with some duct tape. Marking the location on a map, we hid them away for a rainy day. Part of me wanted to shoot a few rounds through the receiver, but they could potentially save lives if the location of the cache was shared with the good guys.

Yeah, good guys.

Was that even me anymore?

Line is blurry.

28 Jan

Tonight was one of the many times I'd risked using HF/shortwave to send a Morse signal back to Rich at Shire Base. We were about ready to leave for the night, which would put some distance between the transmission and our next camp.

The simple message encoded with Rich's codebook read, "Firefight, AT. Chinese insert helo. Pressing to objective."

His response was short, cryptic and terrifying.

"You are compromised via overhead. No more Tx."

After hearing the dire message, I removed the batteries from the HF radio, pulled the long wire out of the tree, and taped the batteries to the outside of the radio. I tossed the small shortwave transceiver and Morse paddle into the bottom of my pack for the last time.

I then asked Maggie to do the same to her HAVE QUICK unit as I did so to mine.

She asked, "Satellites?"

"Yeah."

"What took them so long?" she said rhetorically.

With our batteries taped to the outside, effectively neutering our radios, we kept moving east.

Maggie's shrapnel injury from the fight with the Chinese stormtroopers looks like it's infected. My horse's flank is swollen and she's losing about two hours of travel per night. We're leaving the AT and heading for antibiotics, if any exist.

Sparta
Day

I picked a spot on the map and committed, one of the last towns before we crossed into the Commonwealth of Virginia. Molly was hurting, and I wasn't sure we'd find enough antibiotics and other meds to save Maggie, let alone the horse. Carefully consulting my maps, we avoided the roads leading into the small town for the most part until the map indicated that there was a convenience store a mile up ahead.

We broke cover and rode to the edge of a vast field until the road was in sight once again. I dismounted and clipped the barbed wire fence with the master key and we rode through the severed wire onto the cracked roadway. Up ahead, I could see a Texaco sign reaching up over the trees, our intermediate destination.

I rode ahead, scouting for trouble. Molly complained as I rounded one of the abandoned cars that sat perpendicular to the road.

"Easy, girl," I said to her, hoping to comfort her.

The gas station was trashed, just like I expected, but I didn't need anything here except the one thing that probably still remained under the counter. I dismounted, causing another grunt from Molly, and stepped over the broken glass to the front of the store as Maggie caught up. I looked over my shoulder at her and thought of the pale horse verse from the Bible.

I used the business end of my carbine to clear enough glass to safely get inside. Flipping on my weapon-mounted light, the entire floor began to move and change colors.

Fucking cockroaches.

I suppressed my desire to just burn the whole place down

and crunched over the stragglers to the register. I hopped over the counter and peered underneath. The only thing I saw was a loose shotgun shell and a roll of scratch-off lottery tickets. I stuffed the half dispensed roll into my pocket as an afterthought and continued to search. Digging through the yellowed and torn newspapers on the floor, I hit my own personal jackpot coming across an ad for a vet clinic located "Just off Main Street, we'll see you there!"

I snatched up the ad and left the cockroach nest crunching for the light of day where the vermin dare not swarm. After conferring with my maps, we once again headed down the highway into the small town of Sparta.

We didn't see any movement on the streets as the old stone buildings began to appear up ahead. We passed Persimmon and Olrich before reaching Main, turning right as the road transitioned from regular cracked concrete to older style cobblestone.

Horse hooves kept clicking on the cobblestone as we transitioned down a gentle hill. I saw a horse statue up ahead. Approaching closer, I could see a large stethoscope around the statue's neck and a doctor's head mirror atop its head. A red cross was painted on the ribcage. The sight of the vet office pushed me ahead a little faster as Molly grunted in protest. I was scope-locked on the horse statue, tunnel visioned as I rode.

Maggie's rifle report snapped me out of my focus as her shot ricocheted off the road with a loud *ZING!*

"Don't shoot, don't shoot!" a woman screamed from cover.

My carbine was out of its scabbard before the woman could finish her sentence. I trained the red dot on the group of trees from where her voice had come, flipping over the magnifier to give me a little more clarity on the situation. I pulled the reins and gave Molly the command to walk backwards.

My faithful horse reluctantly complied, not wanting to back into the loud noise she'd just heard coming from the barrel of Maggie's gun.

"Come out, or we're shooting!" I yelled, my carbine leveled to the trees, red dot beaming bright like the eye of the devil.

As the bushes began to move, I was off my horse, taking concealment behind a nearby vehicle. A woman stepped out of the bushes, dirty and disheveled, holding the hand of a young girl. I moved the devil's eye away from them.

"Stop there," I commanded loudly. "What do you want?!"

"Food. My husband is too weak to hunt and my child is hungry. Just food. That's all. What are you doing here?" the woman asked, her eyes searching near Molly, trying to find me.

"We're here for medication; my friend has an infection," I responded.

"I have medication at our house. Antibiotics, ibuprofen, and morphine. If you could spare food, anything . . ." the woman said as she began to beg. "No one is left here. We're not important enough for help. Everyone that lived here left already. We thought we could make it through on our farm."

The woman began to sob and the girl reached her hands up into the air for the woman to pick her up.

I looked over to Maggie to get a read on what she was thinking. As expected, she rolled her eyes and I watched her lips as she mouthed, "Whatever."

I told the woman not to make any sudden movements. I whispered to Maggie that I was going to check the clinic to see what was left inside. I handed Maggie the reins and stepped over to the building, mindful of the woman and the child. If she were to pull a gun from underneath her rags, I'd have little choice but to waste her in front of her daughter.

And then what?

Leave the child to die out here? If I were being honest to myself, I'd probably let the fucking woman shoot and kill me.

The woman didn't skin a gun and remained still as I breached the front door to the vet clinic, negotiating around the receptionist.

"Payment is due upon services rendered" was the sign posted prominently atop the receptionist desk. I made it to a door leading to the back office, which happened to be locked. I breached the door with a well-placed kick, sending it flying so hard that the knob dug into the drywall.

I tossed the place top to bottom looking for drugs. They were long ransacked along with the rest of this town. I realized at this point that I had no choice but to negotiate with the woman outside.

Brenda

I walked into the bright light once more, meeting the woman and child.

"Take us to your place. We need antibiotics," I told her.

Maggie looked at me, but I couldn't read her at the moment. She had the facial expressions of a T-Rex. You could never tell if she wanted to kill you.

The woman turned to walk back into the tree line.

"Don't try anything—don't make me add another demon to trampoline on my soul. I've had enough," I said, not really sure why I took the time to say that.

The woman trekked through the trees for half a mile until everything opened up to a hay field that eventually rounded a bend to a farmhouse and large white barn. The woman asked me to wait outside so she could speak to her husband.

"That's fine, but my friend and I will fall back until you come back out," I told her.

After a few minutes, she came out with her husband leaning on her shoulder for support.

He looked a lot worse than Maggie.

"I'm Brenda, and this is John. This is our farm. The reason you couldn't find any meds at the clinic was because we took them. John was a vet tech there—he had permission."

I got right down to business, telling them that Maggie and my horse had a nasty infection from a gunfight with the Chinese military. They both smiled at hearing that and offered that we come inside.

John looked Maggie over, determining that she probably had some shrapnel still inside her arm. After applying a local anesthesia, he opened her up and removed a small metal shard with a pair of sterilized tweezers. During the operation, the man looked as if he'd pass out from exhaustion. He carefully stitched her back up and asked his wife to help him to the porch once more.

Maggie stayed in bed, waiting for the medication to wear off as John struggled down the front porch steps to look at my horse. Molly was a little leery of the new smell and tried to step away from John, but I comforted her with a pat and a soothing voice.

"She's infected pretty bad. How long you been running her like this?" John said.

"A few days. No choice."

John continued to examine Molly, nearly earning a kick to the leg after the horse reacted to the sharp pain from the check-up.

"Well, mister, the good news is that I have enough antibiotics to kill your friend's infection, but I can't help the horse now. From the looks of the swelling, I'd say she has a few days, maybe a week if you get damn lucky. She's going to be in considerable pain between now and then."

I let that sink in for a long while, petting Molly and kissing her on her nose. She was pleased by the affection, but I could see that she wasn't doing well.

I went back inside the farmhouse to check on Maggie. Brenda had her on an IV drip bag and was already administering antibiotics.

I retrieved some rations from my saddlebag and handed them to Brenda, who immediately began to prepare food for the little girl, who was called Naomi.

After considerable deliberation, I decided to do the right thing.

I asked John to give the meds to Maggie in exchange for enough horsemeat to see them through the rest of the winter, if they prepared it right and didn't waste anything.

I took Molly out back behind the proverbial barn and said my good-byes. Maggie came out to support me and she could see that I was a little torn up over what I had to do, but I didn't want the poor animal to suffer any longer than was necessary. I kissed and rubbed the horse one last time.

Reassuring her that she was a good girl, I put my suppressed muzzle up to her head and pulled the trigger.

The thump of Molly hitting the ground was psychologically louder and more damaging than those of humans I'd sent to the ground over the past year. The horse was loyal to me and was a good companion during our journey from the Arkansas mountains to where we now found ourselves. Molly's death solved a lot of problems for John, Brenda, and Naomi, but they caused problems for Maggie and me. Elvis was a stout horse that could carry Maggie and most of the supplies, but not everything. We'd need to figure it out.

Part of the deal was that Brenda and Maggie harvest the horsemeat, as there was no goddamned way I could bring myself to do that. I spoke to John as the women worked behind the barn and ascertained that he was sick with the flu and malnutrition, and I hoped that the new meat would bring him and his family strength and get them through the winter. I threw in a small bottle of vitamins to go along with the meat. I hadn't even bothered breaking the seal on it since we left and figured that he and his family could use them more than I could.

HOOVES TO HYDRAULICS

Maggie and I took a few hours in the old white barn to strategize our next move. Being down a horse wasn't going to do us any favors. Using our detailed charts, we circled every airfield within ten miles of our intended path through Virginia. After some deliberation and checking of runway lengths, we picked our target airfield and planned our route. We said our good-byes to the family the following evening amidst the heart-stinging aroma of cooking horse meat.

Maggie showed marked improvement since she began the antibiotics. She was still recovering, so obviously she'd be taking Elvis in case we got into some trouble. I doubt that ornery animal would let me ride him anyway. He was used to Maggie; I'd even go so far as to say he was partial to her. As we moved ahead on foot, Elvis's load was a littler heavier, but so was mine.

Every so often I'd catch Elvis looking back for Molly, the travel companion that would never be there again. I'm glad it was dark—Maggie wouldn't notice my watering eyes. I wouldn't have to feel guilty about being devastated over losing my horse, but not over killing men. It was a strange world in which we lived, and every day proved that.

With our radios completely powered down and batteries removed, our chances of being geolocated became exponentially more remote. These chances were even more to our favor if we kept moving at night and sleeping during the day.

About halfway to the airfield, we saw a light on the highway far ahead and disappeared into the brush. A few minutes later, a bicycle pedaled by, its headlight shining brightly onto the road—an older man traveling hard to his destination.

Pedaling as if his life depended on it.

At that instant, I suspected that our previous host had called the bicyclist on the radio about their newfound food. I prayed that they didn't say anything else over the airwaves.

After discussing this theory with Maggie, we both agreed we might have to get off the road quick at the first sound of rotor blades beating the cold night air. One advantage to not having Molly was that I didn't get very cold. I was working pretty hard to keep my forty pound pack from getting the best of me as I tried to keep up with Maggie and Elvis on point. Just before the eastern sky began to change hue, we made it to the top of a hill looking down on the airfield.

We had some work to do.

After arriving at the airfield perimeter, we had to cut the chain link fence to get inside. I didn't want to attempt entry at the terminal side of the small airstrip in case someone was camped out there. After splitting the fence wide enough, Maggie put Elvis in the brush for the time being. If all went well, poor Elvis would be on his own.

The runway was littered with small branches and other debris from suffering a year of zero maintenance. Six aircraft sat evenly spaced apart, with lines tethering them to pad eyes on the ground. We eventually made it through the thick grass and stepped out onto the concrete. An old windsock was swaying in the breeze, half torn apart. Adjusting our NVDs and making our guns ready, Maggie and I moved in on the aircraft, hangars, and admin buildings scattered through the eastern side of the airfield. We purposely didn't choose a larger airfield, as we'd have a much lesser chance of finding a ride out of here.

I checked the first aircraft, an old 172. Her cockpit glass was riddled with small caliber bullet holes and her pilot the same. I opened the door and pulled the shriveled corpse out onto the frosty tarmac. The interior smelled like I imagined it would.

Death.

I thought I'd get lucky and the aircraft would only have damage to the cockpit window, maybe some minor airframe damage, but I wasn't. The controls, glass cockpit, and much of the avionics were damaged. Worst of all, the fuel tanks were ruptured, having long ago spilled their fuel onto the ground. A puddle of oil formed below the engine cowling where another bullet must have struck something underneath. Dozens of 5.56 cases lay on the ground. Picking one up to examine more closely under a flashlight, I observed that they were tarnished and far from fresh, just like the body that was rotting inside the aircraft for months, maybe since the beginning.

I moved on to the next aircraft. One of the tires was flat, but that was a problem that could be solved, unlike the bullet riddled mess I'd just inspected. Much to my frustration, the aircraft passed inspection up until the point I examined the wings. A perfectly round

5.56 hole punctured the wingtip, probably killing this aircraft just like the last one.

Maggie yelled at me from one of the nearby hangars. I got so involved with inspecting the aircraft outside that I'd forgotten about her. I had a couple more aircraft to inspect, but I broke off the search to see what she needed. I stepped through the hangar door into the darkness, letting my NVD adjust to the sight of a business jet sitting diagonally inside.

"Well?" Maggie said.

"I'm not multi-engine rated, Maggie," I told her, pretty sure that this ten-million-dollar monstrosity wasn't what we were looking for this morning.

"Well, I am, you sexist bastard. Flew a few Evergreen sorties in my day, long before you got sheep dipped, young blood," Maggie snapped back, startling me with the tip of her sharp tongue.

You haven't said much more than that since we'd left Arkansas, I thought but didn't say aloud.

"Okay, so you can fly this thing. It's a jet and hasn't had a maintenance check in a pretty long time," I said.

"Yes, I know it's a goddamn jet, but it takes less to maintain this thing than most of those pieces of shit out there. Let me take a crack at the checklist and see what's up. Go get Elvis."

Not wanting to discourage her, I did what she asked, but not before securing the airfield. There were no signs of recent activity in the area. After retrieving Elvis, I rigged up some rope to him and tied off an old tarp I'd found sitting in a stack next to the hangar.

I spent the rest of the morning until sunup leading Elvis up and down the runway, getting rid of branches, rocks, and other bullshit that could get stuck inside a jet intake on takeoff or blow a brittle tire. Halfway back to the hanger with a full tarp dragging behind Elvis, I heard the sound.

A loud, high-pitched engine noise shot from the hangar door out onto the runway. I quickly scanned my surroundings to see if the noise caused movement at any of the perimeters. So far, I saw nothing, no flash of a weapon light or vehicle reflector motion.

I left Elvis where he was and ran over to the hangar to find Maggie's face covered in grease as she held a set of wrenches in her hand. Over behind the jet, I saw a power cart plugged into the aircraft with a fuel hose running to support equipment from outside the door.

The jet door was open, its steps already lowered to the hangar floor.

"Is it serviceable?!" I screamed over the power cart engine.

"Yeah, I think so! Open that hangar door, will you?!" Maggie said, pointing to the large doors.

I went over the control panel thinking that pushing the button would do something, finally realizing that the power cart was plugged into the aircraft and not the building. I disengaged the motor on the bay doors and manually began to retract them up into the ceiling, revealing the morning sun as it spilled over the top of the hangar, casting a large shadow just before the light shone and sparkled from the ice on the ground beyond.

Elvis looked over at us as if we were insane, cocking his head to the side. He didn't dare approach the noise without being led. With the bay doors open, the fumes from the power cart began to thin out, allowing Maggie to work. I took a glance at the manual she was looking at between wrench turns and panel pops. It appeared as if she was doing the monthly check on the aircraft.

My suspicions were confirmed after an engine panel was closed and she stepped down off the ladder.

"Everything looks safe enough. I wouldn't take it across the ocean, but as long as we have a few divert airfields preplanned, I think we'll be okay as far as dying goes. Fuel state will give us about four hours of flight time, way more than we need. I could top it off with what's in the tank outside, but I know the stuff in the jet is still good. I took a sample." Maggie wiped the sweat from her forehead with an oily shop rag.

After shutting down the power cart, Maggie asked when I thought it'd be best to leave. We had a discussion and decided we should at least get a little sleep and figure out what we were going to do about Elvis. With everything shut down, we brought the horse inside and tied him off to the tool cabinet.

I didn't feel safe enough to sleep, as the hangar doors were open wide to the adjacent road. I sat on the wing, eating some of the last of my rations, watching for any signs of trouble as Maggie slept. She'd be piloting, so I wanted her fresh enough for a safe takeoff and landing, the two times that we'd be at the most risk.

I fought the urge to fall asleep while sitting on the wing of the Gulfstream, my back to the fuselage. The flurries started midmorning, prompting me to start a fire outside the hangar. Maggie was asleep in her bag, but I was on sentry duty and freezing my ass off.

I gathered some of the branches Elvis and I cleared from the runway and made a small bonfire. Elvis came sauntering over to warm up. I gave him some pats on the neck and fed him the hay I had shoved in the increasingly open space of my pack. I still reeled with guilt from having to shoot Molly, and the thought of leaving poor Elvis out here to fend for himself only increased the sickening feeling in my stomach.

"When we go, you don't stop for anyone. Head west, back over the mountains, okay?" I said to the animal, hoping it'd somehow understand.

As I fed Elvis the last of the hay, I caught a flash from the corner of my eye on the road through the chain link fence. The same place we'd cut through.

My gun came up quickly but there was no target to engage. Whatever had caught my attention was gone. Trusting my gut, I rushed over to Maggie, waking her up. My kit was already stowed, buckled into one of the leather passenger seats inside.

"I saw something. We probably need to think about quitting this place," I said to her. I swung my gun around to the hangar opening as she crawled out of her warm bag into the freezing air. I heard her toss her kit into the aircraft.

Instead of climbing inside, she walked past me over to Elvis. In a rare showing of emotion, she kissed the animal on the nose and said something to it that I couldn't make out before leading it to the other side of the area, near the terminal parking lot, away from the hangar. After saying her good-byes, Maggie took the saddle off Elvis, tossing it on the frosty ground.

Back at the hangar, Maggie plugged the power cart into the aircraft and started it up just before climbing inside the multi-million-dollar business jet. She signaled for me to wait at the side door.

After a loud compressor type bang, it sounded like she got the APU up and running. She looked back through the cockpit door down the small row of seats and gave me the signal to disconnect. I shut down the power cart and unplugged it from the Gulfstream. The APU was blasting hot exhaust, quickly filling up the hangar despite the open bay door. I decided to open the other side of the hangar to vent more exhaust. I saw Elvis watching from afar, looking apprehensive about the noise.

Maggie left the pilot's seat and came back to remind me to pull chocks and to show me how to stow the cabin door. I performed the last walkaround and then boarded the jet, tossing the chocks to the back of the tube before shutting the cabin door to the sound of rushing air.

I hunched over and walked forward, ducking into the cockpit and taking the right seat next to Maggie. This time, I put on a cushy Bose headset, which was a helluva lot better than the DCs I was used to flying with. The APU noise instantly lowered to the point I could hear Maggie sharply over the ICS.

"Glad you opened the other doors. The jet blast from taxiing might have knocked the wall out and maybe destabilized the whole hangar," Maggie said.

"How's she look?" I asked, gesturing to the jet's master caution panel.

"Nothing critical; we're good."

Maggie worked the checklist startup sequence bringing the engines online with a cough and a lot of smoke. The smoke cleared quickly, shooting out both sides of the hanger from the odd air pressure anomaly created by the exhaust vortices. Maggie hit start on her wrist chrono; about thirty seconds passed before she stuffed the checklist under her leg and edged the throttles forward.

The metal hangar building shuddered and creaked.

Maggie gave the engines more power, bringing RPMs up noticeably on the instrument panel. With nosewheel steering in play, she turned the jet toward the runway taxi lane delta. As she made the turn, the powerful engines swept across a wall on the hanger and all hell broke loose.

Hurricane force winds, focused like a fire hose on the flimsy aluminum siding, sent a section of metal wall paneling spinning up in the air. I saw Elvis gallop off in fright as the metal hit the terminal parking lot and skidded across into an abandoned car on the curb. Maggie began to taxi into position, dodging sticks and other debris that Elvis and I missed on the mile and a half long piece of pavement. The aircraft was in position, nose facing into the wind, as evident by the tattered windsock at two o'clock, five hundred yards away.

"You ready?" Maggie asked.

I didn't say anything, only nodding that I was.

Maggie began the run-up sequence on the jet, sending the engines into proper RPM and internal temperatures for takeoff. Simultaneously, she let off the brakes and pushed the throttles to near firewall and the aircraft jerked forward and began its takeoff roll.

"Eighty knots," Maggie said about halfway down the runway. "Rotate."

The nosewheel left the ground, followed by the main gear, and we were off deck. Maggie climbed rapidly while bringing up the landing gear, reducing the drag, helping us to clear any terrain out there we didn't know about. We didn't have the required FAA pubs, and for all we knew there was a radio tower a mile in front of us and five hundred feet high, ready to cut a wing from our fuselage in fifteen seconds.

"Systems check good. Keep an eye on pressurization for me, Max," Maggie said, gesturing to one of a dozen gauges above my head on the copilot side of the cockpit.

The instrument indicated that cabin altitude was climbing, but it stopped at 2,000 feet as the aircraft shot past that altitude and leveled off at a mile above the earth.

"Gas?" I asked.

"Based on projected burn rate and fuel state on takeoff, still plenty of fuel," Maggie said, tapping the multifunction display on her side.

I pulled out our maps and did a quick scan of terrain near our takeoff airfield. We were good to go at 5,000 feet, but wouldn't win any efficiency awards.

This prompted me to ask, "We're not efficient—why are we staying at five thousand?"

"Look at the road."

Maggie banked the aircraft, giving my window a great view of the scene below. There were people on the road, headed to the airfield. I didn't see any armor, but did see at least two technicals, white pickup trucks with what looked like tripod mounted guns on the back. People on all types of motorcycles were streaming down the road to the airfield.

"If we didn't get out when we did, this jet would have had enough holes in it to look like a cheese grater," Maggie said.

Smoke began to shoot from the barrel of one of the truck mounted guns below.

"Time to go, Mags. They're shooting at us."

Maggie leveled the wings and began to climb, pointing the aircraft east, flying off wet compass.

"I'm going higher, but we still need to see the interstate when we get to it. No GPS, no TACAN or VOR. We are visual direct to DC," she said.

The aircraft cooled off at ten thousand feet and the cabin pressure maintained. Maggie dodged winter clouds, letting us both maintain visual on the road below. I traced our highway with my finger on the map, making sure to calculate time/speed/distance to our next road.

We had about four smaller airports we were going to attempt near Alexandria, but couldn't really count on any one of them. They could have debris all over the tarmac or even aircraft left abandoned. If all our airfields were a no-go, we'd set the aircraft down in some field. Not optimal, but it was either that or run out of gas.

31 Jan
Potomac

I have some purpose. I realize that now. Today. Forever.

I knew that I wasn't destined to go down in history as the guy that crashed the world, not just yet. We survived the impossible, the improbable, and that counts for something.

It has to.

The problem started with our first outlying airfield. Because we were flying lower than the aircraft was designed to cruise efficiently, we burned a helluva lot more gas than we should have. We were at our first airfield option with just over an hour of gas to go. The first airfield had fire trucks spaced at even intervals, blocking the runway from use. When Maggie hit the throttles, climbing out of that aerodrome, we only had enough gas for one, maybe two more airfields.

The rain was heavy over Virginia when we made our low pass over the second runway to survey the field. What we saw sent terror down my spine.

Chinese Flankers.

A squadron of them parked neatly in rows. We were low enough to see the red stars painted on their vertical stabilizers.

As Maggie once again pushed the throttles, the jet began to climb, but not before we noticed two men bust out of one of the buildings, white reflective flight helmets swinging in their hands as they sprinted for their jets ahead of a flock of maintainers, who were also running for the fighters.

"Oh, fuck," Maggie said.

"Weather is bad. Think we can shake 'em?" I asked.

"No. We're on fumes. Probably flame out in fifteen, twenty minutes."

I unbuckled my harness and walked hand over hand to the back of the jet, flipping over seat cushions and opening latched cabinets until I found it.

Life raft.

I buckled the life raft into one of the leather seats near the over wing exit along with our kit before running back up to the cockpit.

"Can we depressurize?!" I yelled over the drone of the engines into Maggie's covered ears.

Maggie glanced up at the gauges and nodded to me that we could.

I ran back to where the sealed life raft was buckled and followed the instruction sticker on the over wing hatch. After a near-death scare, I managed to jettison the hatch, hearing it hit the side of the aircraft as it fell away. We were either getting shot down or we were going to ditch this sucker. It was the only way. We had no time to find a suitable airfield. The safest place to put the aircraft down on short notice was in the Potomac River.

Fast moving air shot through the fuselage, tossing loose papers and small items everywhere. I rushed back to the front and got back in my harness, checking Maggie's, too.

"We ditching?" Maggie asked, already knowing the answer.

"Yep. You know where," I said, grabbing my checklist to make sure we didn't miss anything.

As I scanned the checklist, our radio blared to life on the guard frequency.

"Unknown aircraft, unknown aircraft at four thousand feet on a heading of zero nine four at one hundred and fifty knots, you are in violation of standing no fly zone executive order. You are to change course to zero two four and land immediately at Andrews Air Force Base."

Either ground radar had us or the Flanker radar did. Both would be bad.

I could barely make out the contours of the large river up ahead.

"I think we're losing number two," Maggie said as the aircraft began to vibrate.

Maggie executed a shutdown of engine two, adjusting for the new flight characteristics from the lack of thrust and the new barn door attached to the aircraft outside.

Ten miles to the water.

The altimeter began to tick down and the trees began to get bigger.

"Gear up, flaps set," I said, keeping Maggie focused on setting us down in the river ahead.

We both screamed when the Chinese fighter made its high-speed pass, no more than twenty feet off our right wing. The sonic boom was deafening even through our headsets. I watched the Flanker bank right and then roll, revealing multiple missiles mounted to the hard points on its wings.

They wouldn't bother with another pass. They were no doubt setting up for a perfect aspect shot.

Five miles to the water, Maggie began to configure the aircraft for a ditch. The rain was still coming down and visibility wasn't all that great. The only way the fighters could have found us was with radar vectors or their own onboard radars. Neither mattered.

I scanned the checklist for anything that would kill us if we missed, and held on for dear life.

"Virginia side if you can!" I said into the boom mike with no verbal response.

The aircraft made a slight heading adjustment as the altimeter dropped to fifty feet. We had no idea what the setting should be, so we could be ten feet off the water or thirty. It was difficult to tell, until the aircraft machine gun helped us.

The Flanker strafed, shooting water up into the air next to the

Gulfstream. This gave Maggie the perspective she needed to judge our altitude just before hitting the water.

I'd never ditched an aircraft before and was underwhelmed. The aircraft just slowed down really fast and came to a stop like a boat, pushing a bow wave of water ahead of it. Maggie and I disengaged our harnesses and ran into each other trying to get out.

"Ladies first," I said, happy to be alive.

She punched me hard in the arm and pushed past me to the opening where I'd previously jettisoned the hatch.

"Save the jokes, Max. You think that Flanker won't do another run?" she said, tossing the raft out and yanking the cord to inflate it with one motion.

We threw our gun-strapped packs into the inflated raft and used our hands as paddles, hauling ass to the shore. Much to my surprise, the Gulfstream didn't sink immediately. Also, we were only about a hundred yards away from the Virginia bank of the Potomac. I could even see part of Mount Vernon before we got too close to shore.

We ditched the bright orange raft and disappeared into the thick foliage to the sound of Communist fighter jets buzzing at high speeds up and down the Potomac River.

DELMAY

Maggie and I kept moving inland from the river, navigating via compass and our wet and tattered maps. The foliage was thick and unforgiving and would have been impassable in the summer. Based on our charts, we were only a mile from George Washington's Mount Vernon Estate. As we trekked through the forest, I wondered if General Washington ever hunted in these woods and if he might have followed the ancient trail that Maggie and I traced north to Route 1.

The thumping of helicopters continued for the rest of the day and into the evening, but the sounds were faint and to the south of where we found ourselves.

Moving slowly to avoid detection, we broke through the trees into the back end of suburban Alexandria as we waited for complete darkness to conceal our approach to our CIA front, Delmay Glass. Fighting fatigue and cold, we both took a dose of speed pills that we brought in the event we had to stay awake and make mission.

As we waited for the drugs to kick in, we cached away the heavy Stinger missile. After all, we were horseless and Alexandria seemed abandoned. There was not even candlelight shining through the windows. I could make out the gray/green outline of Route 1 up ahead and saw the familiar specks of abandoned cars probably lined up to cross the Woodrow Wilson Bridge.

The overcast sky concealed the bright moon, providing us enough cover to begin moving at about 2100. Thirty pounds lighter, I sprung to my feet and took point through the empty back-yards, mirroring the curves of Route 1 as it meandered north to intercept the loop. High on speed, we made good time, creeping behind the shadow-box privacy fences, eventually hitting the side street we were looking for.

"Follow me," Maggie said, gesturing us away from the path we were following.

I followed Maggie with the trust rebuilt from trekking over half the country on horseback and being strafed by Sukhoi fighters to-gether. We cut behind a pizza joint and were once again slogging through the type of pseudo woods that existed between abandoned city developments and masses of empty commercial lots.

We moved for some time through these trees and bushes until Maggie stopped at a large gray boulder sitting on the middle of one of the grown-over commercial lots. The large rock was covered with graffiti, MS-13 gang markings, and some lewd interpretations of male appendages. Maggie scanned the area, unmoving. She did this for five full minutes before leaning her gun against the rock and reaching underneath.

A loud click pierced the night silence.

Maggie grabbed her carbine and leaned on the rock, spin-ning it out of the way. Underneath, I could see the massive boul-der was attached to some mounting system and magnetic locking mechanism. I went first down the narrow stairs and watched her petite frame move the two thousand pound rock back into position with one hand. The rock settled down one inch onto the magnetic lock with a secondary click and we were underground.

"Post-9/11 Delmay remodeling. GWOT funded," Maggie said as we moved deeper into the corridor.

"I never knew about it," I said, fishing for a reason.

"You were new, Max. These types of things are reserved for more vetted employees of the Agency. The covered facility is the first layer of the onion. There are many."

I thought about this as we moved deeper into the ground before leveling off. The subterranean passage was solid concrete, with rebar making its appearance randomly along the passage. The emergency lighting had long gone dark and I wondered how the mag locks remained functional as I watched Maggie key a code into a panel next to a large steel door.

With a click, the lock was disengaged and Maggie swung the heavy vault-like door open.

"We're under Delmay now," she said.

Maggie walked over to a bank of dark screens and flipped on a breaker. The machines began to power on and the screens began scanning the drives following an improper shutdown. Maggie skipped the scan and initiated the building's security program after the operating system was done booting up.

Only three cameras were active, covering the lobby and a room marked SCIF in white digital letters on the live feed of the top floor. The other camera feeds had either broken or been otherwise disabled. The lobby looked as if a war had been fought in it, and the SCIF feed looked normal but completely abandoned.

"Well, whoever has been here the past year didn't find the Champagne Room; that's a good thing."

Maggie attempted to bring the other stricken cameras back online, to no avail. They were hard down.

"These two cameras and this terminal were the only ones hardwired to the system and off the grid. I think the computer worm killed the others," Maggie said.

"We're going to have to go topside and reach the SCIF on foot," I responded, not liking the sound of it out loud.

"Yes. The building should be abandoned, though."

"Should," I said.

Maggie released with a click the last maglock between us and the acknowledged area of the building. We stepped through a false wall door before Maggie swung the wall back to its original position. The entrance to the basement was undetectable and, from what Maggie said, the SCIF on the top floor was configured the same way.

We were still on NVDs, as the grid was down in Alexandria, and any auxiliary generators had likely long run out of juice. We moved over an air bridge that overlooked the Delmay Glass lobby. The area was decimated, as the glass was blown out and bullet holes peppered the once pristine white sheetrock interior walls.

We left the lobby view for the stairwell and began to climb to the penthouse, or as Maggie called it, the Champagne Room. Halfway up the stairs, we were forced out onto the fifth floor because the stairs were blocked with likely every piece of furniture from the sixth floor.

As we quietly entered the fifth, we were met with another postapocalyptic landscape. Like the lobby, windows had been blown out, but burn scoring marks and explosive damage replaced the bullet holes from the lobby. Looked like a dozen RPGs went off inside.

We stepped through the rubble of the office, walking over at least two badly decomposed corpses before reaching the other stairwell and eventually the top floor.

Here it was undamaged, with all but one window still intact. A bird had made a home in a cubicle near the open window and was protesting my presence as Maggie and I surveyed the area around the covert entrance to the Champagne Room.

After we were sure all was clear, Maggie went into one of the offices and closed the blinds out of habit. Just like the played out movie trope, she slid a large bookshelf out of the way, revealing a door. After entering her code, the familiar click of a maglock released and we were inside the SCIF.

Maggie slid the shelf back over the opening and secured the SCIF door before flipping a switch, illuminating the dim emergency lights.

"Champagne Room has battery backup, trickle charged by panels on the roof. We are fully command center capable here, but any RF and we get the Flanker treatment," she said.

After clearing the floor to make sure we weren't sharing the SCIF with anyone, we piled our kit in a conference room and sat down for a moment. The speed still had me wired, and I'm a lot bigger than Maggie. I can only imagine how hopped up she was.

"Time to get what we came for. Ready for another layer of the onion, Max?"

Inside the defunct but still secure Delmay Glass company front building remained a few interesting items . . . the last holdouts from the CIA's book of dirty tricks.

One of the items I recognized from Syria.

The box that was carefully placed and wired in with the dozens of other gray boxes at the Syriatel cell and data tower we infiltrated. This one wasn't painted like the one we deployed. I suppose one of the people in the Delmay unit was paid to research the color scheme of junction boxes inside the cell tower buildings of various countries and paint them to match.

Maggie carefully went over the set-up routine for the device. Using a black marker, she wrote the wiring setup on the outside of the box. She stuck the box onto the metal workbench with a clang. I'd forgotten the device had a magnetic strip on the back for easy mounting. After pulling the plastic battery barrier, she switched the thing on and began entering settings, referring to a manual that was inside. Afterward, I watched her carefully enter a code twice before stepping aside.

"Okay, your turn. Enter the exact code you entered in Syria. It has to be exact to work," Maggie said.

I entered my six digit code twice; it wasn't hard to recall, as it was my childhood home phone number minus the first number from back in the day when people still had landlines. The device blinked eights in all six windows before going dark. Maggie secured the power on the box and placed it back in the bubble wrap it was stored in, the Cat6 cables still neatly folded and wrapped with rubber bands.

"Why don't we hook this thing up now?" I asked Maggie.

"Do you want the capital region to have cyber and grid first?" she responded, making me feel pretty stupid.

She placed the device in my pack before summoning me to follow her across the hallway to another storage room. It took a while to get the door open, as my fingerprints weren't as easy to read as Maggie's. The lights in the SCIF began to blink, prompting Maggie to tell me that reserve power was about to deplete.

"We need to get this door open before that happens or our job's gonna be a lot harder," she said as I attempted to press my thumb at different angles onto the glass over and over again.

Finally, the biometric gods relented and a series of thumps indicated that the giant door was unlocked. It took both of us to swing the door open, as under normal circumstances it was assisted by an electric motor.

Inside the vault were stacks of vacuum sealed cash and other odds and ends. The item in the center of the room was what Maggie was after. It appeared to be a piece of carry-on luggage. She extended the handle and pulled it out of the vault and into the conference room with the rest of our kit.

After laying it flat, she unzipped the case, revealing a control panel with Cyrillic markings.

"Maggie, what the fuck is this thing?" I asked, moving in for a closer look under the fading emergency lighting.

"Well, Max, I guess the best course of action is to just tell you outright. It's a false flag weapon. This is a portable nuclear device. The weapons-grade uranium in the core was sourced from Russian uranium mines so that if we ever needed to use it, the core material would trace back to Russia. If our agents were apprehended prior to employment, all the markings would indicate Russian origin. This thirty-kiloton device's only function is to start a war."

"Why the hell didn't someone secure it? How is it still here?"

"Max, there wasn't anyone left to care, or anyone that knew about it anyway. Besides, all the nonproliferation resources were probably focused on the thousands of other first-strike weapons. No one was going to bother with a little suitcase nuke."

"Well, what's our plan now?" I asked, already knowing what she was going to say.

"Very simple. We replace the NAI's C4 with a portable nuclear weapon."

"No, Maggie. That's taking it too far. We're already responsible for enough destruction. Innocent people could die. Children," I said.

"I don't give a shit about their children!" Maggie snapped. "We've come all this way to eliminate those bastards, and you wanna quit over collateral damage?"

She was seeing red.

"Do you know how they disposed of all the bodies, Max? Do you?!"

"No, I don't."

"They pushed them into a fucking landfill with a bulldozer— the ones lucky enough to be buried, that is. The rest they just dumped in the ocean. Millions. That's on them, and that's on me."

I was stunned, numb. The government let so many people die . . . only to dump them in the ocean like common trash? History will remember the entire executive, legislative, and judicial branches as nothing short of war criminals.

So there it was, then. Maggie and I were the ones that started the calamity; it seems somehow fair and fitting that we be the ones to usher in a new era. One where America can start over, without the grip of tyranny and corruption that thrives in this den of serpents.

SUMMIT

Summit Eve

The night before the summit. Using the Delmay tunnel, Maggie
and I exfiltrated into the darkness. At the edge of the empty overgrown lot, I tossed my shortwave antenna, tied to a rock, over a
branch above my head. Making sure the radio would not transmit, I
tuned up the known NAI frequencies for an update.

After a few cycles of gibberish that meant nothing, I heard the
words I was looking for:

"There will be no Christmas this year."

The summit was still happening.

I gave Maggie a thumbs-up and we continued north to the
Woodrow Wilson Bridge. We'd changed our clothes to better blend
into the surroundings. My SBR was tucked under an overcoat and
Maggie rolled our piece of carry-on luggage, playing the bag lady
part very well.

The Woodrow was dark and foreboding, strewn with abandoned

cars on one lane with the other lane cleared off. I could see where someone had tossed the cars off the bridge into the water on one side to clear a passage back and forth between Virginia and Maryland across the Potomac. The concrete and steel guardrails on the side were marred with steel marks and grazes where something had manhandled the vehicles into the abyss. We skipped over onto the cleared lane passing under the Maryland governor's welcome sign suspended across the middle of the span.

I thought to myself how the unregistered short-barreled M4 personal defense weapon with a silencer attached under my coat had made me a double felon—even in the best of times—as I stepped over the invisible state line that separated the commonwealth from Maryland.

Add those two felonies to the hundreds of others the all-powerful, all-knowing state says that I committed. Fuck it. They were going to murder me or bury me under the prison anyway.

It took most of the night to reach the District proper. The Federal Reserve Building was where the summit was going down. New world order powers were meeting to cut up what was left of the United States and they were doing it tomorrow, under the ever-watchful gaze of the money changers.

Maggie insisted on picking a specific tall abandoned apartment building in the grid down area of the District. After her intimate knowledge of the inner workings of the Delmay underground, I didn't question her overwatch choice. Even on the ground from the dark zone, we could tell that the power was still very much on inside the heart of the District.

This wasn't a makeshift fusion center. The Federal Reserve perimeters would have hundreds of cameras trained upon it and would be wired to detect even the slightest movement or seismic activity.

I honed my B&E skills, easily defeating the ground-floor padlock with one of many tin can shims I'd constructed on the way out here as extras to replace my real shims.

We were inside. The place smelled of rotten food and dead animals, and we could see why as we worked our way to the top.

Corpses lay strewn about, frozen in death, clutching fatal gunshot wounds. The bullet marks on the walls inside the stairwell told the story of a gunfight in which both sides sustained casualties. The corpse at the bottom of the steps still had his pistol, along with the one at the top. We stepped over the decomposing mess and continued on to the top, where I had to once again use a shim to defeat a padlock in order to gain roof access.

It was a rather cold February here in DC, but a small fire would have been too risky. Based on our maps, we were five hundred meters from where the powered-up microgrid had been put in place, likely unconnected to the outside. Maggie and I began to surveil what we could, but the distance to the target was a little too far to ascertain watch rotations or other security habits and movements. With my binos, I could barely make out that the perimeter guards were carrying long guns.

The area we inhabited on the top of the building was mostly surrounded by the eerie blackness of a disabled grid, eaten from the inside out by the NSA manufactured super worm. Only the lights from the federal microgrid punctuated the postapocalyptic scene all around us.

One thing that caught our attention was the IR laser activity from the rooftop of one of the buildings adjacent to the Federal

Reserve. Likely a team of night vision capable snipers were nested there, something we'd need to deal with.

Uncharacteristic of Maggie, she asked me to take the first observation period and that she'd tap in after a quick combat nap. She sweetened the deal with a single-serve package of instant coffee she'd been saving since Arkansas.

I gladly accepted her bribe.

Goddamn Maggie.

I awoke to the bright sun of first light, half frost-bitten, near the rim of the apartment-complex roof. I had a splitting headache and the canteen of coffee I was drinking while I stood lookout had tumbled over on its side, the contents spilled out onto the tar roof and frozen solid.

I tried to stand up and wasn't able. Maggie was gone, no sign of her. The only thing left was my kit leaning up against the roof access hatch. I tried to work my paralyzed leg muscles, stretching them to the point of pain. They weren't working right, so I had to drag myself over to my kit, yearning for the extra canteen I kept inside. After reaching my pack, I flipped it over on its side and climbed up on it to get myself off the cold roof for a minute.

After struggling with the bag's zippers, I rammed my freezing hands into the pack, hoping to bust my knuckles on the canteen so I could find it. After a few grueling minutes dealing with the pain of a throbbing headache and near freezing appendages, I found the canteen and drank deeply. This gave me the strength I needed to find the small bottle of ibuprofen. I was so desperate to kill the pain, I popped three into my mouth and chewed them like candy before washing the dust down with another drink.

My legs started to come back after about fifteen minutes of

flexing and massaging. I finally stood, wobbling, and instinctively felt for my short-barreled carbine. It obviously wasn't where I left it, as I'd have felt it crawling over to my pack.

Scanning the rooftop, careful to stay low enough not to be seen, I saw it leaning barrel up against the edge of the roof. Something yellow was attached to the handguard.

A Dogpatch map was affixed via rubber band to my gun. Somewhere Maggie knew I'd find it quick.

I hastily pinched the rubber band from the gun and unfolded the old theme park map.

———

Dear Max,

I know you're angry right now, but you need to understand a few things. YOU are not part of this system. It didn't make you. I am. I knew full well what we were doing in Syria, and accepted it. I am this system, the same system that murdered millions, including my own daughter. You've fought for redemption since the start and have little for which to be ashamed.

The worm device is in your pack. I suggest you activate it in NAI territory. If you follow the instructions I've left for you, the effects of the worm will be ▬▬▬▬▬▬▬▬.

The nuke doesn't have a delay fuse. You know, dead agents tell no tales and all. I never told you, as I didn't want you to try any of your hero guilt bullshit. It's my right. My charge. You're free and clear, Max. Sleep well knowing that this decision was mine and mine alone.

I'd have killed you anyway if you tried to stop me, and you know it.

If you're reading this, you don't have much time. Get out.

—Maggie

I stood atop Delmay as the blast rocked the District. A searing flash, followed by a small but distinguishable mushroom cloud rose up above the trees on the horizon as the sonic boom of the blast eventually vibrated Delmay's elaborate but already fractured glass face.

Maggie had sacrificed herself to slay the beast, along with all of its ticks and fleas, in one fell swoop.

I've read her letter again and again, more than I've read anything in my life. I'd be lying if I said I didn't have my serious doubts over what she had done. Hell, I might have hesitated. Maggie knew. After all, she trained me. One thing is certain: if it was vengeance Maggie wanted, she got it in thermonuclear spades.

I suppose I'll point my boots west and start moving. I'm bringing the grid back online, but I won't start here in the remnants of the hydra-headed beast.

This place will never, ever deserve it.

ARKANSAS TERRITORY

March

Every day I ride.

My life has been a blur since I witnessed the blast on the Delmay rooftop. When I first wake up in the morning, small outlines of high-order nuclear detonation can be seen, overlaid against whatever I'm looking at, burned and scarred into my retinas. Not in my direct line of sight, but just outside—a forever forget-me-not. Something to put Maggie back into my head every time I open my eyes.

A few days after escaping DC, I found an old motorcycle inside a workshop next to a small farmhouse. This was a few miles outside of Quantico, Virginia. It's not much, but it gets me farther west every day. Closer to Arkansas, closer to the objective. Closer to ~~Savannah~~ the Arkansas territory, at least that's what I'm calling it now, as there is no more United States.

I think of Maggie every day. I reflect on her . . . sacrifice. ~~I cry most days~~ I've run into raiders on two occasions.

I didn't even give them a chance.
There isn't much of the old me left hanging on.
Every day I ride.

January 1

Northwest Arkansas Free Press

LIGHTS ON IN NWA

Engineers with the NAI have restored power to the majority of Northwest Arkansas. Washington, Benton, and parts of the adjacent counties currently have power for twelve hours per day, NAI officials confirm. Citing computer performance issues as the main causal factor, engineers were able to stabilize the grid control computer's operating system. Timely for NWA citizens, this windfall comes to us just after the provisional government's unconditional surrender, reverting power back to the individual territories. Incarcerated officials won't confirm the reasons for the unexpected pivot; however, staffer plea bargain testimony points to the nuclear explosion that occurred last February. The attack remains under investigation by adjacent territory officials.

Tune in on 1030 AM nightly at six for more on this, and for provisional government trial coverage.

January 25

Northwest Arkansas Free Press

NO POWER FOR BORDER TERRITORIES

NAI engineers have been unsuccessful in their attempts to bring grid power back online for any of the border territories, sources confirm. Eyewitness accounts of the issue have been streaming in via radio since the NWA power and data grid was restored. Residents of border territories have been bringing their personal electronic devices across the territory border to get them back online. Witnesses report that their devices function as designed while inside the NWA grid zone, but Barbara Kelly of Joplin, MO, tells us her account of what occurred when she recently attempted to take her phone and laptop back across the border:

"They work just fine when I'm in Bentonville, but as soon as I cross back over that line, they start acting up again, just like they did before all this."

Robert Victor of Huntsville, AR, reports, "I brought my dang electric car across the border to charge her up. When I drove her back into Madison County, she just stopped workin', left me stranded all night."

Tune in on 1030 AM nightly at six for more on this developing story, and for continuing coverage of the provisional government trials.

February 10

Northwest Arkansas Free Press

CHINESE TROOPS ON THE RUN

According to the newly elected President Christopher Newmauer of the California Territory, West Coast harbors are being flooded with Chinese troop carriers, but they're not dropping off troops says one eyewitness.

"They're loading those ships down with men like a boat full of Cuban refugees. Surprised they don't sink leaving the harbor," says Michael Shure of San Diego.

With most territorial leaders issuing a "shoot on sight" order on any UN troops operating illegally inside North America, this comes as no surprise. With more than four hundred million guns in American hands before the defunct provisional government's failed attempt at disarmament, the Chinese military has a lot to be worried about.

Tune in on 1030 AM nightly at six for more on this developing story, and for our continuing coverage on the public executions of convicted provisional government officials.

April 23

Northwest Arkansas Free Press

LOCAL FED CONVICTED, SENTENCED TO DEATH BY FIRING SQUAD

Former Special Agent in Charge Lon Peterson was convicted of seven hundred and forty three counts of murder today. The jury only deliberated five minutes in this landmark case deciding the fate of the agent known to many as the man behind the Jailhouse Massacre, among countless other atrocities. He will be awarded the death penalty by firing squad in the Fayetteville town square this Saturday at noon. Patrons are asked to leave children under the age of sixteen at home. A raffle is being conducted to choose ten executioners. Any able-bodied adult citizen may apply. Interested parties are asked to see Sheriff Baker for details or contact her on citizen band channel eighteen.

Tune in on 1030 AM nightly at six for more on this, and for our continuing election coverage of the Arkansas Territory presidential election.

July 4

Northwest Arkansas Free Press

*INDEPENDENCE DAY CELEBRATION
TAKES ON NEW MEANING AMIDST
SINO-TERRITORIAL TENSIONS*

Arkansans take to the streets today to celebrate independence from the former Provisional Government, at times expressing intense outrage on last year's Sino-Territorial occupation. Pressure from newly elected Arkansas Territory President, Jim Sparks, has driven talks with the nuclear capable Dakotas Territory regarding potential retaliatory measures.

Sheriff Baker reminds Arkansans not to discharge firearms into the air in celebration, and to take appropriate firearm safety precautions during their Independence Day celebrations: "Please, people, we've had enough accidental injuries. It is true that all federal firearms laws have been nullified by the Territorial Supreme Court until further notice, but let's try to police ourselves and have some commonsense fun out there tonight. There ain't any more Chinese running around in the Arkansas Territory; just because someone might look like they could be Asian, that don't mean they're a damn Chinese spy. Just keep a level head out there, it's all I'm asking. Long live the Independent Territories."

Although emotions run high as more details are uncovered regarding the circumstances around the Sino occupation, most territorial citizens remain hopeful for peace.

Tune in on 1030 AM nightly at six for more on our coverage of the developing Sino-Territorial crisis.

//END COGNITIVE TRANSCRIPTION

The previous record has been classified as a protected historical document, transcribed from petabytes of text, audio, and video recovered from various sensors that were located in the territory formerly known as the United States of America. Hub records indicate that there were nearly a thousand fragmented personal accounts of the Rebellion of 2021. The Max account clearly stands out from the rest, as it is widely considered by historians to be the most accurate and definitive depiction of how, where, and when the rebellion began and eventually ended. This sixty-seventh edition includes archival evidence that the nuclear device detonated in February 2023 was most likely the single event that triggered the nuclear/EMP exchange of 2025. Although the redacted digital portions of the record outlining the early days of the rebellion survived the nuclear/EMP exchange of 2025, not until 2093, when the yellowed pages of the handwritten volume were discovered at an estate sale in the ArkansasTerritory, was the bulk of the Max account made available to historians. Quantum digital forensics worked diligently for a decade to recover the missing pieces of history that took place before the nuclear/EMP exchange of 2025.

The identity of Max remains unknown as of this printing.

ACKNOWLEDGMENTS

This is merely a work of postapocalyptic fiction; I do not advocate violence. Some may call it thought-crime, but that's exactly where this plotline belongs—in the dark recesses of our minds where we explore the primal side of humanity.

By the time this novel hits the shelves, I'll be walking between the sideboys to the tune of a bosun's pipe, retiring from the United States Navy. I'd like to thank the United States naval service for a wonderful and sometimes challenging twenty-two years of high adventure. I'd like to give special thanks to my agent for his solid and insightful guidance throughout the years. *Serpent Road* would not be possible without the surgical editorial work of my editor (who it turns out was always right from DBDA1 to now—thanks!) and the rest of his great team up at Rockefeller Center in New York City. As always, my family patiently put up with my long hours upstairs in the writing dungeon to bring you this novel, so I'd say they've earned some hearty thanks as well. There would be no professional writers without readers, so, from the bottom of my heart, I'd like to thank you for picking up *Serpent Road* and traveling all these pages with me.

As far as Max goes . . . well, let's just hope he lives out a happy and peaceful life somewhere in the Arkansas territory.

—J.L. Bourne